DEMON BEWITCHED

DEMON ENFORCERS, BOOK 3

JENN STARK

.

1

The New York City goth club Storm Court was rocking hard enough to be heard three blocks away, but not by ordinary humans. This party was for witches and their initiates only, mortals desperate to be transformed into something—anything—else. Vampire, witch, yeti, it didn't seem to matter. They just wanted to become something bigger and better than themselves. It gave a whole new meaning to Ready to Were.

Stefan of the Syx whistled beneath his breath, surveying the debauch. "This is...weird."

"I think you mean unholy."

Stefan stifled a grin as he glanced over to the most taciturn member of the Syx, Gregori. The man was a virtual mountain, the tallest and broadest demon enforcer among them, and by far the grumpiest. If Grigori ever got to choose his own destiny, he'd be perfect as a monk in a mountain cave.

As it was, he stood out in this underground electro-house club like a unicorn in hell.

"Gotta wonder why the archangel sent you here with

me," Stefan said, patting his fellow demon enforcer on the shoulder. "Storm Court is totally not your scene."

Grigori grunted, muttering something about their boss that Stefan didn't need to hear to agree with. When they were sent out on assignment, the members of the Syx had long since learned to keep their mouths shut and their eyes sharp. It didn't pay to complain, not when an archangel of the Lord was doling out your work assignments.

And truth to tell, being a Syx wasn't so bad—or it hadn't been until recently. Having sinned their way out of Fallen angel status and straight into demonhood six thousand years earlier, Stefan and five other demons had been culled from the teeming masses of the damned and had been given a sort of second chance as a demon SWAT team, tasked with routing the worst of their kind. Since no ordinary human stood a chance against the horde—in almost all cases, it took a demon to kill a demon—the Syx had been in high demand since the moment the demon enforcer team was formed.

Now, however, with Earth sustaining a body blow of magic that'd dumped a fresh multitude of demons across the planet, the Syx's caseload had skyrocketed. Jobs that would normally have taken four or five of them only got two, and Michael the Archangel was the final arbiter of who went where.

Stefan drew in a deep, fortifying breath. Storm Court smelled like danger, sex, and witchcraft. He'd never been here before, but clubs like this were exactly his jam. Even if the modern covens were decidedly coed, they were still dominated by women. There was nothing on this earth that Stefan appreciated more than mortal females, especially the ones willing to let their freak flags fly. The crazier they were, the better, as long as they never got crazy over *him*. He'd learned that lesson the hard way, resulting in the sin that'd damned him for all eternity, and justifiably so. He'd spend the rest of his immortality atoning for his transgression.

But that didn't make him immune to women.

Grigori was a different story. The man barely talked to *any* human, let alone a female one. As a result, he was usually tagged with the Syx assignments that were heavy on the brawn, light on the banter. His assignment here made no sense.

Stefan scanned the room, his gaze snagging on a female working her way toward the stage. He narrowed his eyes. She was a witch, but that didn't matter much in this group. Was this the Syx's summoner? The woman definitely had an energy around her that caught his attention, and she wouldn't ordinarily—she was small and thin, her hair cascading down her back in an auburn tumble. While he appreciated all women, Stefan's tastes tended decidedly toward the voluptuous. This chick wasn't that. But she held his attention anyway as she stalked across the room in a body-hugging black leather halter, pants, and high-heeled boots, her biceps wrapped with intricate silver cuffs, her lips painted red as blood—

"So who summoned you?" Grigori grumbled, breaking Stefan's concentration. "It stinks in here, but not of demon. No one's in danger."

"You're half right, anyway," Stefan agreed. There were no demons in the club except him and Grigori, actually, and their glamour was ironclad. Not even the most powerful witch would know that the Syx were demons if they didn't let their guard down, and the Syx's glamour only strengthened when they were within range of someone who summoned them.

Stefan sensed his disguise was nearly perfect—he'd

worked long and hard to build his armor to an impermeable shell. But no one else on the floor even gave off a whiff of demon, which made no sense. He thought back to the call that had brought him here. "Someone on the dance floor demanded aid," he said, "but the summons was muted, desperate. Blocked."

"Blocked because of drugs?" Grigori narrowed his eyes. "Or because they're possessed?"

Stefan shrugged. Either one wasn't a bad guess. "Unknown. But if the latter is what's going on here, whatever demon is possessing our summoner is operating on a whole new level. I can't pick him up, and I just fought a pile of the bastards a few weeks ago. I'd remember the smell. This whole deal feels different, somehow. And different in a decidedly not-good way."

Demons appeared to humans as ordinary mortals and could do anything a mortal could do—eat, drink, procreate, kill. But for some demons, it wasn't enough merely to harm God's children. They had to inhabit them, body and soul. Possessing a human was a form of domination that appealed to the most craven of the horde, because it made annihilating the demon more difficult. To send a possessor demon into oblivion, a member of the Syx or an exceptionally skilled exorcist first had to pull said demon out of the human without causing more damage to the unfortunate host. Easier said than done.

Stefan eyed Gregori. "We need more intel. Why don't you let your hair down and shake your groove thing or something? From their smell alone, these humans are desperate to commune with demons. Maybe you should promise them immortality or whatever in exchange for them giving you the inside scoop on what the hell is going on here."

As usual, Gregori couldn't take the joke. It was one of his charms. "We have rules," the ox snapped back, his eyes going flat.

"Okay, Colossus, then head over to the bar—no, not that one. Over there." Stefan pointed at the elaborate alcohol station at the far end of the room, directly through the writhing crowd.

Gregori focused on the bar. "Why?"

Stefan grinned. "Because you're the biggest guy in the room and the second-most attractive one after me. If someone's banging the drum for deliverance, you're going to look like the answer to their prayers."

Stefan knew immediately he'd gone too far, and he winced as a familiar expression of pain ghosted over Gregori's face. It was too late to call his words back, though. None of the Syx asked too many questions about each other's sins, but Stefan had worked often enough with the big guy to know that Gregori's sin had to do with him not answering a call for aid when it'd come to him. If that kind of call had hit Gregori when he'd been a Fallen angel, ignoring it would have required enormous strength. Something horrific must have gone down for the powerful angel to say no...and now here he was, working as a demon enforcer where he was forced to say nothing but yes, yes, yes, while the cries of the despairing pummeled him from all sides. God definitely had a twisted sense of humor. Or the Archangel Michael did.

Stefan had his money on the latter.

The moment passed, and Gregori straightened. "How will I know who the summoner is?"

"You won't," Stefan said. "Not until I go all kamikaze on whatever demon is possessing them, anyway. But I'm getting the sense we're going to need your demon-killer skills before too long, so don't let this crowd full of humans fool you. Something smells bad."

As he'd hoped, a wan smile creased Gregori's face. Stefan didn't know if it was his attempt at a joke or because the big demon was itching for a fight. That was the only time Gregori could forget who he was and what he'd done. That was the only time any of them could forget.

Stefan watched Gregori head off across the dance floor. As he suspected, roughly two-thirds of the dancers instinctively shifted their gazes to him. The initiates, Stefan knew. Gregori's otherworldly status served as a homing device for humans, but fully consecrated witches were more or less immune to it. Yet another reason why the members of the coven and the members of the horde weren't on friendly terms.

Historically, witches summoned demons to do their dirty work or to get intel on other members of the damned. Witches could control demons, but only if they were careful, and only if the demons weren't very strong. No witch would invite any high-ranking horde member into their presence without setting up hella wards.

Stefan stared around the room, more intently this time. There *was* something set up at five distinct points of the chamber, a febrile flame glowing white in hurricane glass lanterns set up almost casually on red-draped cocktail tables. But though five points generally meant a pentagram was in play, there was no salt on the floor, no arcane figures hastily sketched with chalk. No—

In the blink of an eye, he didn't have to wonder anymore.

A ripping noise tore through the club under the heavy beat of music, as if the fabric of the world was being rent in two. As Stefan watched, the crowd instantly increased by a third, the place suddenly chock-full of some of the most gorgeously glamoured demons he'd ever seen. Big, fancy, powerful demons. Even a few he recognized.

He noticed something else too. Though she wasn't alone anymore, the redheaded witch on the dais now positively shimmered with intensity, her lips moving, her hands out as she surveyed the chaos that spilled across Storm Court's dance floor. *She* was the Syx's summoner, there was no doubt in Stefan's mind. She'd known this was going to happen.

Across the room at the bar, Gregori straightened his shoulders. He could feel it too.

It was time to party.

"SO MANY IN ONE PLACE." The voice was old, elegant. And dripping with censure.

Cressida Frain turned her attention to the former high priestess of the Scepter Coven, the most ancient coven still practicing under its original charter in the world. Its founders had been born in the crucible of the Bronze Age, their coven shrouded in the mists as magic roiled and twisted throughout what was currently known as the Middle East. The Scepter Coven's task, then as now, was a simple one: push back the darkness of Ahriman, the strongest demon ever to lay waste to the earth...and one day, when the opportunity presented itself, destroy him altogether.

The destruction of the great demon was one of the most enduring directives of their sacred grimoire, a responsibility assigned to the First Witches alone. It'd also been a responsibility they'd been able to put off for thousands of years. The next generation of witches would always be stronger, they'd reasoned. The next generation would be more equipped.

But if they didn't act quickly, there wouldn't *be* a next generation.

Ahriman had finally struck. Less than ten days ago in Serbia, seventy-five witches in the Crescent Moon Coven had been slaughtered in one of the bloodiest demon attacks in recorded history. The massacre would be chalked up as yet another military atrocity in the war-torn country, but that didn't change the truth. What the Serbian army had failed to do after nearly a decade of warfare, a legion of demons had accomplished in one night.

According to the accounts of the witches who'd survived, Ahriman had commanded those demons. And so the Scepter Coven would strike him down.

"We needed to summon this many to obscure our true purpose here," Cressida reminded Elysium Gray for easily the thousandth time. "We'll not get a better chance to fulfill the grimoire's requirements than this."

The former high priestess sniffed, but she wasn't the only one who needed the reminder. Behind Elysium stood Cressida's fated mate, Marcus—the only man she'd ever expected to rule by her side. He'd been chosen by the lawgivers, approved by the elders, and blessed by the Goddess.

Cressida grimaced. He'd also just flat-out rejected her tentative amorous advances. Again.

Which was not only mortifying, it was dangerous. Because, not to put too fine a point on it, if Cressida didn't get screwed soon...well, she'd be screwed. A witch's strength in the Scepter Coven increased dramatically upon her sexual awakening, and Cressida's body was still decidedly fast asleep. That wasn't good if she was supposed to be taking on Ahriman in less than a week.

She felt her cheeks flush even thinking about it. What was Marcus *waiting* for?

"They're stronger than I expected they would be," murmured the witch to her right, refocusing Cressida's thoughts. Dahlia, the head of Cressida's personal guard, was the closest friend Cressida had ever allowed herself. Dahlia had stood with her and for her even on her darkest days, no matter how lonely the path of high priestess had become of late.

"We can handle them," Cressida told her. "We need only to choose quickly and cleanly, then return the rest of the horde to their rightful places." The Scepter Coven didn't have the strength to destroy these demons, of course, only summon them. One day soon, the coven *would* take its place as the battle-ax for the global witch community, *would* avenge its fallen, but only after they'd destroyed Ahriman. Everything depended on that.

Dahlia's gaze was focused on the floor, however, her body practically vibrating with intensity. "Our control is slipping."

Cressida scowled. "Our control will hold long enough for us to cull three demons from the herd. Three is all I need," Three demons, one witch, one mortal. No more...no less.

They'd planned it out with exacting detail, after all. She, Marcus, and Fraya, the lawgiver who'd lit Cressida's path from the moment she'd entered the coven as a very young girl. The steps required to defeat Ahriman were mapped out plainly in the sacred grimoire, but those steps were unacceptable. They were also outdated. Together with her mentor and fated mate, however, Cressida had found a better way.

The ancient passages stated that the high priestess of the Scepter Coven must accept a demon consort of highest power to give her the strength to defeat Ahriman.

A demon. As a wedded consort. The very thought was ridiculous.

Demons were the loathsome side product of the conflicting energies between the God and Goddess, energies that had resulted in the creation of the world. No demon would ever be a mortal's equal—let alone be considered a suitable partner to a consecrated witch. And yet, that was what was written in the grimoire. Unfortunately, the ancient ways still held sway in the Scepter Coven, and as the coven's newest high priestess, Cressida was bound to follow them.

So, fine. She wouldn't take on one demon, then...she'd take on three.

Three demons who, together, would be stronger than she was—but who, apart, the coven could control. Cressida would take all three of them as her wedded consorts to satisfy the grimoire's requirements, draw on their strength as the ancient laws demanded...then send them on to the Goddess's final judgment.

Though witches didn't usually kill demons outright, it wasn't enough, in this case, to merely return these demons to their lairs after their usefulness was over. Cressida needed to ensure that no one ever knew what happened here...and especially that no one ever knew a witch had agreed to take a demon as her wedded husband.

But wedded husband did not mean bedded husband. Cressida would *not* be sleeping with any of her consorts... except Marcus, anyway. Assuming he ever agreed to do so.

Her lip curled in self-disgust. He'd denied her again that

very day. It seemed that Marcus was more than willing to rule by her side, but he didn't love her, didn't want her. Hell, he apparently found her so physically loathsome, he couldn't bear to sleep with her even though he knew doing so would heighten her abilities...and despite the fact that everyone in the coven assumed they'd already taken care of such matters.

She wasn't going to tell the coven any differently either. She'd have to level up on her own, is all. Besides, most of the coven *also* assumed that the high priestess would have sexual relations with her demon consorts, simply because the sacred grimoire hinted at such an abomination. She didn't mind such assumptions if they got her people to fight with all their strength when the war against Ahriman finally came. But those assumptions did not equate to actual stated law.

Cressida should know—she'd pored over the dusty tome for months, carefully copying the ancient dictates onto sheaves of fresh paper, the better to study the terms to understand any hidden loopholes or caveats. The grimoire was a minefield of twisting language, but she'd consulted both the lawgivers and the elders of the coven separately on the issue, and the results had been the same. She was within her rights to take on multiple consorts, be they demon, ordinary human, or witch. The demonic power must merely outweigh the abilities of any of her other consorts.

And it would outweigh those abilities, in its fashion. While two demons might not, three demons would easily overmatch a single ordinary magician or a single witch, even one as strong as herself or Marcus. But that demonic power would be split three ways. If Cressida knew anything about demons, they didn't play well together. If the demons remained separate, independent of each other, the combined strength of Marcus and a human magician under her thrall would defeat them. If the demons joined forces, of course...

She pursed her lips tight. The demons wouldn't join forces. She, Marcus, and the coven leadership would make sure of that.

But there were other issues to resolve as well. The grimoire hadn't said *why* a demon's influence was needed to destroy the ancient evil of Ahriman, only that it was. She suspected it was due to the dictate that it took a demon to kill a demon, but that was a rule born in the primordial quagmire of history. Witches had spent the intervening millennia getting stronger, smarter, and far less awed by the natural order of evil. She didn't need a demon to get the job done. She'd be able to handle Ahriman herself, once he came to her.

And he *would* come to her, as soon as she'd fulfilled the dictates of the sacred grimoire and taken a demon as a consort. Ahriman was bound by the same ancient laws as the Scepter Coven. If Cressida fulfilled her part of the bargain, he would be forced to show himself the moment she summoned him. It didn't matter how strong he was, he was still a demon, and she was a witch.

"Who are the best candidates?" she asked as she and Marcus stepped forward, drawing even with Dahlia and Elysium Gray. Together, they scanned the room.

"That one is the strongest," Marcus said immediately, pointing at a leering oaf of a demon surrounded by a half-dozen initiates who could smell his otherness, though they didn't realize the danger they were in.

"No. That one is strongest," Dahlia murmured in contention, and Cressida turned to follow her gaze.

Marcus made a scoffing noise. "That's a human."

"No, it isn't," Cressida countered, her eyes narrowing. The apparent man standing at the elaborate south bar of Storm Court looked a little lost, but there was no denying the power in him. Many would assume that power was because of his mighty build. He towered over the humans around him, a veritable mountain of a man with a face of heartbreaking beauty that looked as if it'd been carved from marble. His glamour was powerful...but it *was* glamour. He was a demon of incredible strength. Which could only mean...

She winced. Had she set her lure so effectively that she'd trapped a Syx?

If so, was there any chance she'd attracted more than one of them? That...would be bad. She didn't want the Syx meddling in her business.

"Cressida!"

Dahlia's shout was her only warning. A darkness so foul that even the clueless initiates staggered beneath it suddenly tore through the room coalescing into a being of pure malevolence. Another demon! Only this one was far, far worse than anything she'd ever seen.

"Hold!" Cressida commanded, her voice rising enough that every witch in the room felt it. Her coven instantly took their positions to obey.

Cressida raced off the dais and into the crowd, making it halfway across the floor before she collided with another figure coming from the opposite direction.

"Pardon, pardon, demon patrol coming through." The lean, sleekly muscled man physically lifted her and thrust her to the side with a strength she wouldn't have thought possible.

Cressida staggered back, and he barreled past her toward the demonic entity that was already swallowing initiates whole, draining them of their life essence like squeezing oranges. Could this new demon possibly be Ahriman?

"Who?" The man suddenly braked and wheeled back toward her as if she'd spoken aloud, staring at her for a moment like she was crazy. "Are you nuts? You *cannot* tell me you idiots summoned that asshat—no, I won't believe it."

Then he was gone again, and Cressida was left racing after him, her witch-spelled speed allowing her to catch up with him—to his clear surprise—so that they both hit the force field of demonic power at the same time—

The attacking demon wasn't Ahriman. She'd studied the ancient scripts enough to recognize the great evil's signature, and this wasn't him. It could easily have been his lieutenant, though, given the hoary filth of age and rage caking the demon's glamour, visible to anyone with the eyes to see. The demon turned and saw the man racing toward him, his eyes wide with surprise, recognition, and...could that be fear?

Once again, it was Cressida's turn to be surprised. For the creature to recognize the man hurling himself forward could mean only one thing. He wasn't a man at all. She, high priestess of the Scepter Coven, had been as duped by his glamour as if she was the meanest acolyte. Like the colossus Dahlia had spied in the crowd, this was another member of the Syx.

The demon enforcer howled a string of ancient, outraged epithets, confirming her suspicion, and launched himself at the creature, at the same time that the towering Greek god from the bar knocked free of the crowd and attacked the demon from the opposite angle.

Their combined strength was great—enormous—and

the larger of the two had the advantage of surprise, barreling into the demon from behind and taking him to the floor. The impact of the two entities striking the hardwood sent a galvanizing jolt through the rest of the room, one the demons in attendance knew all too well.

Dinnertime.

"No!" she gasped. The nearer of the Syx, the smaller one, turned to her with blazing eyes.

"What the hell have you *brought* here?" he demanded. His voice wasn't racked with fear, exactly, but his censure was plain.

"You *dare* speak to me that way," Cressida started. Then she felt rather than saw the rush of ice that swept up on her from behind, as the Syx's face blanked with shock.

"Duck!" he yelled.

2

"What in the actual *hell*!" Stefan roared as three new ice demons as ancient as the first asshat they'd taken to the floor formed in the hole behind the witch queen. Together, the new demons sent out a blast of frozen energy that Stefan barely contained. Whatever summons she'd used to pull these guys out of the deep freeze of the abyss, an area most demons never even heard about, much less were damned to, it was definitely effective. Gregori had already disappeared with the first demon, who was apparently trying to audition for the role of fourth Horseman of the Apocalypse. These three new ice demons could have been that guy's great uncles.

"Cressida." The name floated into the atmosphere of the club, running over and around and along the thrumming music, and Stefan scowled at the young witch opposite him. She was pretty, he supposed, but right now, that wasn't his primary concern. No, really, it wasn't.

"You did this?" he demanded. His breath fogged into the frigid air as he turned on his heel with the witch at his side, keeping the demons in view. After he'd absorbed their first attack, they seemed to be reconsidering their strategy, huffing and blowing like bulls about to take down the toreador. And here he was, fresh out of red capes.

"It's my right to summon demons," she said, with a coolness that had nothing to do with the freezer burn these demons were causing, and he shot her another glance. Still tiny, still fierce, still pointless. "You came, after all."

"I came because there was trouble," Stefan countered, and her scoffing laugh pricked his irritation.

"No trouble, demon," she said, twisting that last word until it sounded like filth in her mouth. "You came because I had the power to call you, the power that has belonged to any witch since the ancient Goddess defied the order that your creator bestowed upon this world."

"He's your creator too, sweetheart." Stefan bit down hard on his tongue. He didn't have time to argue chicken-and-egg theology. "Now, if you'll excuse me, I gotta go clean up the mess you made."

Rather than give her the opportunity to cause even more problems, Stefan shoved the witch to the side with enough force that she went sprawling. Technically, as a member of the Syx, he was forbidden to harm any of God's children. Harming God's children was what had landed him in this predicament in the first place. But witches were, arguably, a little different. They followed a unique path to get to their truth, one that wouldn't find them fans in any traditional church or synagogue, and that path meant that Stefan had the right to keep them out of his way when he needed to, as long as he ultimately did them no harm.

It was a fuzzy distinction, but it gave him the opening he needed.

He blasted into the three ice demons in the room with a rage they weren't expecting—because no one expected it, not from him. His arms and hands glowing with righteous fury, he pounded the creatures into the ground in rapid succession, but no sooner did one fall than another one staggered back up. Gregori was nowhere in sight, and Stefan was beginning to feel the strain when a movement behind one of the demons caught his eye.

It was...it was a human. A dude human, holding what looked like the mother of all crosses, a big shiny silver one with a pointed base. Before Stefan could shout out a warning that humans couldn't hurt demons, and definitely not ice demons, the man shrieked something in ancient Latin and plunged the cross into the back of the first primeval fiend Stefan had knocked silly.

A geyser of black goop shot skyward, making the nearest dancers shriek in a paroxysm of excitement and bloodlust. As the demon staggered forward, Stefan didn't take the time to argue. The man wrenched the cross-spike ice pick free and turned toward the second powerful demon, while Stefan banished the first one back beyond the veil, then drop-kicked the third as well. By the time he got to the second one, it'd turned on the man—some sort of priest? Exorcist?—and had leapt on him like an icicle of fury. The man shouted more Latin at his attacker, but it was a little harder to understand this time given the talons stuck in his neck. Stefan took advantage of the ice demon's distraction and yanked it free of his victim, then beat the crap out of it until there was little left other than black goop-filled ice cubes.

"Thanks," the man gasped from the floor, his face and body covered in black hoarfrost. Stefan reached for him, his touch instantly sealing up the man's wound. "Jim Granger."

"Nice spike."

"I try." Granger grinned as he stood, giving Stefan his first good look at him. The human was tall and sturdy without an ounce of fat, his heavily muscled upper body covered in a tan work shirt tucked into utilitarian-looking jeans. He wore thick brown work boots on his feet, which he stamped to shake off the black ice. His cloud-gray eyes danced as Stefan studied him, lighting up a weathered face framed by salt-and-pepper hair long enough to curl over his collar. "Started out as an exorcist in the Catholic church, but fell away about five years ago and decided to go freelance."

Stefan raised his brows. "Freelance?"

"Yup." Another grin. "Business has been booming."

"Why are you here? You're not a witch, and you're not a demon."

"I—I get dreams, I guess you'd say. Sort of a sixth sense. Gives me the heads-up on what's going down, in a manner of speaking. I find if I can end up at the right place at the right time, I can sometimes help out. I don't get paid for these improv hits, usually, but..." He shrugged. "It's good for advertising."

"I bet." Stefan looked around. The demons on the floor continued milling through the crowd, some of them breaking out in minor skirmishes, but now that he knew what to look for, he could see the net of power that was keeping them trapped. Keeping them trapped and dampening their strength enough they could feel it. They weren't going after any humans, though, so he didn't expect any more trouble from them. The humans, for their part, were back to dancing, clearly buying that all the "fake" black blood was yet another perk of their VIP witch party experience. Gotta love humans. "What'd your dreams say about the clusterfuck going on here today?"

"That's the weird part," the man said, looking credibly perplexed. "I didn't have a dream about this. I simply got a powerful urge to check the place out, so I left my hotel and came over."

"With a spiked cross?"

Granger grinned. "Never leave home without it. Anyway, once I showed up here, I realized I knew a lot of guys in the room. Hanging out the way I do on the fringes of the psychic community, you start to recognize faces. But you've got maybe twelve straight-up magicians in this room, guys you normally don't get within a hundred feet of each other without them strutting around like peacocks. But here, they're mostly getting drunk and thinking about getting laid, if their body language is any indication."

"Body language, huh?" Stefan asked, giving Granger the side-eye. "You sure that dreams are your only psychic ability? There're a lot of power spikes been going around."

Granger's face creased, a speculative gleam in his eye. "Funny you should mention that—"

He broke off as he suddenly jerked, swiveling around toward the front of the room. "What the hell?" he muttered, before lapsing into a low, melodic prayer, but Stefan could feel the spell of compulsion too. Jim Granger was getting dragged toward the collection of witches on the dais as if he were a wayward steer lassoed by a cowboy, and all the Latin lessons in the world weren't helping him.

A second later, Stefan felt a similar tug of energy, also yanking him toward the front of the room. A quick survey of the dance floor showed two other demons—definitely demons, and pretty damned strong ones at that, pun definitely intended—getting the same treatment. What the hell?

He was in no mood to play some witch's party game, however, and the immediate demon threat looked pretty well done for the night. The coven had obviously regained control of their pentagram. Plus, Gregori hadn't come back, and Stefan wasn't about to party without a wingman. He closed his eyes, poofed out of existence, and—

"*No.*"

Stefan sucked in a burst of frigid air, then tried to move —and couldn't. He was trapped in stasis in the formless gray space between Storm Court and his home base back on the Vegas Strip. He wasn't alone either. The ice-white figure of Michael the Archangel stood beside him, a speculative look on his face.

"Report," the archangel said. "Why is the witch child summoning multiple demons to mate with her? That's not what the grimoire demands."

"Doing *what*?" Stefan burst into laughter, cutting his surprised guffaw short when Michael didn't join in. Then again, Michael was kind of a dick when it came to having a good time. But seriously, God's No. 1 wingman needed his halo checked if he thought that was what was going on back in Storm Court. "You got everything wrong about the scene, Captain America," Stefan continued. "One, the witch is all grown up. Not a kid, not even by mortal standards. Second—"

"Hold," Michael interrupted, lifting a hand. Stefan felt the pressure of one of the Lord's most powerful archangels in a way Michael didn't usually impose. Clearly, he was upset. "She's reached her majority?"

"If you mean is she an adult, then yeah. I mean, she weighs maybe a hundred pounds soaking wet, but she's definitely hit puberty. I'm a demon, and we know these things."

That jab made Michael's lip curl in disdain, which made Stefan unaccountably happy.

"She's also not swiping right on anyone in the horde,"

Stefan continued. "She was afraid of a particular demon showing up, if her thoughts were any indication. Ahriman—like that dickhead is even real."

"The assault on the Serbian coven proved he is."

"Well, that attack was in his *name*, yeah. But he wasn't there, no matter how many of his minions had shown up to party. And for the record, we could've taken out the ravening horde *way* before they'd killed all those witches if you'd pulled us all in at once to fight them from the go. Those guys were seriously out of their heads."

"Three of you *should* have been sufficient."

"Well, we clearly *weren't*."

Michael stared at him stonily, and Stefan sighed. The archangel hated to be wrong, and, no matter who was to blame...too many witches had died. Nearly seventy-five of God's children, in all—adults, elders, and children too. Most of them massacred in cold blood before the Syx were even summoned.

Stefan curled his lip. *Pride.* It had been his downfall, all those millennia ago. It had been the witches' weakness here.

He shook off the hollow ache of his frustration, and refocused on Michael. "Anyway, Ahriman was definitely *not* boogying on the dance floor at Storm Court, though it was a virtual roll call of a goodly chunk of the demonic asshole pantheon. Gregori and I took care of the top guns, and there was a human guy who held his own with us—didn't suck at all, in point of fact. I don't suppose you sent him?"

"Name?"

"Jim Granger."

Something shifted in Michael's expression, a look of ineffable sorrow, gone as quickly as it appeared. "I didn't send him. But he came in with these others, you say? These demons?"

"He did. And if you want to give me the rest of the Syx, we can send all those bad boys home to Daddy right now. But one against fifty-seven isn't good odds, even for me."

"The other demons, how are they behaving? Normally? Attacking?"

Stefan made a face. "You really think I would've bailed if they were attacking, fifty-seven to one or not? No. They're chillin' and killin', playing along with the witch's protective net. She pulled a couple of 'em out of the crowd, along with Jimbo. She tried her little voodoo on me too, and that was my ticket to ride."

"So the queen of the Scepter Coven is calling a demon to mate with her," Michael said again, his voice low and filled with quiet wonder. "Multiple demons, it would appear. She believes she is ready to confront Ahriman."

Stefan shook his head. "Duce, Ahriman doesn't exist. Maybe you aren't up on your horde trivia, but he's like Santa Claus for demon kind. A story to keep newb demons in line." Even as he spoke, though, Stefan hesitated. There were those old-ass ice demons who'd appeared on the dance floor, creatures so ancient, he didn't know their names. Their energy harkened back to the time before light itself, when God stirred the primeval magic of the universe to form His earliest creations, twisting and weaving and improving upon His spectacular designs.

Rumor held that it was from that same energy that Ahriman was formed, a creature of such unending evil that God Himself chose to let the darkness made flesh remain extant rather than crush his life essence, to remind Him of the lengths to which He could not go again.

But fairy tale or not, Michael had the Storm Court sitch all wrong. "And again, the witch isn't looking for a demon hookup. That's not how she rolls. Believe me, I'd have picked up on that. So unless you want to give me reinforcements, there's no reason for me to stick around there."

"No," Michael said, his words absolute. "The high priestess has begun fulfilling the ancient requirements to confront Ahriman. She believes he has struck the Serbian witches, and since she leads the Scepter Coven, it's her right and obligation to defeat Ahriman. To do that, however, she must wed a demon. So you need to go to her and pledge your service."

"I *what*? You're in—whoa, whoa, whoa, check it." Stefan took an involuntary step back as he stared at Michael. The archangel's face had gone completely blank, his eyes rolling up until all that was visible was their whites. He was communing with something, Stefan thought, and Stefan didn't want to know what it was.

"She is choosing her consorts, who must...must be... hmm." Michael's voice sounded hollow and timeless. "Two demons, she chooses. A human. A witch. She searches for a third member of the horde. You. But she's not finding you."

"Because I left," Stefan put in helpfully.

"You cannot. You must return to serve as her consort."

"Her *what*?"

"It is your path," Michael intoned, and a moment later, he was back to his usual irritating self. He stared at Stefan implacably. "She is your redemption, Nur-ayya Dadanum."

Stefan stiffened. No one had called him by that name— no one—in more than six thousand years. For Michael to be pulling it out here and attaching the word redemption to it meant he was not messing around.

Michael kept going too. "Accept, and you will be forgiven of your sin, placing you and the Syx one step closer toward your freedom. Reject this path, and none of you will be redeemed."

Stefan blew out a long breath, his shoulders slumping. "Well, when you put it like that—"

A second later, he was back on the dance floor at Storm Court, caught in the witch queer's spell.

3

"He's a Syx," Dahlia hissed.

"I know what he is," Cressida snapped back, her hands low and outstretched at her waist, drawing the demons closer. Not even Dahlia understood the full nature of Cressida's, Marcus's, and Fraya's revised plan, but a Syx would fit in with it perfectly. Cressida would have preferred the first one she'd seen—big, gorgeous, and glowering, the kind of guy who looked like he could squash his enemies like a bug. But he hadn't returned after he'd disappeared the first time, while the second Syx had.

She turned her attention to the Syx, who remained caught in her thrall no matter how impressive he clearly thought he was. Tall—though most demons were tall in their glamour—he topped out at around six foot four, and he was sleekly built, unlike the other Syx he fought with. He had a shock of jet-black hair that contrasted with his cool, fair skin, and his eyes were so dark, they were nearly black, revealing the faintest flare of fiery red glowing whenever he focused. His face was hauntingly beautiful too, with sculpted, high cheekbones, a strong jaw, and that defiant, smirking mouth...

Stop thinking about his mouth.

Cressida refocused on the demon's less intimate details. Definitely strong, even powerful, his body was remarkably compact compared to his fellow enforcer's giantlike build. The kind of guy who would bend long before he broke. The kind of guy that any intelligent woman would want in her bed.

Not helping.

Cressida frowned, disloyalty tugging at her. She shouldn't be thinking about bedding anyone other than Marcus, she knew. He was her promised mate and the witch who would help her defeat Ahriman once and for all.

Only—oh, that's right: Marcus had rejected her. Rejected! When he knew full well that Cressida's powers would never fully blossom while she remained a virgin—yet another ridiculous dictate of the sacred grimoire, but one that had been proven again and again.

No one knew the truth, of course—and no one could know. Cressida's position as high priestess was tenuous enough. Fraya had made it clear that any hint at all of Marcus's "hesitation," as she'd called it, would reflect poorly on Cressida, no matter how strong she already was. Witches liked their traditions, none more so than the Scepter Coven. And after everything Fraya had done for Cressida—rescuing her from destitution after the death of her parents, raising her within the coven, teaching her the sacred arts, and finally sponsoring her unstintingly when it came time for her to be consecrated as a full witch—Cressida couldn't ... *wouldn't* let her down.

Besides, it had been a foregone conclusion that she would have consummated her relationship with Marcus the same day she'd risen to her new role of high priestess—but he'd denied her. That day and every day after, up until this morning. He still planned to rule by her side, he assured her, still planned to help her defeat Ahriman, still planned to wed her in accordance with the sacred grimoire—to stand first as part of this trumped-up retinue and then as her sole consort. But...their relationship stopped there.

Which left Cressida stuck between a witch and a hard place.

And staring at a demon so overtly sexual that it made her toes curl.

Cressida watched Stefan as he strolled forward. Unlike the other demons, he seemed to know he was being compelled, but he was covering it well. His smile was easy, almost amused, and his body was loose, his saunter both cocky and relaxed. She got the feeling that cocky and relaxed was the Syx's general state. It'd be easy to convince the coven he was the right demon for the job—as a Syx, his power was undisputed, and he wore his sensuality like a second skin. No one would question that choice, except for perhaps Marcus, and he didn't get a vote.

As for the other consorts...

She turned her attention to the two demons, who were already sniffing at each other with curiosity, clearly sensing the compulsion on the others but not themselves. As the Syx approached them, they turned and bared their teeth.

"Relax, brothers," the Syx announced, *sotto voce*. "None of us are going to get eaten tonight." He slowly and deliberately shifted his gaze until he met hers. "Not unless we're very, very lucky, anyway."

Cressida's eyes flared wide at the obvious inference. Did he somehow know what was going on here? That couldn't be possible. Her summons to the demons had been beyond generic, and there was nothing in her compulsion spell that even hinted at her plan. Nevertheless, the Syx's grin only deepened as he stepped past the confused demons and collared the human ex-priest. Dahlia had been responsible for that choice, but Cressida didn't mind. The human was the least of her troubles. He was perhaps forty years old, but clearly a magician of significant strength, and that was the only necessary requirement. Once again, despite their honorary role as her consorts, she *wasn't* going to have sex with any member of her retinue. She merely needed to tap their strength—in a decidedly nonsexual way. Marcus would be the only consort to share her bed.

Or at least, that'd been the plan.

Cressida glanced to where the strongest male witch of the Scepter Coven stood on the dais, well back from the trio of Elysium, Dahlia, and Cressida. His power was contributing to the strength of the coven's pentagram, but it was time to remove the other demons from their midst. She waited to catch his eye, to nod that they could let the other demons go—but he wouldn't look at her. Instead, he stared at the two demons he'd selected from the throng, pride and domination rolling off him like a thick tide.

Cressida frowned. Why was he so proud?

"These are your choices?" Elysium Gray demanded, and once more, Cressida refocused. Three demons, a human frozen in wonder, and her fated coruler. It was exactly what she needed, but that didn't make her feel any better. She wanted this business over with.

"They're my preliminary choices," she hedged. "Should they fail in their duties, I will seek others."

"As you say, we don't have that kind of time," Elysium countered. "We must prepare for Ahriman with all haste. If you cannot best the ancient demon with the consorts you've chosen, we should choose others. As soon as the ritual is complete, he'll come to us. We need to be prepared."

"We will be prepared," Cressida said. "I've studied the requirements more closely than you have. I know what's expected of me, and when. We can begin this night, but not until we clear this hall."

"Agreed." Dahlia's voice was clear and strong beside her, and Cressida sensed her captain was also tracking Marcus's reactions across the dais. "We need to focus on clearing the hall."

"No." To Cressida's surprise, it was Marcus who spoke. He stepped forward, one hand extended to indicate he was keeping his focus on the pentagram restraining the demons. "Elder Gray is right. You must ensure your selections are to your satisfaction without delay, High Priestess Cressida. We may not have an opportunity this clear again, and if the demons talk..."

Elysium blew out a harsh breath. "If the demons talk, then there's no question Ahriman will know what we intend."

"There's no question of that regardless," Cressida snapped. "Do you really think he's not aware the Scepter Coven is rising to take him on?"

No one responded to that for a long moment, and then a totally different voice rang out, carrying easily above the pounding music.

"Not to interrupt your powwow, princess, but your little pentagram of doom is starting to lose some of its mojo. Whatever it is you think you need to do, you'd best go ahead and do it before the horde starts the mother of all food fights."

It was the Syx who spoke, of course, and Dahlia muttered something derisive beneath her breath as Cressida's glare switched to him, then sheared away just as quickly. The Syx was watching her with open curiosity in his gaze, and, if anything, the intensity of his sexual interest was increasing, not decreasing. Probably not surprising given her spell of compulsion, but—

"Do it," Dahlia said, her voice holding a warning tone for the first time. Cressida could hear the concern beneath her sharp words. Dahlia also didn't know if the pentagram would hold. They'd never attempted to restrain so many demons in such a small space before, certainly not for any period of time.

In the end, it was Dahlia's concern, not Marcus's, that made Cressida move. Stepping forward to the pair of demons who stood to the left of the human, she forced herself to lock eyes with the first one Marcus had selected. This was a heavy, swarthy creature with a prominent jaw and dark, angry eyes. And his magic was undeniably strong.

Cressida hesitated. He was *very* strong, actually. Too much so? Could she take him as a witch not fully ascended to her own powers?

She could, she decided. She must.

"I'm Cressida Frain of the Scepter Coven, first among all witches," she said. "You will be my consort. Tell me your name."

At first, the demon stared at her, clearly taken aback, whether by her words or by the compulsion those words carried with them, Cressida didn't know. It didn't take long for the creature to jump to his own conclusions, though. He grinned at her with pure carnal delight, his heavy lips stretching wide to bare surprisingly white teeth. Then again, Cressida knew she shouldn't be surprised. She and Marcus had crafted the compulsion spell quite deliberately to ensure that she wasn't paired with any of the more repugnant members of the horde. A demon's glamour was his own construct, and the more attractive the glamour, generally speaking, the more civilized the demon. Sexual partners or not, there would be no ugly demons in the high priestess's retinue.

"I am called Boltar," this one announced in gravelly tones. "I am the strongest demon on this floor."

The snort that sounded far to the left of Boltar, on the other side of the human, was by now so familiar to Cressida that she didn't need to turn her head. She merely nodded to Boltar. He was certainly strong. He also reeked of less pure evil than she would've expected for someone who simmered with such obvious power. She wondered if she would need to learn his story before one of the other demons destroyed him. She hoped not. She didn't have time for any more drama than that which Ahriman would provide.

The next demon was more what she'd expected to catch in her net. Thickheaded, thick necked, and squat, this creature exuded far more malevolence than Boltar—and he was equally strong. Once more, dismay curled through her. What was Marcus thinking, choosing demons of such power? He more than most knew Cressida harbored deep doubts about her abilities. Was he trying to test her?

Before she could open her mouth to speak the ancient words, the demon's lips quirked into a harsh, cruel sneer. "You pull me into your machinations at your own risk, *priestess*," he rumbled. "When I fill you with my seed, you'll learn the error of your ways."

Cressida's patience snapped. "You won't *touch* me, demon. That isn't your purpose here." She lifted a hand crackling with power, the sight of which merely caused the demon to hoot softly with pleasure.

"Oh, I don't think so. You'll scream my name, I promise you. It is Zeneschiah."

"She is *not* going to be screaming your name," commented the Syx from the end the line. "I am totally out if I have to hear that ridiculous word even one time more than necessary."

The smug derision of the Syx managed to accomplish what Cressida couldn't on her own, breaking the momentary surge of energy from Zeneschiah that seemed to reach out and throttle her. She knew she didn't have to worry long-term about any of the demons attacking her. When the ritual was completed and all five of her chosen were verified as consorts, they'd lose much of their free will to oppose her. But then again, Zeneschiah wasn't actually opposing her, which was a little more concerning. Despite all the research she'd done on the horde, coming face-to-face with their depravity was more alarming than she'd anticipated.

The next of the chosen was the human, who was already showing the wear of the continued hold on his soul. He was a Connected of some power, a sensitive, and she didn't miss the spiked Christian cross he held in his grip. Why had Dahlia chosen him? It didn't matter; he was the least of her concerns. "Tell me your name, mage."

"Jim Granger," the man said, his voice low and resonant, the voice of a man of experience, even understanding. She sharpened her gaze on him, but he looked back with blank eyes. He wasn't trying to break her hold on him. He wasn't trying to understand it or fight against it. He was bending to its sway, which was exactly his strongest move if he wanted to preserve his energy. She frowned. Maybe she would have to worry about him after all.

"You will be my consort, Jim Granger," she said. "Do you understand?"

He quirked a smile. "Not even remotely. I look forward to being educated."

That earned another snort from the Syx, but Cressida didn't need to confirm him as her choice. The two demons and the human were the question marks. She only needed the Syx to dispatch the other demons at his earliest opportunity. She didn't think it would take much, particularly with Zeneschiah.

When she would have turned away, however, the Syx had the gall to clear his throat. "Your lapdog back there wants the full show, princess," he murmured beneath his breath. "Probably a good idea to give it to him."

It was only then that Cressida became aware of Marcus's stare. He was focused on her with almost laser-like intensity, though there was no trace of compulsion in his gaze. He wasn't strong enough to compel her. Still, she longed to glance his way, to understand what he so desperately wanted her to do, but she was the high priestess of this coven now. She couldn't afford to look weak, especially when so many of her fold were working hard to keep the veil steady, restraining the demons within the confines of the pentagram.

"You may as well get it over with," the Syx taunted softly. "What'd you say your name was? I didn't quite catch it with all of Hellboy's heavy breathing."

Cressida's gaze snapped sharply to meet that of the Syx's, and once again, she fought the urge to step back. Not because the Syx was leering at her, though. The quality of his stare was different—far more powerful, far more dangerous.

"I am Cressida Frain," she said slowly and distinctly. "High Priestess of the Scepter Coven, first among witches. You are my consort. Tell me your name."

"My name is—"

For a moment, all the magic in Storm Court froze, and the world fell away. There was no Marcus or Dahlia or Elysium with her on the dais. There were no dancers writhing on the floor or demons panting for their energy. There was only Cressida and the Syx, and an aching maw of pain that seemed to open up and threaten to swallow her whole. The Syx maintained his glamour, looking as dark and dangerous as ever, but the word that came out of his mouth was no word at all. Instead, it was a howling wind that blew up between them, so bleak and desolate that it sounded as if it contained the wail of a hundred thousand souls, each trapped in their own personal, ice-bound hell. The sound of it was agony to listen to and stopped the breath in Cressida's throat, the blood in her veins. Her bone's very marrow turned to crystal as she stared at the beautiful Syx, his eyes holding hers in a fierce, unholy challenge.

Then his grin stretched farther, and the spell was broken. The dais was back, Marcus and Dahlia and Elysium holding firm, as if nothing had happened in the intervening seconds.

"But it'll probably be easier for you to call me Stefan," the mighty demon of the Syx said. "Since we're being so neighborly and all."

4

S tefan felt the power of the Scepter witches close around him, and it took every ounce of his training to let it happen. He kept one eye on the two demon thugs that Cressida had inexplicably included in her cohort of consorts, and the other on the human, Jim Granger, who seemed particularly amused to be along for the ride. Normally, it took humans far longer to obtain that kind of perspective, if they obtained it during their lifetimes at all. He would need to rifle Jim Granger's thoughts to understand exactly what this man had seen in his thirty-odd years on this earth to allow him to transcend the here and now so easily, detaching from what was right in front of him.

It would no doubt be interesting research.

For the moment, however, Stefan had other issues. He kept working until he could finally feel his body relax enough to slump forward, faking the twilight sleep that was the closest he was ever going to get to being fully knocked out in this world, at least by a force other than simple exhaustion. Demons didn't sleep like normal humans did, because they weren't normal humans. Their bodies didn't run down or give out; they simply stopped—until they started again. It took very little time for a demon to recover from most damage inflicted upon its corporeal form, and its glamour could maintain the effect of perfect health through all but the worst attacks.

It was the glamour that Stefan manipulated, allowing himself to appear to sink into a nearly somnambulant state, which was what he assumed the witches were after. The other demons succumbed much more quickly, but there was more to being a Syx than simply having the stones to knock out other demons. He wasn't so sure he wanted the witches of the Scepter Coven to understand the finer points of his transformation into one of God's most dangerous hired guns. He'd never had much truck with witches, and he saw no point to trust them now.

The moment he shut down, however, the witch's pentagram blew a fuse.

He saw it happen as if in slow motion, the wave of energy that flowed through the room an almost palpable wave. First the minihorde of demons still assembled on the dance floor of Storm Court remained static, almost confused, and then they jerked into action, their energy moving quickly into full and aggressive force.

"*No.*" He heard Cressida's shout—not a screech, not a panicked yelp, but an aggressive denial of what was happening in front of her face—but he couldn't react at first. He could feel the force of multiple witches striving to keep him in check, and Michael's orders had been clear. He was to obey this little wisp of a witch and bow to her every wish until he was faced with Ahriman. Then the gloves could come off again.

Nevertheless, he'd spent the past six thousand years protecting humans from demons, and it was maddening to watch the worst of his kind take chunks of flesh out of God's children, biting and tearing and—

"Stop them." Cressida was suddenly in front of him, her voice clear where everything else was muted. She obviously was the primary witch subduing him, which surprised him. He'd thought the male witch on the dais would've done the honors, with all the big swinging-dick energy he was exuding.

He focused on Cressida. "Stop them, how?"

"However you can," she said. "I waited too long. The spell is breaking, and I don't want the mortals hurt. They believe they're initiates with a chance to learn the sacred arts, but they're not. They're merely bait."

Stefan scowled at her. "That's not cool."

"I know—I know. We were desperate, though. We had to draw in demons without them suspecting why." Another cry sounded deeper within the throng of dancers, and she paled. "Please, go. As—as a favor to me."

Stefan's brows shot up. A favor was something entirely different from a compulsion. A far more interesting something. "I can do that."

He swung around, the spell of submission falling off him like boxers on the bedroom floor, and instantly identified the problem. A gang of demons had crowded around one corner of the pentagram, all but blocking out the hurricane candle that served as the symbol of the ward the witches had created. They couldn't stamp the light out, but there were so many of them—far more than would typically be called forth for a spell like this—that they were blunting it enough for an unexpected pivot: while typically demons would be eager to depart the witches' pentagram, in this case, more demons rushed in. That continued to overload the spell, wearying the Scepter Coven witches and breaking their hold.

But the demons didn't know much more than that they were crashing a party. They certainly didn't know a Syx had been invited too. And where there was one...

He weighed his options. Michael would be pissed, potentially. But Michael had stuck him in the middle of this mess without any information. And the moment this trouble was past, he was going back into the witch-run Zombieland, cut off from his brothers. That wasn't cool either.

"Knock 'em flat. The humans. Can you do that?" he asked Cressida.

She stared at him, obviously perplexed. "Why?"

"Because I need the place cleared from about three feet up. If you can do it, tell me. If you can't, stop being such a sissy about it."

His taunt had the desired effect. With a twist of her lips, she slapped her left hand to her right wrist. Instantly, all across the room, the nearly seventy-five mortal initiates dropped, boneless, as if their legs had been knocked out from under them. Before the first head connected with the first puddle of spilled vodka, Stefan moved.

The witches had chosen fire as the grounding points of the pentagram—normally, they would use salt or blood or a spelled rock or something. But fire, Stefan knew well, was a far more flexible tool when it came to demons. Fire was the symbol of the one place in the universe they least wanted to be, and for a Syx, it was a tool of inestimable proportions.

He lifted his hands, and all five points of the pentagram exploded upward and joined together, making a molten dome that caught the demons in place. They jolted, staring upward, their faces transfixed in fear. Stefan knew he would have only a moment to act, but a moment was all that was needed.

He summoned the Syx.

In another instant, the world snapped tight, and five other figures burst into the room. Warrick, the leader of the demon enforcers, barely gave Stefan a grin before he and Gregori shoved their shoulders into the nearest demons, sending them flying in an explosion of black blood. Finn, the youngest of the Syx and newly redeemed, showed no sign of the incredible trials he'd endured a scant three weeks earlier, but instead rushed forward with a gleam in his eye and, apparently, a song in his heart as he singlehandedly took down another knot of demons. Raum and Hugh, the last of the Syx, saluted Stefan briefly before they too raced forward, roaring with bloodlust. It wasn't often anymore that the entire team of the Syx could fight at once, and it was a good feeling.

It was more than a good feeling.

Even as he continued to fell his own demons, Stefan watched with interest the progress of his fellow Syx. There was a difference in them, without question. Warrick and Finn fought with less intensity but greater effect, as if they'd unlocked some mystery of their opponents that had been withheld from the others. Was this why the archangel had been so reluctant to let them fight together? Was their obvious shift in abilities important?

He fought his way over to Warrick, who was plowing through demons like he was pulling weeds out of a row of green beans.

"They're summoning Ahriman," Stefan shouted when he got close. "They're going to attack him. Think it's their right."

"They've been misinformed." The leader of the Syx

glanced over, dropping his voice as Stefan neared. "Ahriman wasn't even in Serbia. The horde got it wrong."

"They don't seem to care. There's some old-ass grimoire they're quoting about how to take him down, and according to Michael, I'm supposed to help."

Warrick scowled. "I know the Scepter Coven grimoire."

"Figured you would. So tell me how to fix this."

"Well, it's been a while...but if I recall correctly..." His eyebrows suddenly shot up. "Wait a minute. You've got to marry a *witch*?"

As he howled with sudden laughter, Warrick caught another demon by the throat and hurled him to the ground. The demon's snarl of surprise turned into a cry of terror as he exploded in a geyser of black spray, then disappeared completely to the other side of the veil.

"Try to focus," Stefan pressed. "There's got to be a reason they need a demon. Because based on the assholes she chose as candidates besides me, any demon will do. So it's not about me being a Syx. What can a witch and a demon do together that they can't do apart?"

Warrick's grin only deepened. "Besides make little demon-witch babies?" He lifted his hands as Stefan tossed a demon at him, punching the creature beyond the veil. "I don't know, honestly. But you're right, there has to be a reason the grimoire demands a demon. But I can't think it will be a reason you'll much enjoy, if there are witches involved."

"Agreed. Witches are a pain in the barbed tail." Stefan turned, then turned again, taking in the carnage. The demons were all but ended, and Raum and Hugh were making their last rounds, knocking down the ones who struggled upright like whack-a-moles. As always, the fight was over too soon. "Thanks for coming, man."

"Felt good to work together," Warrick said, clapping him on the shoulder and grinning. "Now you'll have to name your firstborn after me."

And then, as quickly as they'd arrived, the Syx vanished.

Stefan straightened, looking around the room. There was a hiss and a crackle, then the music came up again, and with it the dancers—except now a good third of them were covered with goop. But as he braced for the inevitable screaming, Cressida strode forward, her red hair practically on fire beneath the bright lights, her silver cuffs gleaming.

"You have passed the test and survived the trial!" she announced, her arms arcing wide. "Celebrate as initiates of the Scepter Coven!"

The music pounded even louder then, and a cheer went up, those dancers covered in the thick dark liquid looking like they'd suddenly died and gone to heaven, though they literally had no idea what that meant. Stefan watched them, stupefied. As part of his payment for his sin, he couldn't remember what heaven looked like, but he was pretty sure it wasn't filled with people stained with demon blood.

Cressida turned back to him, her jaw set. "Thank you. The pentagram was fully broken as the attack continued, and there would've been far worse casualties than a few ruined bandage dresses without the help of your team."

"No problem, princess." Stefan grinned, then staggered forward as the now-familiar wave of magic hit him once again. This time, it didn't come from Cressida but from behind him, on the dais. He watched her eyes narrow as she took in whoever it was who'd delivered the blow, but it didn't take a genius to figure it out.

"Who *is* that dickhead?" Stefan gasped, and Cressida's mouth tightened.

"My prime consort. Marcus Frost."

"Consort." Stefan breathed through his nose. Whatever Marcus was leveling at him, the witch was definitely frosty. "You seem to be racking up quite a few of those."

"I figure among all of you, I should find at least one who can get the job done."

Stefan managed a laugh beneath the surge of power being leveled at him. "I guess that depends on what your definition of the job is."

"Cressida."

Stefan swiveled as another young witch approached, the pretty blonde from the dais. He hadn't caught her name yet, but she seemed to know Cressida well. "The others are below. We need to move before the club's management investigates all the screaming."

"Agreed." Cressida nodded, though in Stefan's book, the screaming hadn't sounded all that different from the music currently thudding through the sound system. He didn't complain as she reached out and took his arm, though he also didn't miss the intensity of the pressure on him increasing.

"So this Marcus guy. If he's your consort already, why the nonsense with the rest of us? What do the rest of us have that he doesn't? Besides balls?"

"Stop it. He can hear you," Cressida said beneath her breath, but Stefan didn't need her to point that out. The intensity of the compulsion spell jacked to a higher level, well past the point of pain.

"He better not be pulling this shit on the exorcist. I don't give a damn about the demons, but he dicks with one of God's children and he's done."

She gave him a sidelong glance. So did the blonde. "Marcus is one of God's children as well," she observed. She wasn't wrong, of course. Technically. The witches of Earth had chosen a path at the dawn of history that dog-legged a hard left from Judeo-Christian religious belief, positing the Creative force of the universe was equally shared between a male and female deity.

Their magic derived from the energy of the elements and all living things, but it was their faith that took them beyond ordinary Connected humans. They believed in and honored the sanctity of their spiritual path as incontrovertible truth, and that gave them a unique strength among mortals...as well as the power to command demons. Some witches were born, but most were made, brought up through a ritualized training or converted after highly emotional events not dissimilar to the Storm Court rave he'd just witnessed.

Another stab of pain sliced across Stefan's brain, and he winced, trying to shake it away. No question about it, Marcus was an ace spell caster and an even more impressive asswipe. And he'd better not be doing any of this to Granger.

Stefan glared at the tall, slender witch. His hair was as white as snow, his eyes an ice blue, his mouth pulled tight in a sneer. He was attractive enough, Stefan supposed. For a dickhead. But the witch was seriously getting on his nerves. "You know, we've had plenty of opportunity to come up with special treatment for those of God's children who need a time out," he muttered.

"Shh," Cressida said, and Stefan felt an overlay of her power on top of Marcus's. With the weight of both witches on him, he felt like he was being smothered under a lead blanket. Good to know that while one powerful witch was an irritant, two were damned near debilitating. He didn't know what three would do to him, and he was pretty sure he didn't want to find out.

With very little choice otherwise, he allowed Cressida to escort him off the dance floor of Storm Court, back past the bars and into a short hallway that led to an elevator bay. The other witches followed behind them, including, he presumed, Marcus. The male witch's pressure didn't let up even after they exited the dance floor, but Stefan breathed through it. Better to get used to the oppressive weight and adapt than to be caught by surprise later, when it mattered.

The doors to the elevator opened, but to his surprise, there wasn't an elevator on the other side but another corridor, this one lit with a strange green hue.

"Security," Cressida said beside him.

He nodded, figuring as much, but security against what? None of the witches lit up, and he was the only nonwitch in his small group. As far as he could see, he also didn't trigger the security measures, but with Marcus's pressure bearing down on him, it was difficult to tell.

The doors shut abruptly behind him, cutting off the rest of the witch's group, and Cressida turned quickly. Stefan stumbled forward with the release from Marcus's hold, his brain instantly clearing.

"There isn't much time," she said. "It's a thirty-second break before the others come through. You can't break Marcus's hold on you. You'll need to be more careful with him."

"I don't need to break his hold," Stefan retorted honestly. "No matter what he thinks, he's not that strong. I simply need to make sure he's the only one on me. That means you, princess."

"Not only me. Dahlia and Elysium—"

"Aren't as strong as you are. Unless they're working together, and believe me, I'm not going to give them any reason to do so. So you lay off me, and we'll be good. Deal?"

She pursed her lips, then nodded. "Deal."

"And another thing," he said as her gaze jumped to the far doors. "You owe me big-time for the favor you asked of me."

She jolted. "We have no *time* for that."

"Yeah, we kind of do." Stefan breathed out, stopping time for a precious moment. Then he leaned forward and captured the witch's lips with his.

Oh. He felt more than heard Cressida's startled reaction, right along with the spike in her blood pressure, the swell of heat blooming in her core, the thudding of her heart, the shock and wonder and outright amazement at something as simple as a kiss. If he didn't know better, he'd have thought the human had never been kissed before, never been desired, never been touched—

But surely that was crazy.

Stefan pulled away as quickly as he'd leaned in, leaving Cressida staring at him in utter shock and confusion as time rebooted and the doors opened behind him. Cressida whirled around, dazed, while Marcus's choke hold on him returned with a vengeance, taking Stefan from pleasantly jacked up to flat-out pissed. Just how badly did he need this job?

Badly enough.

He gritted his teeth and kept moving.

5

"How are you feeling, child?" Lawgiver Fraya murmured beside Cressida, before hurriedly correcting herself with a soft, self-deprecating sigh. "Though not a child anymore. Far from it. Forgive me."

Cressida slid her mentor a warm glance. They stood together in Cressida's apartment, waiting for the other lawgivers, and Cressida cherished these moments with her mentor more and more—particularly as they grew less frequent, given Cressida's new role as high priestess.

"There's neither forgiveness needed nor formalities between us, lawgiver. You know that." Even Cressida's use of her mentor's official title had always been a misdirect. Fraya had been the only mother Cressida had truly known, though the older woman had always been careful to impress upon Cressida that her own mother had loved her very, very much before she'd died. However, from the first moments that Cressida had found herself welcomed into the coven, Fraya had instructed her to always address her mentor as "lawgiver," to ensure the coven understood Fraya's role was simply as Cressida's sponsor—nothing more.

Though of course, Fraya had been so much more to Cressida. She'd been Cressida's sole supporter, her root and her tree, helping to both ground Cressida and to allow her to stretch to her highest potential until—finally—she'd reached the pinnacle position of high priestess. Fraya had assured Cressida she was ready for the position, but Cressida privately had her doubts.

Doubts she wasn't about to betray to Fraya, of course. The lawgiver had done everything she could to prepare Cressida to take on Ahriman and lead the coven. There was no way Cressida would let her down.

That said, Fraya was never one to sugarcoat the truth.

"You should know, your choices are already coming under fire," her mentor murmured, reminding Cressida of the value of not sharing her fears with Fraya—or anyone except Dahlia. There were more than enough people willing to voice their misgivings about Cressida's new role.

"Then they should be pleased I'm following the dictates of the ancient grimoire to destroy our ancient foe." Cressida returned her gaze to the large screens lining one of the walls of the tastefully decorated sitting room of her New York City apartment. There were two dozen screens here showing various positions around the witch compound, a vast network of rooms beneath some of the city's most prized real estate. While not entirely soundproofed from the rush and rumble of the subway trains that ran nearly constantly around them, it remained the safest, most secure holding pen for untested threats. That was part of the reason the entire coven had assembled here rather than in their usual location in upstate New York.

The other part of the reason had to do with the city itself. New York City was a cauldron of ancient magic, but not because it, in and of itself, was particularly magical. The land had simply been the land hundreds of years ago when travelers sought opportunities and safety in the New World. But many of those travelers had been witches, psychics, and adherents to the occult. Some had been outlaws, some refugees, but all of them converged on the city in a great tide of magical strength. The city, in turn, had adapted.

There were many magical places in the world, but New York was one of the few that could absorb an influx of magic with no more than the lift of one aristocratically arched eyebrow. The old-world cities in Europe could as well, but they were across the ocean, not a short train ride away. For what the Scepter Coven needed, New York City was perfect.

What was not perfect was having her very first decision as high priestess of the coven second-guessed. She only had a few minutes before the others arrived, so she pressed Fraya for more information. "Have they shared specific concerns?"

Fraya thinned her lips, clearly uncomfortable, as if betraying a secret. But, as Cressida suspected she had since Cressida was a young child, the lawgiver decided in favor of her charge above all else. "There are those who feel that Marcus could overcome you in a fight," she said. "That he has grown too strong."

Cressida blinked. This, she hadn't expected. "But Marcus is my ally. There'd be no reason for us to fight." True enough, Marcus was uniquely powerful among the male witches of the coven, and he'd grown only stronger since a wave of rogue magic had swept across the world several weeks earlier. That wave had also let loose a horde of demons who were even now marshaling their forces, demons who had swelled the ranks of the beasts who had attacked the witches of the Serbian coven.

Which meant the attack Cressida was preparing against

Ahriman couldn't be better timed. Too many demons had been set free upon the earth, too quickly. The balance of power between witch and demon had decidedly changed.

But that ripple of magic had not been an entirely unhelpful turn of events for the witches of the world. With so much raw magic to work with, accomplished witches like Marcus had found themselves with new and better tools at their disposal. Given his dedication to the dark arts, he had quickly ramped up his own abilities to wield those tools. It was the sort of initiative Cressida appreciated in a man. And, unlike the other witches of her coven, she didn't fear it. She welcomed it.

That said, she couldn't discount the concerns of the coven out of hand. While the Scepter Coven historically had been run by women, there was no dictate that this must always remain the case. Male witches of sufficient strength could take over the coven. Marcus would be the most likely candidate to do so—though he'd never given any indication that he wanted that. Despite not wanting her physically, he appeared to want them to rule together, not apart.

And she was stronger than him, still...wasn't she?

Either way, she sensed the worry rolling off her beloved mentor, and her first and fiercest thought was to put the older woman at ease.

"There'll be an accounting of the consorts I've chosen," she said. "Marcus has given no one any reason to doubt his loyalty to the coven and to the ancient dictates of the grimoire. You know that as well as I do."

"I do," Fraya said staunchly. "But I didn't wrap you in the mantle of priestess so he could wrest it from you."

"Of course you didn't," Cressida agreed, startled by Fraya's show of loyalty. Marcus was the lawgiver's protégé as well...her preferred protégé, Cressida had often thought. To feel Fraya's unequivocal support straightened Cressida's spine as a knock sounded at the door to her apartment.

She turned as the other members of the coven's ruling council filed into the room—a half-dozen elders and lawgivers, all female, all passionately dedicated to the coven. Like her, they all also owned high-ticket apartments in New York's West Side. The apartments had been coven property since the 1800s, managed by families who'd been loyal to the witches since they'd first lived together in the old world. It gave a whole new meaning to rent control.

Now the coven leadership gathered in the airy salon of Cressida's apartment, their eyes on the multiple screens that extended down from the ceiling, covering the seventeenth-century artwork. Watching them, Cressida drew in a deep breath. It was time for her to reveal at least part of her plan, since it had been set in motion.

Whenever a marriage was arranged for the good of the coven, the consort—or consorts, in her case—needed to be approved by the coven leadership. Later, there would be the grand ball where her consorts were presented to the coven as a whole, but this far more intimate look was on a need-to-know basis only. And she would give them a full accounting.

"We are here to present my consorts for your review, but before we do, there is something you must know." She met the impassive gazes of the lawgivers and the elders, including Elysium Gray, the most recent high priestess. Cressida had no doubt Elysium was one of the witches sowing concerns about Cressida's fitness to rule, despite the fact that Elysium had acknowledged her own inability to adequately take on Ahriman. "There is much that the sacred grimoire assumes, but little that it mandates. I will pass the sacred cup with the five members of my retinue, and we will be joined in power, such that I may draw on their strength to defeat Ahriman. But none—*none* of my consorts will share my bed. You need to know that, even if no one else does."

An audible rustle moved through the women surrounding Cressida—some sighing with relief, some dismay. To her surprise, Fraya spoke first.

"Then it's good that you've consummated your relationship already with Marcus."

Cressida blanched. Fraya knew very well she hadn't done any such thing. She'd been the one to comfort Cressida after Marcus's first rejection. "Well, I—"

"You have. You don't need to be shy," Fraya said, her measured tones drowning out Cressida's reply. "The witch who confronts Ahriman must be fully prepared. You are. These others"—she gestured airily to the screens—"are necessary only for you to draw upon their strength."

More murmurs from the older women, and even Elysium nodded. "That makes...much more sense," Elysium said. "No one would wish you to be forced to lie with a demon, no matter what the ancient grimoire assumed."

"Then we are—" But before Fraya could finish her pronouncement, Cressida held up her hand. The lawgiver fell obediently silent, though Cressida couldn't understand her flat, wary expression. Why did Fraya want her to lie?

Regardless of the reason, she clearly did. And so...Cressida would lie. It was as simple as that.

"The matter is settled, then," Cressida said. "When you view these consorts, don't consider them as anything more than power sources, and focus on what spells we should construct to direct that power."

She turned to the screens. "Boltar," she murmured, and the voice-activated console flashed and whirred, the first screen filling with the image of Boltar's immense form sitting at the table of platters and goblets demolished of food and drained of drink. Even sedated, the demon maintained his glamour, as all demons did in the presence of humans unless they were under extreme duress. Not that demons didn't enjoy scaring the pants off humans, but a human sufficiently frightened by the sight of a demon was extremely likely to summon a Syx. No demon wanted that.

Certainly not this one. Boltar's large, bulbous, but very human-looking head was flung back, his mouth open in a snore, his heavy arms hanging at his sides.

"Remove the filter," Cressida said without preamble, following that order with the murmured invocation of the spell of revealing. Some things were better handled quickly. From the gasp of her sisters, she was correct in assuming this was one of them.

Boltar's glamour fell away. It was one of the Scepter Coven's most powerful spells, and a critical one to be able to correctly identify the most ancient of the horde. With it, they could see Boltar as his god had made him. His god, and his own depravity.

Smaller than his glamour indicated, he was a singularly ferocious-looking beast, with spikes that stuck out from every square inch of his skin and a heavy brow lined with three more sets of spikes, the tips of which glistened with what had to be poison. Cressida leaned forward, unable to control her interest.

"It's a secretion like tetrodotoxin," Elysium said, her voice tempered with professional curiosity and maybe even a little interest. "We could distill that, use it as a weapon."

Dahlia snorted. "We could, but we'd have to milk him like a cow. I don't relish the thought of that."

"He's a demon," Cressida said. 'He would give it up to us willingly—or not willingly, but he'd give it up—if we demand it of him."

"And you are to be his consort." Another voice sounded in the room, the eldest of the lawgivers, dressed in dark ceremonial robes. "Now that you've reached your full strength as high priestess, you can command all of them. It's a very powerful weapon you've drawn to us."

Cressida winced. This was why she'd wanted to tell them the truth about Marcus's change of heart regarding the two of them, but that was clearly a discussion for another day. For the moment, only Fraya knew the truth. And, of course, Marcus.

But the elder lawgiver was clearly waiting for a response. "I serve to strengthen the coven," Cressida finally said, then switched her gaze to the second screen. "Zeneschiah."

The screen flashed to life, and a second demon presented himself, this one smaller in size and not gorging on the food that was laid out for his delectation. Cressida tensed. They had prepared all the temptations a demon could want, save those of a sexual nature, but they needed the demons laid out and asleep to unmask them. And Zeneschiah was asleep on his bed—or he appeared to be.

"Closer," she murmured.

The camera dutifully zoomed in, and then she saw it. Zeneschiah's head had fallen over onto his arm, an arm that was tied off with a strap, one of the sleeves rolled high. She couldn't see the hypodermic needle, but she didn't need to. A drug strong enough to knock out a demon was difficult for ordinary humans to come by, but the Scepter Coven had been cooking such pharmaceuticals for the past fifty years. There was no stronger magic than that which the Scepter Coven could wield against the demon horde...but humans were not so well prepared. The coven had planned on releasing the demon-debilitating drugs into the pharmaceutical pipeline later that year, but Ahriman's arrival on the scene, and his deadly rampage against the ancient Serbian coven, took precedence.

Cressida ordered the removal of the filter, and once again, the glamour of the creature on the screen changed drastically. This time, instead of a demon covered in spikes, she was faced with a fire drake. A slender white-hot creature made of fire, drakes were among the most instantly deadly of demons, used for killing entire swaths of the damned. They were of less benefit in the mortal realm, and Cressida grimaced. She didn't want to go through another summons to pick up a demon of greater worth.

To her surprise, the elderly lawgiver strode forward. "How in the world..." she muttered, peering at the screen. She slanted a glance to Cressida.

"Explain to me the nature of the summoning spell you made," she ordered.

"It was in accordance with the ancient ways." Elysium surprised Cressida by chiming in. "We followed the exact prescription in the grimoire for the summoning of consorts."

"Did you mention Ahriman by name?"

"No," Cressida said. "I had no interest in him knowing of our plan before we were ready to execute it."

"Then he doesn't know that you have one of his own here?"

Cressida blinked. "I'm sorry?"

"Fire drakes are very specialized demons. We took notice of the ancient ones you drew out with your summons, but ascribed that merely to your strength as a new high priestess. But a fire drake, especially one as powerful as this one, whom we did not identify until this moment, that is something else again. That will take more study." The old woman's gaze slanted to Cressida. "And more control. You will drain him of his life force first. We can't allow his power to go unchecked."

Cressida barely avoided expressing the disgust she felt as she studied the limp and flaccid lizard, lost in drugged delirium on the bed. "So you're saying we should keep him?"

"Keep him?" snorted the lawgiver. "Trapping a fire drake makes you one of the most powerful witches in all the covens. You'll be famous when word of this gets out— assuming he doesn't overpower you."

"Word of this will never get out," Cressida muttered. "And he won't overpower me."

She hoped.

Cressida turned away from the snakelike demon and focused on the third screen. "Jim Granger."

The screen on the wall wasn't the only thing to snap to attention in the room. Beside her, Dahlia stiffened as a man's figure took form in front of them. Unlike the two demons, he hadn't touched any of the food or drugs that lay before him. Instead, he sat on the edge of his bed, fully clothed, staring down at the spiked cross he held in his hands. He looked like nothing more than a man consumed in prayer, though his lips didn't move. Nothing moved, in fact, until a brief flash fell from his face and splashed off the bright silver crossbar.

Cressida's brows rose. Jim Granger was crying.

"Remove filter," she ordered.

Granger was human, not a demon, but that didn't mean that he didn't shield his true nature from the world. The witch's spell worked differently on humans than it did on demons, but it still worked. A moment later, Jim Granger's psychic ability was laid bare for the witches to see. And what they saw was something remarkable. A line of gorgeous crystalline bursts of light extended through his body, from the ruby red of his base chakra to the stunning purple light of his crown chakra. The crown chakra stole the immediate show, scattering its lights around the room and indicating Jim Granger was a psychic of impressive strength. But it wasn't the most powerful of his chakras.

"Who is this man?" murmured one of the lawgivers, and Cressida could well understand the surprise in her voice. She glanced at Dahlia only to find her captain staring at Granger with an equal level of surprise. Surprise...and something else too. Something Cressida couldn't quite define.

The lawgiver was waiting for a response, however, so Cressida stepped smoothly into the gap. "He was the most powerful Connected we could catch in our net when the pentagram was compromised. He is easily replaced if need be."

"No." The lawgiver's rejection of that idea was quick and absolute, but it also wasn't alone. Dahlia had spoken as well, her voice soft and strangled. An admission, Cressida suspected, Dahlia hadn't meant to make.

"He'll do well enough," the lawgiver continued. "We'll be seeing more of this level of Connected, not less, I fear. It will be good to study someone who has clearly been affected by the recent increase in magic. You can sense he is struggling to come to grips with his abilities. We can use that struggle to our advantage."

"Agreed," Cressida said, more to get the lawgiver to shut up than anything, as she sensed the flare of irritation surging from Dahlia. For some reason, her captain had connected with this human, which explained why she'd chosen him out of all the psychics in Storm Court—some of whom Cressida expected were quite a bit stronger than Jim Granger.

And yet there was no denying the power she could see on the screen, particularly in the bright, pulsing green star in the center of the man's chest.

"Stefan," Dahlia announced, making Cressida smile. She too had obviously been focusing too hard on Jim Granger's heart chakra, wondering what its unusual strength could mean, and she wanted the other witches' attention off the man.

Nevertheless, Cressida dutifully turned her attention to the fourth screen, frowning as it snapped to life.

There was no one in the room. Cressida straightened, ordering another view, then another, but nobody was there. Not at the table filled with food, not collapsed on the bed, not at the ornate writing desk, not—

A loud rap sounded at the door to her apartment.

"Room service," Stefan of the Syx called out.

6

S tefan grinned as the door swung open on the palatial penthouse room. He might be the prisoner of the Scepter Coven, but that didn't mean he didn't have resources.

These witches needed to understand that.

"Demon." The woman who stood at the door wasn't Cressida Frain, though she could have been her great-great-grandmother, twice removed. She stared at Stefan from the depths of a gray cowl and made no move to grant him entry. She also made no move to take him out at the knees, and Stefan could tell at a glance she had the power to do so. Unlike most humans, witches were impervious to a demon's ability to read minds unless they specifically gave their permission. Sort of a gift with purchase that they got after crossing over the Sisterhood bridge. But women were women no matter how powerful they got, and Stefan, for good or ill—okay, mostly ill, in his experience—understood women. Like anyone, women liked to be given credit where it was due, yet all too often, that credit was swept up by someone else.

"Hellraiser." He nodded back. The woman's eyes lit up, then narrowed, but she still didn't move. "You don't have to be shy. I can smell the fire and brimstone on you, but I didn't see you on the floor at Storm Court. That means that you were either helping to spell from afar or using the energy of that spell for your own purposes. Very crafty of you. But I guess craft is what you guys specialize in."

With a decidedly unladylike snort, the old woman stepped back. "You think very highly of yourself, Syx."

"If I don't, no one else will. Hazard of being the scum of the earth."

She didn't say anything to that, but the look in her eyes grew, if anything, more speculative. Stefan wasn't sure he liked what he saw in the old witch's expression, so he nodded to the brightly lit room off the foyer. "You're not going to force Cressida and me to hook up in front of an audience, are you?"

That merited an eye roll. "I don't think the high priestess fully understood what she was doing when she caught you in her net. I don't envy her her future."

Stefan's brows went up with that. "Is telling the future one of your party tricks? Because I got to tell you, I have a lot of questions."

"Go," the old woman said, but it was clearly more diffi-cult for her to keep her mouth in its narrow, disapproving line, and Stefan noticed she didn't immediately follow as he stepped into the bright parlor. "Idiot." The word floated softly on the air behind him, almost too faint to hear. Almost.

To his surprise, the elegant, feminine space was occu-pied by only one woman, Cressida Frain. He looked around, taking note of the empty screens, the gathered chairs.

There'd definitely been a gathering in this room up until a very short time before.

"Was it something I said?" he offered, leaning against a wingback chair as Cressida turned to look at him. It was only due to his thousands of years of advanced training that he didn't react to seeing her up close and personal for the first time in a well-lit room.

She was stunning. While he'd picked up on the red hair and porcelain skin in the nightclub, now Stefan could see that her eyes were a snapping green, her lips blessed with a deep rose hue that she managed without any apparent makeup. Her lashes were dark and lush, and her brows arched defiantly as he stared at her. She also radiated a psychic energy unlike most any human he'd ever met, and he'd met his share of powerful psychics over the millennia.

As busy as the Syx had been in recent months, he hadn't given much thought to the value of tracking mortal sorcerers. But seeing Cressida Frain, he found himself wondering how many other humans were out there running around, thinking their abilities had been augmented enough to face the dangers the world offered them. Stefan was a demon and Cressida a witch, but unless he was standing in her magical pentagram, she didn't have the kind of power over him she thought she did. Unless she'd created a pentagram that extended the length and breadth of New York City's West Side.

Probably something he should figure out sooner rather than later

Then Cressida folded her arms beneath her understated but still quite impressive breasts—he'd missed them in his first survey, so he made up for lost time—effectively distracting him. "How were you able to get out of your room?"

"That sounds an awful lot like something my mother would say, and believe me, that is not the vibe you should be going for here."

"You don't have a mother. You're a Fallen angel turned demon."

"And, what, you know everything you need to know about the horde? Because you sure as hell need an update on your 'How to Train Your Demon' chapter. Fortunately, I'm happy to help."

Cressida's jaw tightened. "While I appreciate your need to turn everything into a joke, it's neither necessary nor especially appreciated right now. I need to understand how you broke through our wards. Happily, as my consort elect, you are bound to answer me."

"Fair enough. I like being tied up as well as the next person." Stefan ambled forward nonchalantly, but he didn't miss the powerful tug of Cressida's compulsion spell on him. That answered that: there *was* a pentagram under the city, large and effective enough to contain a demon or three. Had it always been there? He wasn't a huge fan of New York City, but he hadn't avoided the city on principle, at least up to this point. Or was this simply the go-to pentagram that the witches of the Scepter Coven carried with them, packed up with their bed knobs and broomsticks?

Either way, Stefan didn't feel like fighting the compulsion, not for this particular question.

"I got out because your little witch spells are pitched to a demon of a different color," he explained. "Boltar and Zeneschiah are sealed up nice and cozy, but I'm a member of the Syx. You can be excused for not knowing exactly what that means, beyond the obvious superhero-like skills and spiffy haircuts."

"I know you've been chosen to take down the worst of demon kind," Cressida snapped.

"Correctamundo. By extension, that means I can also take down any mortal who sets about controlling demons, kind of a 'let's save the humans from themselves' corollary. Pretty much any connection you have with the horde gives me leverage against you."

"Leverage," Cressida echoed.

"Yep. Which, I got to say, makes me a little surprised that your buddy Marcus was down with pulling me in as one of your bachelors. Because I gotta tell you, if it comes to sheer hocus-pocus ability, I got the rose ceremony all wrapped up." He grinned. "Come to think of it, I got everything wrapped up no matter what the criteria are."

Cressida raised one of her perfectly formed brows. "You think so?"

"I think you'll be very interested to find out," he assured her. He didn't miss the flash of annoyance in her eyes, but neither did he miss the rise of color in her cheeks, the blush of—what? Irritation? Embarrassment? Arousal?—making her that much more attractive to him. He wondered if it was possible that this was part of the compulsion spell. Was Cressida actually manipulating him as some sort of seduction gambit? The idea pleased him far more than it should. He needed to dial it down a notch.

"Very well, next question. How much do you know about why you were summoned here?" she asked.

Once again, Stefan felt the pull of her compulsion spell, and once again, he found himself not willing to care. He weighed his options. He needed her to trust him, but more than that, he needed her to confide in him. The archangel had been clear on that point. Whether he went along with the Scepter Coven's game and helped Cressida take out

Ahriman or simply delivered him up to Michael, he'd not only lock down his own redemption, he'd get all the Syx closer to their Independence Day. He needed to make that happen.

To do that, he needed Cressida Frain.

He gave in to the compulsion—once again, it was easy to do. "I know enough to be dangerous, I guess you'd say. You drew to you some of the most powerful demons in the northern hemisphere, dangling humans as bait for it to look realistic. Once you got a quorum, you picked a couple out of the crowd. You also snagged a random human, for reasons I have yet to figure out, but rest assured, I will."

"You think very highly of yourself."

"I get that a lot. Anyway, after poking around the barest amount, I pulled a name out of the air I hadn't heard since I was a wee little demon trussed up in flame-retardant blankets. The kind of badass monster even we were taught to fear in the fiery cradle. Ahriman." He lifted a hand as she sharpened her gaze on him. "Before you ask, I don't know as much as you do about the guy, since you all seem to have a hard-on for him, but I know enough. In the beginning, there was the Light and there was darkness, and darkness had a form and a face. It was a form and face not pleasing to God, so when he created Earth and all its wonder, there was no place for such a creature."

"He should never have been allowed to exist," Cressida said, her voice harsh.

"Yeah, well. Creation is a funny thing. It grows in the gaps, and it never forgets. So when the opportunity arose for angels to be tempted into interaction with humans, God allowed it. Welcomed it, in fact. There was so much He wanted to teach his children, so much He wanted them to understand. And so His Fallen did so teach, and did so interact with the children of God, and eventually, some of those angels gave in to the temptation of the darkness that they found on Earth, allowing that darkness to swell and take physical form in their hearts."

"Ahriman."

"Yep. The black beast himself, caught in the lining of God's finest creation, and waiting for his chance. When sin was first created, Ahriman was there to embody it, and with each new transgression, he grew in power, until God turned His angels on themselves in the first angelic war and the Fallen were banished from Heaven. After that, Ahriman disappeared into mist and magic, never to be seen again."

"Until now."

Stefan made a face. "Maybe, maybe not. The attack on the witches in Serbia was in his name, but the demon himself didn't actually make it to the field. So you can't actually know he was the architect of that particular atrocity."

"You're wrong," she snapped. "The witches who survived claim they heard his name howled upon the legion who attacked them. And while your tale makes one heck of a bedtime story, it's not quite the one we tell within the covens."

Stefan spread his hands. "I await my education."

"In the beginning, there was light and there was darkness, there was good and there was evil, there was night and there was day. And each balanced out the other. The grace of the Goddess encompassed all. Each energy had its place in the warp and weft of the world, and each knew and honored its place. Until the energy of darkness sought to overcome that of good. And that energy took the form of a demon. Not any demon, but one that was made up of all the evil that has ever been or ever would be. Ahriman."

"This guy really needs a better press agent."

"Because the Goddess creates nothing in a vacuum and there is always a balance that may be restored, the Scepter Coven, first witches among all witches, was given the tools to eventually return Ahriman back to the Goddess. Such a battle was not to be undertaken lightly, however. The reality was that if the Scepter Coven failed in its attempt, Ahriman could then potentially destroy the covens, for their strongest sword would have been blunted. Once the witches were defeated, one of the last barriers to controlling demon kind would be removed. After that, only the Dawn Children would remain—and there are precious few of those."

Stefan grimaced. The Dawn Children were also not as strong as they thought they were, though good luck getting them to believe it. What was it with humans' belief in their own invincibility?

"So let me guess, you needed to wait until such time that the witches could reasonably be stronger than the greatest demon who ever lived. And that time is now."

"Don't get ahead of yourself," Cressida said. "There've been many opportunities over the years, many witches and coven leaders who have grappled with the decision about whether to go after Ahriman. In the end, it's never been worth it. He's very strong, but he's been relegated to the dregs of society. He doesn't venture too far out of his hole, in other words. We didn't feel the need to go scrabbling after him...until he came after us."

"I'm telling you—"

"And I'm telling you, you're wrong," Cressida said. "But the situation was dire even before the attack on the Serbian coven With the recent influx of the horde, there's been a great deal more fear that he will take an active role on Earth. We cannot allow that. Ahriman isn't the only ancient evil who has sensed the shift in the world. He is the first, however, and arguably the worst."

"Fair enough. So how exactly does your penta-bridegroom plan come into play?"

Cressida held his gaze steadily. "The sacred grimoire of the Scepter Coven maps out a process by which Ahriman can be defeated. But it involves the collaboration of a witch and demon."

Now it was Stefan's eyebrows' turn to dart up. "Collaboration? Or marriage? Because those are two very different things. We could've easily done without the flag football team if you were simply looking for a few good demons to back you up. I know a couple who owe me."

She pursed her lips. "The grimoire was written thousands of years ago, when the relationships between men and women were more open-minded."

Stefan snorted. "Yeah, because the Bronze Age was known for its tolerance."

"Nevertheless, the grimoire states that the demon must be the witch's consort. It assumes a great deal about the nature of that relationship, but does not codify it. All that's required is that I'm able to tap the strength of a demon stronger than I am. I wasn't willing to do that, so instead, I split the demon quotient by three, while bringing in a human and witch to cover all my bases. No one can say I didn't do everything I could to fulfill the requirements of the grimoire."

"You plan to get married but not put out."

She grimaced. "In a manner of speaking."

"Then why do you need five of us—including three demons? Because I'm stronger than you all on my own, sweetheart. You could've just asked me that up front."

Her lips twitched. "I don't *need* a demon at all, no matter what the writers of the sacred grimoire believe. I only need a partner of strength and ability."

"Also covered—"

"Marcus Frost is that partner," she said quellingly. He's one of the most powerful witches to exist in the covens, and he's completely dedicated to the cause of the Scepter Coven and to me. I trust him with my life."

Stefan eyed her, trying not to laugh in her face. "He sounds like a great guy."

"He isn't, however, a demon."

That did make him laugh. "Never thought I'd see the day when that was considered a problem."

"I didn't make the rule, I simply have to get around it," Cressida continued. "But to satisfy the letter of the law, again, I required not just any demon, but a demon who is stronger than I am. As I said, I wasn't willing to go that far. But I was willing to take on three who altogether were stronger than me, and then let their natural order assert itself."

Stefan frowned. "Natural order. That's pretty much mutual annihilation when it comes to demons."

"As you say," she agreed. "Then Marcus and a Connected could round out the retinue, in case there were any...complications."

"Meaning in case the demons decided to work together against you instead of eating each other."

She nodded, and Stefan blew out a long breath. "Well, it sounds like you've got everything figured out except one small issue, princess."

"What's that?"

He winked at her. "I'm one of your consorts. And I'm a hands-on kinda guy."

She jerked back, exactly as he expected she would, but

he didn't miss the flare of heat that passed across her face. "I told you. Your services in that regard are not required."

"And I'm telling you, you might want to rethink that." Stefan didn't know why he was laying it on so thick, only that he felt an impossible need to have this woman in his arms. In his arms—and in his bed. And since Cressida had by now fully dropped her compulsion spell on him, this desire was all him. "There's got to be a reason for a demon-witch coupling that goes beyond a simple power exchange; otherwise, your little spell book wouldn't have been so insistent. What if your power jacks up when you, you know, get jacked up?"

Cressida's delicate brows snapped together so quickly, he knew he struck a nerve, though he wasn't sure which one. While he had the basics of the coven's history down, his modern witch education was woefully lacking. "It does, doesn't it?" he pressed. "You're stronger when you've—"

"I'm not having this conversation with you," Cressida cut him off. Then she moved so quickly, he couldn't react in time. The spell she called down upon him was most assuredly *not* the work of a single witch, but an amalgam of several sorceresses' power, all condensed in a single archaic line. It was a great and powerful force.

But his need was great and powerful too.

Stefan lurched toward Cressida, driven by a hunger he couldn't quite define, but by the time her first word reached him, her beautiful voice desperate and stressed, he could already feel the tug on his body, his lungs. By the second word, he'd lifted his hands to her face, while fireworks shot across his vision and his head swam with dizziness. Still he fought through it, leaning close, his lips brushing hers as she breathed the third word—

And he blacked out.

7

"Why did you tell him so much?" Dahlia demanded, her nimble fingers affixing the triple-moon headpiece to Cressida's hair. "He's not your ally in this battle, he's a demon. His primary goal in life is to deceive and destroy anything human."

Cressida slanted a glance to her captain, watching her in the elegant mirror. She could still feel the demon's mouth on hers, and she knew in her bones he'd kissed her not once, but twice—both in her apartment and before, when time had seemed to stop in the corridors stretching away from Storm Court. He'd *kissed* her. And then he'd wanted to kiss her again, so fiercely that he'd battled through one of her strongest spells to do it.

Now her emotions were completely in chaos, a state that hadn't been helped when Marcus had swooped into her apartments like an avenging angel and whisked Stefan away. Cressida had been so overwhelmed with need, her lips burning from the demon's touch, that she hadn't trusted herself to look at Marcus, let alone talk to him.

This was all his fault! If her prime consort had actually behaved like the red-blooded male she knew him to be, Cressida wouldn't have been so tempted by Stefan, wouldn't have been so desperate for his mouth on hers, his hands, his—

"Um, Cressida?" Dahlia prompted, her tone concerned.

Cressida yanked her fingers away from her mouth, which tingled from Stefan's kiss. "He's a Syx, not an ordinary demon," she countered. "I presume that makes him different."

"Not different enough." Dahlia stepped back from Cressida, surveying her critically. "With all your hair, we need more pins to hold your crown in place. And maybe some tape to keep your mouth closed too."

Cressida snorted. "If you're going to ply me with tape, use it to keep this dress closed."

The tiara and scepter were the two royal pieces that denoted rulership of the coven, and neither was particularly delicate or feminine for all that they were usually carried by women. But the rest of Cressida's outfit made up for that. In a dictate presumably written by a teenaged boy one ancient winter's night, the sacred grimoire had prescribed that the high priestess who would stand against Ahriman must go to her consort wearing a long, flowing robe open from the neck to waist and floor to thigh. There was very little way to get around that decree, even with the most enlightened of modern dressmakers, and Cressida's gown fit the bill. Made of white silk, it lay gracefully against her skin, with long sleeves, a high collar, and a neckline that plunged all the way to her abdomen. The edges of the neckline were held in place on her torso with body tape, but the entire upper part of the gown looked like it might slip free at any time.

The lower part of the dress was little better. Two thigh-high slits bisected the floor-length white skirt and would have revealed more leg except for the thigh-high boots Cressida had chosen to wear, bypassing high heels or, even worse, going without shoes altogether, which was typically expected of witches during high ceremonies. She'd be dancing with demons tonight—she wouldn't be doing that in bare feet.

Speaking of demons... "What have you discovered about the consorts?" she asked. "What can I use?"

Dahlia transitioned easily back into her role as captain, a role much better suited to her than that of royal hand-maid. "Boltar has never been summoned by a coven, but he's done most of his work on this earth as a summoned demon, bent to the service of warring factions primarily in the Middle East since the earliest wars tore through those countries. He's consumed with battle lust and hasn't lacked for work in six thousand years. He responded to your summons so quickly because he was on a private security detail of one of the Saudi entourages in the city."

"Will he be missed?"

"He's already been missed, but the current thinking is that he was killed or kidnapped by a rival faction. No one will work too hard to find him, lest they draw attention to the fact that their security was so well and truly breached, but there will be eyes out. He can't be seen until the battle with Ahriman is finished, or we'll have more attention than we wish." Dahlia watched her in the mirror. "If the Syx could dispatch him to the other side of the veil once our need for him is through, that would also suffice."

Cressida nodded. In theory, she could compel any of the demons to destroy the others, but playing that would be complicated. The most obvious approach would be to demand Stefan do the deed. However, he'd already proven prone to zig when she needed him to zag. She couldn't allow that in the crush of battle. "What about Zeneschiah?"

"We have nothing on him other than what the lawgiver revealed. He's a seneschal for Ahriman and has never walked the Earth, at least not at the behest of mortal summoning. He came because you summoned him, nothing more. He's made no attempt to breach the bonds of the wards, no attempt to reach his master, no attempt to do much of anything other than stay doped to the gills. He's upright, but still juiced with a barbiturate concoction that has left him...remarkably relaxed. I would warn you that his abilities as a deceiver are likely quite strong, however, if he's even remotely in service to Ahriman."

"A spy in our midst," Cressida said, frowning. "That feels like something we may be able to turn to our advantage when the time comes."

"When the time comes, he could serve as the beacon for Ahriman to follow. The lawgivers are adamant that the great demon already knows you are preparing for the battle, so it may amuse him to have Zeneschiah planted here. But as far as we can tell, the demon hasn't reported anything to his master."

"There's nothing to report. He's done nothing but get captured and get high."

"As far as we know, yes," Dalia agreed. "Meanwhile, the Syx has been transferred to his new quarters."

Cressida looked at her sharply. "What new quarters?"

Dahlia's brows went up, and she pursed her lips briefly. "Marcus said you ordered the transfer of the demon to the upper floors of your domain, specifically to the chamber next to his. He's reallocated his own security detail to enforce the wards on the room, ensuring the Syx doesn't leave."

"I made no such order."

"I didn't object," Dahlia said frankly. "We don't have the power to keep the Syx held if he doesn't want to be, but Marcus seemed to have a plan in place, and so far, that plan is working."

Cressida frowned. If what Dahlia was saying was true, then she should welcome Marcus's intervention and not react as if it was actually interference. But it felt like interference all the same. Granted, she wouldn't need private access to the Syx. Their relationship was a sham, the installation of Stefan as a member of her retinue merely part of the farce, and the battle with Ahriman was set to occur within a few short days, when the moon was full. She wouldn't need Stefan for more than window dressing to convince the coven she was playing by the rules of the sacred grimoire, and yet...

It still felt like interference.

"Marcus is not yet my wedded consort," she said coolly. Even to Dahlia, she wanted to project that she was in control. Never mind that with each passing moment, she doubted that control more. But Dahlia was more than her friend, she was a member of the coven that Cressida needed to lead. To protect. She owed this coven her life, and she could never falter in her service...ever. "He presumes too much."

"He is your head of security," Dahlia countered. "He presumes exactly the right amount."

Then again, Dahlia could also be a pain in the ass when she wanted to be.

Irritation flared deep in Cressida's belly, right around where the vee of her neckline finally stopped. "You believe he's acting in his role of security and not in the guise of my future husband?"

"If he's smart, he's doing both. There's no denying the alluring glamour of the Syx, and you've never lain with a man."

Cressida stared at her. "*Dahlia.*"

"I knew it," her captain retorted. "But you play a dangerous game, Cressida. You should have consummated your relationship already. Go to him."

"I *tried.*" Cressida slapped her hand over her mouth, but she was too late to recall the words. Dahlia froze in place, staring at her.

"What are you talking about?" she whispered, as if Cressida had just revealed that Marcus had beaten her with chains. "He *rejected* you?"

Heat flooded Cressida's cheeks. "This is impossible." She whirled and stalked away a few steps, her cape flaring around her. She clenched her hands into fists, but there was no denying her need to tell someone, anyone, other than Fraya. The lawgiver had seemed supremely unconcerned about her trouble with Marcus, but Cressida was the high priestess. She was endangering the entire coven by not completing these rites.

She drew in a shaky breath. "I first went to Marcus two months ago. There were already rumors of Ahriman stirring, though nothing concrete. I... was coy. Flirtatious. Or I thought I was." She grimaced, reliving the shame of that first time. "He looked at me like I was insane, until he realized what I was about. Then he was, ah, kind, I'd guess you'd say."

"Kind." Dahlia's tone was neutral, and Cressida winced. She knew how ridiculous this all sounded.

"He truly didn't seem against the idea, but he said it wasn't the right time. That he would come to me when it was. He made me feel like I'd overstepped my bounds."

"Overstepped your..." Dahlia's words were less neutral this time, and Cressida glanced back to see her captain had moved several steps closer to her. "This is Marcus Frost we're talking about here. He rejected your sexual advances. The advances of a future high priestess."

Cressida gritted her teeth. "I think I've made that clear enough—"

"That doesn't make sense, though. His abilities would be augmented too—and that witch would dry-hump a dog if it would get him to the next level."

"I know." Another wave of embarrassment crashed over Cressida. Marcus had made no secret of his interest in the sexual path to the mastery of his magic. Which rendered his rejection of her that much more acute. "I eventually pressed him on that very point."

"And what did he say?"

"By then, he...had become less kind," Cressida said hollowly. She didn't know what was worse, her own mortification or Dahlia's pity and concern. "He informed me that he'd already achieved the levels opened by sexual gratification, that he could choose his partners by choice and not necessity."

"You're *kidding* me."

"I'm not. I thought he must be in a relationship, and challenged him on that score as well, but he made it very clear. He was my consecrated consort, approved by coven leadership. That would go forward. He simply wouldn't sleep with me until—I guess until it was required of him after our wedding."

"But you can't marry him, Cressida, not after he did something so—"

"Can't I?" Cressida's voice was harsh as she turned back to Dahlia. "He's the strongest witch in our coven. He's been blessed by the Goddess. And he's the key to this ridiculous retinue I've been forced to assemble to ensure I have the support of the coven in confronting Ahriman. No one knows that I haven't had sex—they assume I have. They assume I'm at the height of my power. I can't afford doubt to creep in about me. Not now."

"But if you marry him...you're bound for life. There's no getting away from him."

"I'm aware of that. And he would be bound too. I even offered to complete the marriage ceremony immediately, before the attack of Ahriman, and he said no to that as well. I think..." She shrugged. "Honestly, I don't know what to think anymore. Other than I'm not at my strongest because I'm somehow not appealing to the most sexually promiscuous witch in the entire coven. You can imagine I'm not feeling really good about that."

"I'd throat-punch him," Dahlia agreed, and her tone had shifted again, this time to wariness. "There has to be a reason he's doing this—or not doing this, rather."

Cressida sighed. "If there is, I can't find it. His powers would be augmented with our union—it's what I kept holding on to, in the beginning. That surely the promise of power would trump any physical distaste. But he seems to have found some other path—yet he continues to act as if he's my fated consort. I can't exactly approach another man within the coven—"

"No one would dare touch you," Dahlia muttered. "So what's Marcus's game?"

Cressida blew out a long breath. "Whatever it is, I have to keep on playing it. I need his help, especially since we've captured the demons. I can't control them without his strength—at least not all of them at once—and I can't release them until we've confronted Ahriman."

"True. We'll—we'll figure something out. Does Fraya know?"

"She not only knows, she seems completely okay with it. Something else I can't understand. Like, she acts as if Marcus's delay is no big deal, like I'm some love-struck teenager desperate for validation, when she of all people should understand the importance of this."

"That's...weird."

"I know!" Cressida gestured helplessly. "And now you know too. Tonight there's the cup ceremony, where I have to convince the coven I'm meeting the dictates of the grimoire while trying not to throw up every time one of those demons gets near me."

Dahlia eyed her. "I don't know, Stefan didn't seem to make you throw up all that much."

Cressida felt her cheeks heat again. "That was...a momentary lapse. He's still a demon."

"Yeah, but he's a hot demon." Dahlia grinned. "Which I guess makes sense."

"I'm getting a headache." Cressida lifted her hands to her temples. "And I need to keep Marcus on a leash, apparently. Has he done anything to the ex-priest?"

Now it was Dahlia's turn to hesitate. "Ah...Jim Granger has also been moved to the upper floors."

"Why?" Cressida demanded. "I didn't give that order either."

"You didn't." Dahlia had the grace to look abashed. "I did."

That caught Cressida up short, and her usually stoic captain rushed to close the sudden silence that stretched between them. "Jim Granger is a Connected of remarkable and untapped abilities, one of the few we've been able to study at any length. You saw the same thing I did when the filters were stripped away. He's more powerful than easily three-fourths of our coven, and he's wandering the world without affiliation. More to the point, he can kill demons."

"Not all demons, not all the time," Cressida said, thinking of Stefan's words. "He's also not a witch nor likely to become one."

"But if men exist out there like him, and we can turn them to our service—then we should learn how to do that," Dahlia insisted. "We summon demons because we can trust them to the extent that our compulsion is strong. But they're not willing participants in those arrangements. Working more closely with Connecteds outside our coven may quickly become preferable to commandeering demons, especially given the overwhelming response to your last summons. Or, if working with such people proves untenable, they could at least be put to service as an extra security force, one that isn't bound by the restrictions of our order."

"He's only one man," Cressida protested.

"He's the first man," Dahlia countered. "We don't know who else is out there like him."

"I get the feeling there aren't a lot of men out there like him." Cressida shook her head. "So where have you put him? Also near Marcus?"

"No." Dahlia's chin came up. "In the west wing."

"Near you, in other words."

"Marcus will be distracted with Stefan, and I didn't think

it wise for two of your consorts to be so close to you without protection, particularly once the spell of bonding is underway."

Cressida fought not to grind her teeth. The sacred grimoire had been unreasonably specific about that protocol too. "Three, you mean. Marcus is also one of my consorts. Presumably, he'll be caught in my thrall as well once that spell gets underway. So you'll have three moony-eyed consorts roaming the upper halls, including the head of security, and you're my sole line of defense?"

"You won't have any problem subduing Jim Granger," Dahlia scoffed, but there was an edge to her voice that hadn't been there before, and it was all Cressida could do not to burst out laughing.

"Dahlia!" she accused. "You've got a crush on him!"

"I do *not* have a crush on him," Dahlia replied hotly. "I am your captain at arms. I won't be taking a husband."

"You're not interested in him as a husband, though, are you? You reacted to his psychic abilities, his big pointy spike, and the twinkle in his eyes. You saw him and you finagled him into the coven, and now he's three doors down from your rooms." Cressida grinned as Dahlia's cheeks turned bright red. "What in the world are you going to do if he's affected by the bonding ritual more than we expect him to be? It's never been applied to a nonwitch."

"I'll be delighted for him to be your consort," Dahlia said staunchly. "That's why I suggested him. He's strong, and he can combat demons. He'll protect you."

Cressida shook her head, utterly confused. "But that makes no sense."

"It's also irrelevant," Dahlia said. "There's also the matter of the Syx. You've not asked about our intel on him."

"Fair enough." Cressida put the question of the former

exorcist to the side for the moment, though it bore careful thought. Why in the world would her captain—whom she'd known since they both were children—suggest a man to Cressida that she secretly wanted for herself? Who did that?

She refocused, gesturing for Dahlia to continue. "So what do we know about Stefan of the Syx?"

"Most of the information we have is on the Syx proper," Dahlia admitted. "And it dates back further than the establishment of our own order. They respond to mortal summons—and are very rarely, if ever, called by witches, though it has happened in times of great need. Their tactics are brutal and quick, and then they're gone again. They don't linger."

"Hmmm. Stefan is definitely choosing to linger here."

"And he's proven he can escape all but our most powerful and focused wards. Which means he wants to be here. We would do well to understand why. Another concerning detail you should know is this."

Dahlia reached for the tablet on the table, swiping the screen to life with a few quick, efficient finger jabs. She swiveled the tablet back to Cressida. On the screen was a video capture of the dance floor of Storm Court, cavorting dancers all around. In the center was a blur of indistinct shapes—the dark forms of Ahriman's lieutenants, the brighter forms of Stefan and Cressida. "What am I looking at?" Cressida asked.

"This was taken, obviously, midbattle with the ancient demons that entered the pentagram and were confronted by you and the Syx. This..." She swiped the image forward, "is immediately after."

Cressida's brows went up. "No Stefan."

"Correct. Like the other large demon from his team, the one who looked like a statue from the original Parthenon, he winked out with the effort to remove the worst of the demons on the floor. Unlike his fellow team member, he didn't stay gone. He returned in time to be a part of this."

She flipped to the next picture, showing Stefan with a decidedly curious expression on his face, standing shoulder to shoulder with Jim Granger. In the next shot, both males were closer to the dais, where Cressida waited, her hands lifted.

"And your thoughts on this?" Cressida prompted Dahlia, though she knew what conclusions her captain would draw. She was drawing the same ones.

"Stefan wasn't trapped in your net, Cressida. He came back here by choice and willingly allowed himself to be caught. We've not contained him effectively since the moment he made that choice, though presumably Marcus is having better luck keeping him put. So that begs the question: why? Why did he come back to assist us?"

"The archangel," Cressida said thoughtfully.

"The archangel," Dahlia agreed grimly. "The one creature on heaven and Earth the Mother Goddess has decreed that no one may speak to, no one may approach, no one may draw the attention of. And we've not only drawn his attention, we've inspired him to send one of his most precious lieutenants to our aid. Why?"

Cressida sighed. "I guess that's something we need to find out."

A knock at the door recalled their attention. At Cressida's command, it swung open. A young white-gowned initiate stood in the doorway, practically glowing with her budding power.

"It's time, High Priestess," she said breathlessly, reciting the summons as carefully outlined in the sacred grimoire. "Your consorts await you in the Grand Hall, ready to surrender all they are so that you can become all you must be."

Cressida grimaced. Put like that, she was forcefully reminded that she didn't have much choice here. Ready or not, in command of her full abilities or not, she was about to be wedded to five different males, including three demons.

"It's time," she agreed.

8

"**D**id you learn how to become such an asshat at some kind of boot camp program, or were you born that way?" Stefan asked, giving Marcus his best glower. The male witch had him in a thrall that wasn't exactly painful but didn't feel all that great either. Stefan was suspended up against the wall, hanging from restraints that Marcus had thoughtfully screwed into the studs. Ordinarily, not a bad thing, except that Stefan's feet couldn't quite reach the floor and the manacles were spelled with a deadening energy that would eventually sap his ability to maintain his glamour. He wasn't about to drop his pants around this jackwit.

"You should be silent," Marcus observed, his tone speculative, and Stefan gritted his teeth. He knew that. He could feel the compulsion spell tweaking his vocal cords, but he never was good at playing by the rules.

He was also getting bored with this game. Since Marcus had come to collect him from the delightful Cressida Frain's rooms, the man had been acting decidedly off his nut.

Stefan knew women, not men, so he couldn't figure out what Marcus's glitch was. He could simply be the jealous lover. Having stood next to Cressida on multiple occasions, Stefan could attest to how ravishing the redhead was, and how distracting. Marcus gave every indication that he was her betrothed, and so having a demon like Stefan sniffing around his main squeeze had to chafe. Even more than Stefan's wrist manacles.

At this point, however, Stefan had gone nearly thirty seconds without speaking, and that seemed like more than enough.

"So how obnoxious is it knowing your honeypot is going to be shared with four other Pooh Bears?" he asked in his most casual, insolent voice. "Because I gotta say, I'm not sure how I'd take it."

Marcus narrowed his eyes at him, but though his manner betrayed his irritation, it wasn't...it wasn't the right kind of irritation, Stefan decided. Marcus was pissed at something, but he wasn't jealous. "You know nothing of our ways, demon. You can't presume to judge, given the filth you are."

"Well, I can, sort of. I've been around a hell of a lot longer than you have. Pardon the pun. This isn't my first witch harem."

It was, of course, but the fact that Marcus hesitated gave Stefan a twinge of satisfaction. It was almost worth the spikes that suddenly burst from the manacles, piercing Stefan's forearms. Not quite, but almost.

"Pretty sure you're not gonna want me to bleed all over your girl's dress," Stefan said, glaring at Marcus. This asshole was about to get dead, he decided. It would be super helpful if Marcus did something to justify his death, but it wasn't entirely necessary. Stefan was bound by the charter of the Syx not to harm any humans, but for Marcus, he was pretty sure he was going to make an exception.

"You'll heal," Marcus said crisply. "If it's one thing that demons do well, it's repair their own glamour. Even when their wretched forms beneath remain broken and defiled." His lips twitched, and Stefan felt the first sliver of actual concern. Fear would be overstating it, but a nice healthy blob of unease was growing in his belly as Marcus's grin stretched wider. The archangel hadn't told him he'd be going up against some kind of sadist, but Stefan knew he shouldn't be surprised. The male witch was the head of security for the oldest coven in witchdom. He probably had a long history summoning demons and making them suffer, and for every torture he didn't know himself, there was probably a dusty old blood-spattered tome somewhere that could give him lots of ideas. Good to know.

A sharp, eager rap at the front door of Stefan's suite shattered the moment, though, and Marcus turned, gesturing sharply to one of his stone-faced goons. The goon turned and opened the door, and a bright-eyed blonde witchlet in a spotless white gown stepped into the room, her voice high and clear. "It's time, Stefan of the Syx," she sang out triumphantly. "Your high priestess will join you in the Grand—"

The girl's voice cut off and her eyes rounded as she took in the whole of the scene. Stefan, naked, scourged, drenched in sweat, and hanging from the wall. Marcus standing in his Sunday best, a defiant smirk on his face; goons one through three lined up and ready for goon duty, staring at the young witch as if she was their afternoon snack.

"Captain Frost?" she asked uncertainly.

Marcus murmured another few lines of incantation, and the manacles sprang free—the manacles, not the spikes. The sudden weight of Stefan's body on the skewers caused them to tear a little more deeply into his demon form, and it was all he could do not to howl in legit distress as his body slid sharply to the floor.

"The demon will follow with a retinue of soldiers to ensure he finds his way. I believe you have something to say to me as well?"

The girl brightened again, glad to be returned to her exalted task. "It's time, Marcus Frost," she announced as Stefan straightened. "Your high priestess will join you in the Grand Hall, ready to accept all that you are, so she can become all she must be."

"No way," Stefan protested, shaking out his hands. "You did not just say that."

"Keep a civil tongue in your head," Marcus said casually, not turning to look at him. "Or I'll happily cut it out."

"Yeah, I'd rethink that one, buddy," Stefan shot back. "Unlike you, I know how to use this tongue in ways your high priestess is going to appreciate."

The young witch gasped, but before Marcus could snarl anything back at him, a loud gong sounded from somewhere deep in the building, the sound strong enough to send a tremor of energy through the floors and walls.

"Please, sir," the young girl said, her eyes on Marcus as she took a step back. "You should be first among all."

"I will be." Marcus strode for the door, gesturing to his goons. "Get him ready."

Then he was out, the three remaining soldiers remaining as blank faced as ever.

"Guys, as much as I'd normally look forward to the idea

of you dressing me, I've got this," Stefan said. All the magic wards in the room had lessened significantly in their severity the moment Marcus left the room, and it was the work of two seconds for Stefan to reach out and rifle through the thoughts of the guards. They also did him the favor of having their next task uppermost in their minds.

Stefan glanced to the room he suspected was his bedroom. In there, he'd find whatever ceremonial getup was required for this little presentation that Cressida had lined up for him. Also in there was a jeweled torque the witches were supposed to affix around his neck, essentially rendering him a zombie. One thing about Marcus, he sure loved his toys.

"You don't really think I'm going to let you put that thing on me, do you?" he asked. The men attempted to move forward, and Stefan lifted a hand, effectively freezing them in place. Unlike Marcus, these witches were not spell casters by training, but instead foot soldiers chosen because of their willingness to follow orders. Stefan knew the type. They could be dangerous if not handled correctly.

"The law is clear," the center man said, a bright, eager, intense-eyed kid barely twenty-one years old. "All consorts wear the torque."

"Marcus didn't."

"Marcus Frost is the head of coven security," interjected the second man. They didn't seem to realize they couldn't move yet. Stefan got the feeling they spent a lot of their time standing at attention. "He cannot allow himself to be restrained in any way."

"Noted," Stefan said with a grin. "So we're going to play this my way. I'm dressing, I'm putting on the torque with my own two hands, and you're not touching it or me. Savvy?"

He didn't give them a chance to express any concerns

with that plan. He moved quickly into the bedroom, stripping off his clothes and wiping away the worst of the blood. Marcus had been thorough, scourging Stefan to his knees with a barbed cat-o'-nine tails before fixing him to the wall. Stefan had sent an irritated query out to the archangel when the abuse had started, but he'd received no response. Typical.

Now as he swiped away the blood, the skin that comprised his glamour quickly knit together and healed. By the time he reached the folded-up clothes on the bed, he was more or less back to his normal appearance. A sheen of sweat stood out on his skin, but there was nothing he could do about that. Healing himself was not always an easy task, and there'd been poison of a decidedly magical sort on those spikes as well as on the barbs of the whip that Marcus had used. The man wasn't doing anything by half measures.

The outfit that apparently had been chosen for the Bachelors Most Wanted looked like something Elvis might have worn, or at least one of the hundreds of Elvis impersonators that Stefan had seen since first coming to the Las Vegas Strip, the most recent headquarters for the Syx. Trying not to let his judgment slow him down, he slipped into the white trousers, skintight white shirt, and high-necked white cape. All he needed now was a pair of sunglasses and a microphone, and he could totally croon "Love Me Tender" at Cressida all night long.

He considered the torque, bracing himself to pick it up —then paused in surprise.

The torque was clearly an artifact of some power, but that power was not currently in effect. It was as if someone had forgotten to switch the thing on. Was that some kind of trap? Was Marcus deliberately trying to fool him into wearing the thing, only to strangle him with it?

Either way, he didn't have much choice. The torque was part of the costume, and the only part that wasn't dead white. It gleamed a bright platinum, inset with precious stones. It was pretty enough, he decided. At least until someone pulled out a matching leash.

Before he could talk himself out of it, he slid the torque around his neck, settling it against his collarbone. Other than the barest whisper of magic when the cool metal touched his skin, he could feel no immediate compulsion emanating from the device. Something to monitor.

He returned to the front parlor, where the three witches remained, looking decidedly more agitated as they tried to move. Stefan waved off his restraining spell, and they burst into action, stumbling forward a few steps before regaining control of their bodies.

"Geez, get a hold of yourselves," Stefan chided. "The party hasn't even started, and you're already hitting the booze. And another thing, boys."

He turned and waited until all three men faced him, and then he dropped his glamour, just a bit, displaying his true soul-curdling face. "You tell your little lapdog that I held you in place for even a second, and I will hunt you down and rip your guts out through your nose, then light them on fire as you watch. You know I have the power to do that, and I know your faces. Do I make myself clear?"

It was a cheap shot, threatening a human like that, and ultimately an empty threat. But the three witches didn't know that, and Stefan needed to secure himself some breathing space. The torque around his neck suddenly seemed to weigh more heavily on him, and he gritted his teeth. *Here we go.*

The witch entourage led him down a hallway to an elevator bay, and they entered the elevator carriage for a quick trip deeper into the heart of the building. When Stefan stepped out of the elevator, he could already hear the music playing in the room beyond. From the look of the sky outside the windows at either end of the corridor, it was nighttime again, though he had no true sense of how long he'd spent in the witches' domain. Probably no more than a full day, he decided. So this was most likely Sunday night, four days before the full moon. If he knew his witches, that was when they would strike Ahriman. He only had to get through the next four days.

When he stepped into the great ballroom, however, those four days suddenly stretched before him like a lifetime. Which, for a demon, was saying something.

The room had been decorated as a winter wonderland. Glittery fake white snow covered everything. It was piled up along the tables, dusting the floors, even scattered on the curtains that were pulled back to reveal a brightly lit cityscape below. Stefan could see Central Park beneath him, stretching out in a velvet black canopy surrounded by lights, and he tried again to orient himself. They were in a relatively unprotected building in a densely populated section of one of the busiest cities in the world. Why had Cressida Frain chosen this location to make her stand against Ahriman? Was it simply because it was the most convenient?

Stefan quickly scanned the room. He could see the two demons Boltar and Zeneschiah, each with a three-strong security detail, though the witches needn't have bothered. Both demons were high as a kite, more than happy to go along with the foolishness of mortals as long as they had their deepest vices indulged. Jim Granger was also on the floor, looking relatively ridiculous in his white Elvis getup, yet somehow managing to pull it off. He was no longer carrying his spiked cross, and Stefan grinned. It was hell having a costume with no pockets.

But his focus on his surroundings was shattered as a familiar voice rang out.

"Stefan of the Syx, welcome," announced Cressida Frain, her voice low and sultry as it was projected over hidden speakers. He turned, trying to sort out the location, then he saw her. His breath stopped in his throat. Cressida was more undressed than dressed in the flow of white silk that seemed reluctant to cover her body. Stefan could sympathize. His own physical reaction was powerful and immediate. He wanted her...all of her. And he wanted her now.

Was this a new compulsion spell she had on him? Or... Stefan shot a glare to the other consorts, but none of them were regarding Cressida with anything more than passing interest. So why was he the only one suffering from this knee-buckling need? What was going on here?

It didn't matter, he decided in the next moment. One way or another, she was going to be his.

Cressida continued, clearly oblivious to his claim on her. "With your arrival, the full complement of my retinue has come to celebrate this most powerful of bonds. Be merry and let us dance."

Stefan felt a pull of compulsion so intense, it almost drove him to his knees. He could no sooner ignore it than he could avoid taking his next breath. He turned to Cressida, his eyes flaring wide, and moved forward as if in a dream. For her part, she waited for him, watching him with an intensity that took his breath away. He covered the real estate between them in a dozen long strides as the music flared to life around them. He pulled her into his embrace, more roughly than he intended, unable to deny the surging need in his blood, the pounding of his heart, the heavy ache of his shaft.

"Cut the spell casting crap, princess," he gritted out. "I'm playing along."

Her eyes went wide. "There's no compulsion at play in this room, save for that ensuring the coven's protection," she said. "I'm not forcing you to feel anything."

9

Cressida studiously ignored Marcus's glare and Dahlia's startled stare as she allowed Stefan to pull her out onto the dance floor. The dictates of the grimoire required her to dance with each of her consorts in turn. It didn't specify the order or give any indication of primacy of place. There was absolutely nothing wrong with her dancing first with Stefan, even if that was not at all what she had intended when he walked into the room. She merely wanted to greet him as per protocol, the same way she'd greeted Jim Granger, Boltar, Zeneschiah, and of course, Marcus.

And her first thought, of course, was to dance with Marcus. He was her prime consort—her only true consort, in fact. Everyone knew that. They'd been inseparable since they were children. He'd been chosen by the lawgivers, approved by the elders, and blessed by the Goddess.

Yet here she was, being turned around the floor by a creature so powerful, she couldn't even pierce his gorgeous exterior to see the monster beneath.

"Are you also wielding some form of compulsion spell?" she asked him quietly—less angry than curious. She'd never encountered a demon so strong and yet so curiously at his ease among humans. "Are you forcing my hand against my will?"

"Seems to me you were the one who asked me to dance," Stefan protested, the side of his mouth quirking up in a grin. "I was just a poor wallflower, wondering if I'd ever catch a lady's eye, then you came along. Was it my cape? It's a very nice cape."

"It is a very nice cape," Cressida agreed, smiling despite herself. "You wear it so well."

She got the feeling the demon would wear anything well. Though she knew what she was looking at was a glamour, and not his true form, Stefan's beauty struck her even more forcefully now that she was only a few inches away from him. His dark hair was swept back from his fair skin, his eyes glowed with a fiery intensity that only deepened as she noticed the hints of red that glowed in their depths, and his lush, mobile mouth smiled even more broadly at her regard.

He towered over her, and both his height and his obvious strength once more took her by surprise—though it shouldn't. She'd been in his presence several times, after all. Why did all of this seem so different? Why was she so affected by him? He wasn't actually this gorgeous human-looking male before her, pushing all her buttons and sending her into sensual overdrive...he was a demon.

A *demon*.

Yet she couldn't help wondering...

As Stefan moved her gracefully around the floor, Cressida registered with a jolt that other than their all-to-brief kisses, this was the first time she'd touched the demon, skin to skin. Or skin to glamour, anyway. It certainly was the closest they'd yet been to each other, their bodies pressed close, though he was so much taller than her that she had to crane her neck a bit to meet his gaze. He stared down at her with a strange mix of emotions in his eyes that called to that same place deep inside her that had been awakened when he'd first told her his name.

"So how'd you end up as a Scepter sister, anyway?" Stefan asked, the question so unexpected, she blinked up at him. "Because, no offense, you really don't fit here."

"Of course I fit here, I've been here practically my whole life," Cressida replied, anger surging to the fore—anger that was completely out of proportion to the demon's casual question, she knew. She struggled to school her expression back to one of flirtatious interest to satisfy anyone watching them, but Stefan didn't make it easy.

"Yeah, but, witches aren't born, usually," he observed, his stare unflinching as they moved across the dance floor. "They're made. Even when both Mom and Dad are in the coven, it's not a foregone conclusion that the witchlet is raised that way. Most often, in fact, the child is sent off until they can make their own decisions. So you're saying your parents are witches?"

"No," she gritted out through clenched teeth. "I'm saying my parents are dead. I was rescued by a lawgiver from a hospital waiting room where I was about to be shuttled off to child services. Instead, she brought me here."

"And raised you to become high priestess. That seems pretty nice of her."

"She saved my life," Cressida said simply. "I owe her everything."

"Uh-huh. Including going up against the biggest bad in the universe, it seems. And on that note, explain to me the nature of the spell you'll level against Ahriman. Why does it require a demon?"

She instinctively pulled away, but he kept her close, turning her tightly as other dancers joined them on the floor. "I don't need to tell you any of that."

"You don't technically need to brush your teeth every day either, but it's the polite thing to do," Stefan observed mildly. "I can't help you if I'm flying blind."

"You're not here to help me at all," Cressida retorted, unreasonably nettled by his tone. "You're here to look pretty and impress the coven. And you do a credible job of that, for which you have my thanks."

"So you *do* think I'm pretty."

Cressida barely stifled her laugh, but she couldn't help answering Stefan. She *wanted* to, she realized, and in truth, he probably could help her. She might not fully believe the old maxim that it took a demon to kill demon, but Stefan had spent the last six thousand years blasting demons back behind the veil. "Honestly, I don't know why the grimoire dictated a demon's assistance. The spells we will employ against Ahriman all draw upon the power of the coven. The demon's role in the actual takedown of the beast seems to be merely as window dressing."

"Window dressing." Stefan snorted. "You sure you aren't missing a few pages?"

"Of course we aren't." Unbidden, a new worry snaked through Cressida. "I mean...no one would alter the sacred grimoire. Ever."

"Those who control the present, princess," Stefan offered neutrally.

Cressida narrowed her eyes at him. "Are you deliberately trying to undermine my confidence without me realizing it?"

"Oh, rest assured, if I wanted to undermine your confidence, I'd start with your taste in boyfriends. I don't know where you found ol' Marcus, but I'd throw him right back into the pond, if I were you."

"And you're better?"

"I'm certainly more fun."

"You are that." Cressida spun for a few moments more in Stefan's arms, debating the spell of compulsion flitting through her mind. "I can make you do what I want, you know."

"You can try. You'll find I'm a relatively open book, though."

"Oh, really. So tell me—what is your sin, demon? Why did you fall?"

Stefan gave a grim, knowing chuckle. "You know, everybody always wants to skip to that chapter."

He turned her again on the floor, his glamoured body seeming less like human and more like liquid light for a moment, before he spoke again. "The short answer—and trust me, that's all we've got time for since Bachelor #2 over there is waiting in the wings, is that I did not take enough care with one of God's children."

"A woman," Cressida guessed. She caught the demon Zeneschiah's movement at the edge of the dance floor, but she had no interest in cutting her time short with Stefan.

"A woman," he agreed. "She fell in love with me when I was a Fallen, and I ignored her entreaties to return that love. I thought her unworthy of me, and didn't understand how fragile either she or her gift was."

His voice was hollow, filled with long-held pain, but

Cressida frowned. "You wouldn't be the first to reject a woman's love. And you were an *angel*. How could denying one human's love possibly lead to your damnation?"

Pain lanced across Stefan's face, but before he could respond, the music shifted, and another voice sounded over the loudspeaker. "Zeneschiah, son of darkness, welcome." It was one of the lawgivers speaking, Cressida knew immediately. Cressida turned and saw the fire drake approaching in his blocklike human glamour, his body cloaked in white and a platinum torque at his neck, studded with rubies. He was grinning, first at his captors, then at her.

"I like this game you play, witch," he said.

Cressida stepped away from Stefan, then bowed to Zeneschiah. "With your arrival, the full complement of my retinue has come to celebrate this most powerful of bonds," she said, repeating the ancient words. "Be merry and let us dance."

Allowing the leering demon to sweep her away from Stefan was far more difficult than Cressida would have expected. But though Stefan let her go easily enough, he watched her as she danced first with Zeneschiah, then Boltar, then Jim Granger—and finally Marcus. By the time her prime consort claimed her for a dance, however, Stefan seemed content to stand with the ex-priest, the two of them talking as if they were long-lost friends. Goblets had been distributed among the crowd by then, and both men drank deeply. She wondered what they were talking about, but she couldn't tell, other than whatever it was, it made them laugh.

"You don't need to stare at them," Marcus informed her, sounding bored. "I can tell you precisely what they're discussing. It isn't you."

She flashed him an angry look, taking in his thin

features, his perfectly brushed silvery-blond hair, and his pale skin and pale eyes. Everything about Marcus paled in comparison to Stefan, she realized abruptly. Where Stefan's fair skin gleamed with vitality, his eyes flashing with energy and passion—Marcus simply hovered like a ghost, watching, waiting, manipulating.

Like he was trying to manipulate Cressida, right now. "I wouldn't expect them to be talking about me," she said tartly. "But I also wouldn't expect you to know what they're —oh, the torques. You've bugged them."

"Of course," Marcus said. "No need to waste energy on an enhanced ward when there's a simple electronic solution."

She eyed the platinum torque around his own neck, studded with sapphires. "And your own? Is someone listening in on your conversations?" She kept her tone light, but her mind was already rushing over the brief words she'd exchanged with Stefan. The torques were ceremonial objects, intended only for the most formal of occasions, but she already wanted to cast them aside. Marcus had tainted them...even though she supposed it was for a very good reason. Namely, her protection.

As if he could read her mind, Marcus smirked. "Nothing I do or say is for any reason other than your utmost security, Cressida, and solely for your highest good."

There was something in his tone that grated against her, and she studied his thin-lipped face more closely. "You chose Boltar and Zeneschiah. Why?"

For the barest moment, Marcus looked almost surprised. Then his expression returned to its habitual smug assurance. "They're strong, and strength was required to satisfy the dictates of the grimoire."

"The strength of three demons *combined* was needed to satisfy the dictates of the grimoire. These three would outstrip nearly every witch in this coven save for you and me. So why? What is it about them that interested you?"

She hadn't given the question much thought, actually, since up to now, she'd been considering the demons as pawns. But as pawns went...these were a dangerous choice. When Marcus didn't answer, she pressed. "Help me understand. Boltar is a walking pincushion of poison, and Zeneschiah is potentially a minion of Ahriman's. You're the head of coven security—why put us at such risk?"

"Risk?" he shot back. "You're the one who invited a Syx into our midst. What were *you* thinking? He could ruin everything." As soon as he spoke this last, Marcus shook his head hard.

Cressida blinked at him. She hadn't seen him do that since he was a young boy—it was one of his earliest tells that he'd revealed something he hadn't wanted to. But there was nothing outrageous in his comment. Though the Syx were bound to protect God's children, they were still demons—and incredibly strong demons.

Why *had* she chosen Stefan?

Marcus glowered at Stefan across the room, looking for all the world like a jealous lover. Though she knew better than to believe that.

"I don't trust the Syx," he muttered, more to himself than her.

Cressida pressed her lips together. She knew from long experience it was better to soothe Marcus's ruffled feathers than allow him to continue to stew. She couldn't afford him erupting during the middle of the ceremony, tipping off the rest of the coven to the tension between them. "Well, you would be the first to tell me that you shouldn't trust any of them. The Syx is no different from the others."

"Not true," Marcus countered, and his voice turned suddenly hard. "The Syx is the most likely of the three to get you to spread your legs for him. That would have disastrous consequences."

Cressida recoiled as if she'd been struck. "That's none of your concern. As you've made abundantly clear." She tried to pull away from Marcus, but he held her tight.

"Just because I'm not willing to fuck you, doesn't mean you should let someone else do it. You're practically panting for him. It's disgusting."

"You *dare* to talk that way to me." It was all Cressida could do not to spit with fury, but she felt more than one set of eyes on them.

Marcus seemed to know it too. His smirk grew even oilier. "I absolutely dare. I know you're desperate for it, but it isn't *time* for you to ascend to your full power, High Priestess. That's why I've held off. You should defer to wiser minds."

Fury lit along Cressida's nerve endings, racing beneath the surface of her skin. He had no right to treat her like this —no right.

He kept going too. "You're not a child anymore, Cressida, for all that you seem willing to act like one. But you must be more careful. The exorcist wouldn't be so bold as to touch you without compulsion. He admires you. He's even a little in awe of you, but he's no threat. The demons Boltar and Zeneschiah would as soon maul you to death as look at you, but they're safely held within the bounds of the pentagram. They're a threat, but they're a threat that can be managed. The Syx is an unknown quantity. It was a mistake to pull him into the net."

"It was a mistake that has earned the blessing of the

lawgivers," Cressida informed him sharply, but inside, her mind was awhirl. Marcus was a fine one to talk about threats. He had moved Stefan without Cressida's tacit approval, and he'd bugged all four of her consorts, listening to their every word. Listening, but not specifically reporting to her, or even letting her know that it was his plan until she'd irritated him enough by staring at Stefan and Granger. What if Marcus himself was the threat, a threat that needed to be managed? She trusted him with her life, and she always had. But in the wake of this sudden, new heavy-handedness, could she still trust him with her freedom?

The answer to that seemed simple enough. *No.*

"I no longer know what you're thinking, Cress." At this new shift in Marcus's voice, Cressida looked up to see her longtime comrade staring at her in the way that had started taking her breath away when she was sixteen and he was a newly minted spell caster, one of the earliest the coven had ever allowed. Now, suddenly, he didn't look pale. He looked tired. Haunted even.

Despite her better instincts, Cressida's heart quivered a bit, and her tension eased. Marcus was one of her oldest and truest friends, after all. One of her only friends in the coven, it seemed, beyond Dahlia. He wanted the best for her. He always had.

But she had become the high priestess of the Scepter Coven, and she couldn't afford his jealousy to rule her. She couldn't afford anyone to rule her. "We'll drink from the cup this night, all six of us," she said. "Then we can begin preparing for Ahriman."

"You'll remain careful around the demons?"

"Of course," she said, her words immediate and absolute.

She could sense Marcus relaxing a fraction at her

unqualified agreement, however, and that bothered her. Ever since he'd begun casting spells, he'd grown stronger and fiercer as a witch—attributes she admired, along with half the female population of the coven. But he'd also grown sharper. Harder. And there were the whispers that had started up a year earlier, knowing murmurs from the older witches with darker proclivities, questions about where Marcus's true future lay. As his consort and the high priestess of the coven, Cressida could bend Marcus's considerable energies to her will. But was she truly strong enough?

All of this would be easier if she'd just been allowed to reach her highest abilities—and yet, Marcus had warlock-blocked her from that. Granted, he wasn't Cressida's only option anymore, but sex with Marcus, someone she'd known practically all her life, *had* to be preferable than sex with...ah...

I'm a hands-on kind of guy.

Stefan's words struck her out of the blue, at once nonchalant and pointed, and her mind instantly became a whirl of conflicting emotions.

"There's much we can learn from the Syx," Cressida said into the silence that suddenly stretched between her and Marcus, trying to refocus her thoughts. "We haven't successfully summoned a demon of their company in all the centuries of our order. He can teach us about who ruled the demon realm in ancient times, and who rules there now."

"He can," Marcus agreed grudgingly. "But the cost of that conversation may prove to be too great."

She flashed him a look she hoped contained one tenth the level of irritation she felt. Marcus seemed unmoved.

"You're a delicate soul, Cressida, unused to the ways of the world, while the Syx has spent several dozen lifetimes perfecting the art of manipulating humans. Do you really believe you would be able to stand strong against him, should the worst happen and your wards fail?"

"My wards won't fail, against him or Boltar and Zeneschiah," Cressida said, hearing the truth in her own declaration. "And I will do what's best for the coven both in the fight against Ahriman and for our continued strength."

Another flurry of bells rang, and then Cressida did break away from Marcus.

The ritual of the cup was the first and most important requirement of the sacred grimoire. It allowed the coven to designate the starting point of Cressida's marital activities, so long as she agreed with the designation.

The five members of her retinue joined her in the center of the room. Five coven representatives stood there, each with a cup. The head lawgiver Fraya, who had been Cressida's mentor since she first came to the coven, stood forward with her chalice. "By the grace of the Goddess, our high priestess has chosen five consorts to secure the strength of the coven. With this ritual, we validate her consorts and help create the path to her happiness. Let us choose the first consort."

She turned to the remaining representatives. The first coven appointee, a foot soldier on security detail, turned and gave her cup to Marcus practically before the lawgiver had stopped speaking, and the coven burst into applause. A consort had been chosen.

Then the second coven member stood forward. It was the oldest of the lawgivers, and she moved forward without hesitation, stepping straight up to Stefan and handing him a cup. The response from the coven was more startled than celebratory this time, and whispers rustled across the group.

Dahlia was next, and Cressida found herself watching her far more nervously than she would've expected. Nerves that proved warranted, as her captain stepped up to Jim Granger and handed the startled ex-priest her cup. The two exchanged a long look, though as per protocol, Dahlia didn't speak.

"I...ah, I don't know what this means," Cressida clearly heard the exorcist say before he was shushed to silence.

A second lawgiver strode forward and handed her cup to Marcus, her choice earning a sigh of relief from half the room. But only half, Cressida realized warily. There were now so many whispers that the room seemed flooded with them.

Finally, Fraya lifted her cup. She surveyed the consorts before her, human and demon alike. Then she made her choice. She handed her cup to Stefan.

Cressida stared, rooted in shock as her mentor turned to her. "High Priestess, we have arrived at two worthy consorts. It is up to you to choose the consort who will start your path to full marriage and happiness within the coven. Marcus Frost, spell caster of the Scepter Coven, or Stefan of the Syx, demon enforcer. Which do you choose, as leader of the coven?"

Cressida blinked, her mouth going dry. Marcus stared at her with self-important satisfaction, Granger with unabashed confusion, and Stefan with something approaching boredom in his eyes.

It was the boredom that got her in the end. Stefan didn't know how this process worked, but he had to have his suspicions, even though those suspicions were probably dead wrong. Did he really care so little about her that he was willing to let her go through formal courtship procedures with another man after announcing so boldly that he didn't like to share? Had he meant what he'd said at all?

It didn't matter, because she didn't care. She didn't need

a bedmate, she needed answers, and of all the males before her, Stefan could give those answers to her.

"Though five are consorts of the high priestess, only one is chosen this night," she announced, her voice high and clear. "I choose Stefan of the Syx."

10

The rest of the night passed by in a blur for Stefan. After drinking the entire contents of both his ceremonial cups—which had to have been laced with some deeply narcotic technoceuticals for them to affect a freaking demon—he felt like the top of his head was going to come off. He must have been introduced to every single member of the coven, and danced with all of them as well, male and female alike. It didn't seem to matter much to the members of the Scepter Coven, now that he was apparently first chosen. According to what he could pull out of the elderly lawgiver on that score, however, being first chosen wasn't really all that impressive. It simply meant that he would be the first to undergo a series of courtship rituals with the high priestess, none of which involved actually having sex. Which seemed to be a highly inefficient process as far as he was concerned.

Even more interestingly, Marcus Frost was treating the turn of events as if Cressida was about to be handed over to a group of bikers on fight night. From the moment of her announcement, he'd cornered Cressida no fewer than four times, growing angrier with each altercation. Stefan could tell because Marcus's movements and expression grew more controlled, not less, every time he spoke with Cressida. Having seen firsthand Marcus's icy stare, Stefan suspected the man did his worst when he didn't have to flicker an eyelash.

At last the evening came to a close, however, and a cadre of initiates appeared around him in a circle of smiling faces. "It's time," they murmured, their high, light voices sounding eerie in the—

Stefan knew nothing more as he slumped to the ground.

He came to what seemed like only a moment later, but he was no longer in the ballroom. Instead, he'd been returned to Cressida's parlor, propped up in a large wing-back chair.

To his surprise, however, it wasn't Cressida opposite him. It was the ancient lawgiver, the first lawgiver to give him a cup.

"Don't tell me you're our chaperone," Stefan asked, struggling to sit up straighter in the chair. His body still didn't seem to be working right, but he wasn't going to slump in front of this witch.

The lawgiver's brows lifted. "Cressida is being prepared to meet you. I expect you to comport yourself with the highest dignity you can muster, whatever that actually means for a demon."

Stefan grimaced, resisting the urge to cradle his pounding head in his hands. "Yo, you were the one who gave me the cup of hook-up back there."

Amusement flashed across the woman's face, quickly replaced by stoic seriousness. "This room has been carefully warded against your strength, Syx. That, combined with the elixir you've consumed, is what's causing you discomfort. I warn you not to test its bonds. What Cressida does with you is her choice and her choice alone."

"You know, this isn't how I envisioned marriage going at all."

"You would do best to remember that you're the consort of a witch, and you are, at your core, a demon. Witches have controlled demons since the dawn of time."

"Well, witches have summoned demons and drawn a pretty star around them, you mean, and demons have gone along with it because they like pretty stars." Stefan flashed her a dangerous look. "There's a difference."

The elderly woman's gaze narrowed on him. "Cressida Frain chose you," she said. "Why?"

"My body's to die for, my demon-fu is strong, and I make a mean crème brûlée," Stefan said without hesitation. "The real question you need to ask yourself is—why'd she choose a nutcase like Marcus? Or if she didn't—who chose him for her?"

The old woman's hard gray eyes sharpened, even as a voice sounded from the far door.

"Lawgiver," came the soft murmur. Stefan tried to keep himself from looking, but when he saw the change in the lawgiver's expression, he couldn't help himself. He turned in time to see a young woman bowing out of the way, clearing the path for Cressida to step forward.

She...she took his breath away. Perfectly poised in a long, intricately embroidered sky-blue robe, she gazed at him with just enough trepidation in her composed expression it made his heart tug hard. Her gown was belted at the waist with a corset that could have doubled as Kevlar, and Cressida's riot of thick red hair was tortured up in a mass of ringlets and complicated braids.

With her flashing green eyes, haughty brows, and stern,

repressed pout to her mouth, she looked like the Mother Superior of Do Not Touch—which was too bad, because all he wanted to do was touch her. He longed to thread his fingers through her hair, undoing every carefully pinned lock. His body reacted so forcefully, he was surprised he didn't jolt out of his chair, or use his powers of illusion to turn this room into an exquisitely outfitted sex palace where time would stop and only the two of them would continue until he had mapped every inch of her skin and committed it to his eternal memory.

She was *his*. Totally his.

She just didn't know it yet.

"I leave you to your conversation," the lawgiver said, standing and brushing nonexistent lint from her robes, as if leaving a high priestess alone with a slavering demon was the most natural thing in the world to do.

He opened his mouth to say something—anything—but he didn't have enough control on his reactions not to betray the desperate need surging within him. Cressida walked the lawgiver and her aide to the door. After they exited, she locked it tight, then turned back to him and lifted her hands to her hair, pulling out maybe three pins. He gaped as the beautiful mass of her hair tumbled over her shoulders, but before he could speak, Cressida dropped her hands to the neckline of her robe, pulling what looked like delicate twin cords—and the gown collapsed around her ankles.

Stefan's eyes nearly crossed.

As a demon, both during his tenure as a Syx and before it, he'd given pleasure to thousands of mortal women at their tacit and incontrovertible request. He'd seen the female form in all its permutations, from lush and full to lean and athletic to frail and delicate. Never before this moment had he witnessed a woman at once lush, strong, and exceptionally compact all at the same time. Cressida Frain stood in front of him with her hair flowing over her shoulders, clad in a simple shift that reached her knees. It would have been the most modest of adornments—except it was *sheer*. As in see-through.

She stepped out of her ornate gown and left it in a heap on the floor, strolling back to him as Stefan stared at her. "Ah...princess?"

She settled herself on the couch, then smiled at him. He didn't miss the triumph in her expression, and his curiosity leapt. Did the lawgiver or her aide—or anyone in the coven, for that matter—know she'd planned this little surprise for him? And how far did she intend to go with it?

"Do you know what's required of you here?" she asked him in her haughtiest tones. "Did the lawgiver explain your obligations?"

"The lawgiver didn't give me bupkus. She certainly didn't tell me you—"

Stefan broke off abruptly as Cressida raised her hand. She gestured to the torque around his neck, then laid her finger against her lips. Stefan's eyes widened in sudden understanding. The torque was bugged? Of course it was, if Marcus the sniveling weenie was behind it. Stefan waved his fingers in front of his eyes, and Cressida shook her head, smiling broadly.

"Can I get you anything to drink?" she asked, reaching up to push her hair behind her shoulders. "We have so much to discuss."

Stefan found himself staring at her breasts as they strained against the sheer fabric. She was totally doing this to him on purpose, but why? What could be the possible value in goading a demon past his limit—let alone goading her chosen betrothed as well, who was surely listening in?

"I'm good," he said, clearing his throat as Cressida nodded. She dropped one hand, then the other to her lap, her fingers playing with the hem of her garment. Then starting to inch it up.

"So what's the point of this little soiree, princess?" Stefan asked. "Assuming I'm not supposed to simply nail you to the wall."

Her gaze shot to his, suddenly panicked, and Stefan leaned forward. Two could play the game of tease with a blind voyeur, but Cressida was insane if she didn't realize he could make her squirm far more easily than she could do the same to him. "No? No nookie tonight? That's a pity. So, spill. What do you want me for?"

As he spoke, Stefan reached out easily and drew his finger down the neckline of Cressida's shift. Then, just as nonchalantly, he dropped his hand and tweaked the peaked bud of her nipple. Cressida's eyes snapped wide, her mouth falling open, but she didn't allow herself the shocked intake of breath. Because Marcus would be able to hear that and might take matters into his own hands. Might even burst in on them, and that would be a pity. Especially since Stefan was rather enjoying the soft brush of his fingers over the tip of Cressida's breast, back and forth, back and forth. "Well?" he prompted.

"Information," Cressida said, and though her pupils were dilated and her hands clenched into fists, she spoke with a credibly calm tone. "By drinking from the cup, you are bound to me. You must do exactly what I say and answer any question I put to you."

"I like the sound of that," Stefan said, moving his hand to her other breast and palming its weight. For such a fit woman with a small frame, her breasts seemed to swell perfectly to fill the curve of his hand. He squeezed gently and continued. "And since you seem far more interested in what I have to say versus how I can make you feel, why don't you get to it?"

She laid out her requests in tight, brief sentences, her tone growing sharper as he brushed her hands away from her legs, giving him a tantalizing glimpse at what lay beneath the sheer mesh of her shift.

"I need you to tell me every truth you know about Ahriman," she said. "He's a demon as ancient as time itself, and the legends about him are long and twisting."

Stefan shrugged. "That's the downside of legends, yeah."

"I also need to understand how mortals can kill demons, beyond those who act as agents of faith, like the exorcist."

Stefan's brows climbed. "Demons in general, or Ahriman in particular? There's a difference. And you witch types don't typically kill demons, last I heard. You use them." More to the point, he didn't like the idea of spilling his candy to Cressida on this score, whether or not Marcus was listening in. There were some things humans didn't need to know.

"You don't deny it can be done."

He could feel the compulsion of honesty on him, and irritation whispered through him. He didn't like being ordered to do anything, particularly by magical means.

"It most definitely can be done." It was only the truth, and as Cressida had pointed out, he was bound to tell the truth. He dragged his hand down the swell of her breast and spread his fingers wide against her belly, kneading the soft, rounded curve of it. The movement was incredibly intimate, and she froze beneath his hand, her mouth tightening in surprise. "The descendants of the Fallen and humans can do it, princess. Straight-up humans, that's a different story. Those who pull it off have the might of God on their side, like the exorcist does. But another human lining up right beside them, doing the exact same move? No dice. The demon lives."

"What of the children of humans and demons—demons, not the Fallen?"

"Those are spawn," Stefan said matter-of-factly. "They aren't blessed by God, and they usually don't survive the pregnancy. If they do, they generally don't turn out too well, though they have their chances. There's no joy in that path, princess, but if you really want to give it a try, we can see how it goes."

He moved his hands down to grab the edge of her gown, then pushed it up her thighs. He could practically feel need coiling within her, and it called to him, an answering desire building as his cock stiffened further. This was going to be a really long night.

"But there would be no point in us having sex, is what you're saying. Your seed would bear no fruit within me, no matter how much you filled me up."

Stefan could feel the blood draining out of his head at the images she was conjuring—all of that blood pooling in points farther south. "Well, there'd be plenty of point. It just might not make a baby. If you don't have a problem with that, I certainly don't. Anything else you need to know?"

Cressida blinked quickly, as if she'd lost the thread of the conversation. Stefan took advantage of her hesitation to brush his fingers against her legs once more. He inched the hemline up farther, nudging her legs apart. They opened easily, exposing creamy flesh that looked far too soft for the roughness of his hands as he pressed his fingers into her thighs, probing the sensitive skin. When he dragged one thumb across her sex, the moist, delicate skin shuddering beneath him, Cressida stiffened beneath his touch, panic crossing her face. If he didn't know better, he would almost think...

No. There was no *way* the high priestess of the Scepter Coven could be a virgin. He was almost certain that little milestone had to be reached before they were even allowed to take higher office. Marcus should've unlocked that achievement well before they'd started preparing for this little level of Whack-A-Demon.

"Will you sacrifice yourself for me to banish Ahriman?" Cressida asked suddenly, and he supposed the question was important enough that anyone would excuse a little breathlessness. So he could be excused for taking his time to answer it. He brushed his thumb the other way, then shifted his hand up, his fingers unerringly finding the nub of nerves at her center. He hovered directly over it, not touching, as he pretended to consider her question.

"Probably not," he said at last. "Anything else?" As she opened her mouth to speak, he dropped his finger the bare fraction of an inch to brush against her. She sucked in a breath that sounded more like a startled gasp.

"One more thing," she said, when she could manage speech again. "And this is nonnegotiable. You must swear fealty to me for the duration of our marriage."

"Our marriage? I kind of got the idea that wasn't a real thing." Stefan longed to touch her with his tongue, to taste her, but he didn't want to tip off Marcus. Not yet. The guy might be an idiot, but even he would be able to figure out the sound of his supposed betrothed getting the best oral sex of her life while he was sitting in a dark room somewhere, huddled beneath his earphones.

"The requirements of the sacred grimoire have been met," Cressida countered, reclaiming his attention. Her cheeks were flushed, and energy seemed to leap from her, electrifying the air. Once again, Stefan had an almost irresistible urge to sweep her into his arms and pleasure her till she begged for mercy. That definitely would get picked up by Marcus's bug. "The marriage doesn't need to be consummated for it to be real."

"And that's a crying shame, wouldn't you say?"

"Well, yes—I mean no."

Stefan smiled. "You certain about that?"

Her eyes widened, her lips parting—

And then...

All hell broke loose.

There was virtually no warning for the hellspawn's arrival, but Stefan heard them the barest breath before Cressida did, heard them and went flying through the air, hitting the first wave of demonic insects with a snarl of fury, and—

And then he was caught, ripped out of Cressida's chambers and once more suspended in the ephemera of space and time, the vise grip of the archangel around his neck.

"Will you *stop* doing that!" he protested, shifting and twitching in the gray netherworld between Earth and the abyss. Mortals who knew about the veil thought of it as a thin net separating Earth from the endless realms of spectral creation, but it was both more and less than that. It was —a nothingness. A moat of endless fog. And it was Michael's favorite spot for his little fireside chats with the Syx, chats Stefan had managed to avoid for most of his term as a demon enforcer. He very much wanted to go back to avoiding them.

"No, I will not. You must let her stand on her own," the archangel said, punctuating his command with a burst of electricity that nearly fried Stefan's nerve endings. The torque around his neck shattered into a dozen pieces, but Michael didn't so much as glance at it. "Cressida has been building her power for the past twenty minutes. She needs to be tested."

"I hate to break it to you, buddy, but I've been with her all that time. Whatever she's been doing for the last twenty minutes, it wasn't building her power."

"Perhaps not intentionally, but that doesn't change the fact that she was drawing on an energy source heretofore unknown to her."

Stefan grimaced. "Okay, that I can buy. But in case you didn't notice, those demons attacking her in her cute little New York apartment are *hellspawn*. As in the insect swarms of hell. There's no way she's fought them before. They're going to sting like a bitch if she doesn't protect herself." He stared at the archangel. "Do *not* tell me you dropped those on her ass."

"I didn't. They were summoned by someone else in the coven. To test her."

"Wait, *what*?"

"She will never know her own strength if you step in unnecessarily," the archangel continued, talking over him. "How long do you have to exist among humans before you will finally understand that? They cannot evolve unless they put themselves into the fire willingly. She's ready for the test. You must be ready to let her take it."

Stefan scowled. "Duly noted, *after* I take out the hellspawn. Maybe it's not her being tested here, maybe it's me. I haven't had to deal with the little ankle biters for a long time either."

That stopped the archangel, and Stefan pressed his point. "While we're up, what's this shit with Ahriman? Do you seriously want me to let her stand in front of him when he shows up? Because she'll be one crispy human if I let her do that, and that's going to be on you, not me."

Michael regarded him stonily. "You told her you wouldn't sacrifice yourself for her."

"I won't be sacrificing myself. I can kick Ahriman's ass without her help. But she doesn't need to know that."

"You may not, in point of fact, be able to defeat Ahriman alone, even with the witch's bond to aid you," Michael countered. "You've never faced a demon that strong."

Stefan placed a hand on his heart, staggering back. "O ye of little faith. You wound me."

Michael rolled his eyes. "Very well, you may protect her with your strength and your fire should she confront Ahriman. But your primary goal must be to destroy the—"

A scream cut across the veil, cutting him off. A vaguely "Stefan!"-sounding scream.

"That's my cue," Stefan said, and he hurtled back to Cressida's side.

11

Cressida stood in the center of her apartment, fury rolling off her in waves as she worked dual spells of attack and self-protection. The demons should never have gotten this close to her. She was high priestess of the Scepter Coven, and there were so many layers of wards on the coven's New York fortress, most of which she'd set herself in a flurry of redundant spell casting, that even the idea of hellspawn hitting her inner sanctum strained credulity.

Yet here they were. The insects of the underworld. She'd never seen them in the flesh before, but the sacred grimoire considered them one of Ahriman's first lines of offense. Smaller than she would have expected, faster, and there were so many of them, it was all she could do not to get dizzy trying to track them as they whirled around the room. She didn't miss the fact that half were gradually getting closer to her—while half were pressing outward, looking for any means to escape her apartment.

No way was she going to allow them to roam through

the rest of the floors in this building, none of which were as well warded as hers.

"Hold!" she shouted, and five points of fire erupted to life at the edges of the room. It wasn't real fire, but its spectral nature made it no less intense. The creatures reacted immediately, recoiling from the five points of the pentagram, perfectly contained. But that meant all of them were headed directly for her.

Who'd summoned these horrible creatures? They flew like they were born to, not as part of some affected glamour. They were also horribly misshapen, long and slender, their joints distended into sharp angles capped with sharper prongs. She was instantly put in mind of Boltar, his body covered in spikes. Had the dampening spell they'd laid upon him failed? Had he summoned these creatures? Or was Zeneschiah to blame? He was the presumed foot soldier of Ahriman himself, to hear the lawgivers talk. And surely—surely it wouldn't have been Stefan, right? For all that he'd disappeared, surely he wouldn't have sprung these creatures on her and fled.

Right?

It didn't matter. They were here now, squealing at such a high pitch that Cressida flinched back every time one got too close to her face.

"Begone," she ordered in Latin, then Sumerian, and then Akkadian, but the demons paid her no heed. She could feel power building inside her, and she knew her capabilities and her potential for greater strength—why couldn't she command them?

Then the first one breached her wall of protective fire, raking across her face. The pain was so abrupt, so intense, Cressida staggered back—and that was all the invitation the other creatures needed. They pounced on her in a fury of wings and claws, scraping, tearing, rending, and worse than that, they focused all around her head, some of them small enough they flew into her mouth as she inhaled to issue another spell. With a bleat of real fear, she doubled over, putting her arms above her head. She knew—*knew* she was stronger than any of the other witches in the building—but there was one wielder of magic she suspected was stronger than her, one she hadn't seen since the onslaught of this attack. Cupping her hands over her face, she cried his name.

"Stefan!"

Nothing happened, and a renewed flare of panic scorched through her. What if Stefan *had* been the one to summon these creatures in the first place? What if she *hadn't* been directing the last thirty minutes between them, the way she'd thought she'd been, but he'd been running the show? She'd wanted to conjure up a deeper magic, leveraging the demon's obvious bent toward overt sexuality, and he'd seemed completely on board with that plan. But was he on board because he was planning to dupe her? Had she truly misread him that much?

Another of the stinging creatures assaulted her mouth as she drew breath to scream again. Pain hissed across her lips as they were slashed by what felt like a firebrand. The strike was so unexpectedly intense that tears sprang to her eyes, and she grabbed the offending creature with a darting swipe, focusing all her anger on it—

It dissolved in a puff of smoke.

The air suddenly snapped around her, like a sheet flapping in the wind, and Stefan's joyful laughter cut through the whirring, biting cloud of insects. "Boom! You got there before I even told you. I knew you could do it!"

Another birdlike creature bit her in the shoulder, and Cressida snarled with rage, batting it away. The moment her hand connected with it, the demon exploded. It was larger than the thing that'd attacked her face, so instead of shattering into dust, it burst into an oily residue of black goop and ashes—these things were definitely demons, but exceptionally small and nasty demons.

"Why—How—?" More of the creatures leapt on her, and she had to work to keep her focus on rage, like a lick of fire exploding moths that got too close.

"Hellspawn don't need an invitation," Stefan offered helpfully. She tried to focus on his voice, but he was too far away from her, and she dropped to her knees and began sweeping her arms wide, keeping her mad burning hot and bright. With each square foot she cleared, it seemed that half again as many of the creatures flooded back toward her, nipping at her ears, her cheeks, her bare shoulders—and the even softer skin they could easily latch on to through the fine mesh of her nightgown. She'd wanted to surprise Stefan, to catch him off his game. She'd wanted—if she was being honest—to surprise him so much that he would throw her back on the couch and make love to her before he even fully understood what he was doing. But this was a demon, a Syx. Of course she hadn't taken him by surprise. Instead he'd turned the tables almost immediately, driven her to a level of sexual need that'd nearly made her explode...and then all hell had broken loose.

And now she was fighting off the horde in a nightie.

"Dammit!" One of the creatures latched on to the soft skin of her heel, and Cressida howled in real pain as it sank its pincers into her.

A second later, something ripped it free. "I like those feet," Stefan growled, and she rolled over on her back, shielding her face as a blast of heat rolled over her. For the first time since she'd ordered the hellspawn to remain within the pentagram, she could draw a deep breath, albeit a very smoky one, as Stefan practically exploded with fiery rage, incinerating every demon caught in her thrall...which was a lot of them.

The burst of fire blew out almost as quickly as it started, and Cressida sat up automatically, looking around. Stefan stood with his back to her, and she gaped. This wasn't Stefan as she knew him in his beautiful glamour, but a Stefan encased in a broken, shattered body—not twisted and gnarled and grotesque, but horribly abused. His back was covered with crisscrossed scars that looked like they went all the way to the bone. Parts of his skin were bleached white from acid; while other sections were black as tar. He had no hair, and his ears had been cut from the sides of his head—

Then he turned, and Cressida blinked. His glamour was back in place—minus the torque, somehow—his black hair swept back, his dark eyes flashing with desire, his smile once again brimming with confidence. He was...perfect. Absolutely perfect.

"Hello, beautiful." He grinned, his manner so relaxed that she inexplicably wanted to burst into tears.

Instead, she whirled away, trying to compose herself as he approached her.

"Where's the torque?" she rasped, and Stefan halted behind her, snorting with satisfaction. He clearly didn't realize what she'd seen beneath his careful glamour, and she didn't want him to know.

"That was deactivated right after the hellspawn showed up. Consider it an extermination special—two bugs for the price of one."

Cressida sagged with relief. Marcus couldn't hear them, then. Had he detected the swarm of hellspawn? Surely not. Surely, her head of security would have already been here, no matter what privacy the ancient grimoire demanded be given to the high priestess and her consort, if he'd thought her life actually at risk.

Wouldn't he?

Stefan's next words were impossibly gentle, drawing her focus back. "Whoa, you got the crap bitten out of you," he said, whistling.

He wasn't wrong. Cressida gasped as she held out her hands, turning them over. The skin on her arms alone was marred with easily two hundred bite marks, some of them bubbling with a fizzing sort of goo. She lifted her hands to her face, remembering all the attacks there, suddenly rigid with mortification of how she might look.

"My face," she whispered, and Stefan took her hands before she could touch herself, chuckling as she jerked away from him. A few tears leaked from her eyes, stinging against the slashes, and her mouth started to tremble despite her best efforts to keep it still.

"Relax, princess. These are the marks of hellspawn. They hurt, but they're not permanent. And anything wrought of a demon, I can fix faster than your fancy spells. Which is a good thing, or ain't no way you'd be getting your cleaning deposit back."

"But—"

Stefan cut her off by squeezing her hands, then turning them around so that Cressida could see her own palms. While before her hands had been a mass of overlapping bites and scratches, now the skin was clear and blemish-free. She watched, spellbound, as he slid his hands up her arms, his touch as cool as water, leaving a trail of unbroken skin behind, everywhere he touched.

Then he reached for her face, murmuring something soft and archaic when she flinched away again, but following her motion with his hands. He drifted his fingers down her forehead, her eyelids, brushing away her tears with soft thumbs and trailing farther down her face and along her jaw and neckline. He spread his fingers wide against her collarbones, and she shuddered as the physical sensation of his healing caught up with his movements. Her skin felt electric where he passed over it, a shiver of life rolling along her nerve endings, rushing in her veins. He dropped to his knees in front of her, then his hands were on her thighs, her knees, her calves. He picked up each leg in turn, whispering something she couldn't make out as he brushed every exposed inch of her, then setting down her feet as delicately as he'd picked them up.

Then he sat back on his heels, looking up at her. "There's more damage," he said simply. It was an observation, but also a question, and Cressida didn't hesitate. She reached down for what remained of her tattered shift, then drew it over her head. With another hushed murmur, Stefan leaned forward, drawing his hands back up her thighs, around to her hips, and along her waist. He stood and stepped closer to her, pausing again until she nodded. She could no more keep this man from touching her than she could fly, and she found she didn't want to. Every time he lifted his fingers from her skin, she missed his touch like a physical ache that had nothing to do with her few remaining injuries. When he returned his hands to her body, it was like he was coming home.

Until he stood in one quick, graceful motion and cupped her backside, his fingers splaying wide as he arched her back, angling her toward him.

"Oh," Cressida murmured, a new sensation swirling in her belly. It made her feel dizzy and filled with expectation at the same time, and was vaguely familiar—which was impossible. She'd never been touched like this in her life.

"They were very thorough,' Stefan murmured. Cressida sucked in a sharp breath, but seemed incapable of exhaling when he slowly, deliberately moved his hands to the small of her back, then up farther, sliding them across the skin of her torso until they rested against her rib cage. He held her gaze steadily with dark eyes as his fingers crept higher, easing up the soft swell of her breasts.

He'd touched her breasts before, through her mesh shift, but this was different.

This was...better.

Stefan's lips twitched in a manner she couldn't read as his hands squeezed her breasts lightly, her nipples trapped between his long fingers. She sighed despite herself and arched against him, causing him to rumble deep in his throat. The sound was irresistibly sensual, and Cressida found herself quivering with anticipation.

"Cressida," Stefan murmured and she blinked her eyes open to find him staring at her. This close, she realized that his eyes were not like the normal eyes of a human. They were a rich dark chocolate—she'd known that from the start, but deep within the irises, there was also a hint of fiery red. Had that glow always been there? Or was it only coming out because of the fight, or the healing he was doing...or because of her?

She realized he was waiting for an answer, and she belatedly attempted one. "What?"

"Your mouth—is injured," Stefan said. "Inside and out." He sounded like the admission cost him, and she frowned as he dropped his hands from her breasts to rest again on her waist. He was deliberately holding her away from him, and she didn't know why.

She also couldn't see her own lips. He'd cleared the other wounds with a brush of his thumbs but—maybe her mouth was different?

"You can't heal it?" she hazarded. "Should I try a spell?"

His own lips tightened in response, along with his hands on her waist. She loved the feel of them there, steady and sure, but she didn't like how he was planting her to the floor, keeping her from touching him. She felt that was important.

"I can heal you," he said. "I'll have to kiss you, though."

Her eyes flared wide, and a new wave of heat suddenly blossomed inside her at the idea. She'd been wanting him to kiss her for the past five minutes—she'd arguably wanted him to kiss her since she'd first seen him on the floor of Storm Court, but now the moment was taking on a greater importance, one she couldn't quite understand.

Stefan clearly saw her confusion, and his eyes drifted shut, as if he was steeling himself against a terrible battle. "You'll have to give me your permission," he whispered. "The permission of a witch to allow a demon to kiss her is not one that should be—"

Cressida didn't wait for him to complete whatever tortured sentence he was trying to construct. She leaned forward and pressed her lips to his.

Instantly, her body caught fire.

Literally.

A bright rush of purple-and-red flames burst around Stefan, leaping immediately to her skin and running down the length of her arms and legs, before circling back up again, surrounding her in a corona of blazing heat that somehow didn't scorch her. She reached for Stefan with a strength well beyond what she knew she was capable of and yanked him to her, before he seemed to come back to himself and pushed her away once more.

The fire disappeared in a puff of smoke as she did, and Cressida dragged in a long, searching breath. Then she stared as Stefan balled his fists at his sides, looking like he was about to spontaneously explode.

"What..." she finally managed. "Was *that*?"

12

S tefan was breathing hard, his heart rate completely out of control, every inch of his body clamoring for him to take Cressida and pound her into the ground. He deserved that. He deserved her. Every job for every human over the past six thousand years shouted defiantly in his mind, every demon he'd ever bounced to the other side of the veil, every indignity he'd willingly suffered—every single abuse he endured, he'd endured for this moment, this woman. He knew it in his body as surely as he'd been forged in the fire of God's creation.

The need within him to take her, to fill her with his shaft, his seed, nearly overcame him with its primal force.

"What's wrong?" Cressida spoke again. He'd heard her the first time, barely, over the roar of his own blood pounding in his head, and Stefan gasped at the sound of her voice, desperate to regain his hold on his own rampaging lust. He was a demon, not a human. He could control the way his glamour responded to the female touch—had controlled it, in fact, for millennia. He was no saint, like so many of the other members of the Syx. He didn't deny himself the touch of a woman when it was offered. But he'd never so much as spoken to a witch before. No witch had ever had the strength to summon him to her pentagram, for any purpose, sexual or otherwise. He'd only got pulled into this one's thrall because she'd been endangered—no. Because he'd thought she'd been endangered...

No.

Because the archangel had sent him here.

Stefan tried to focus on that very important point, but he couldn't seem to get a fix on anything but the pheromones pouring off the witch like a lure to a wild animal. Cressida was everything to him: food, water, light, oxygen. He couldn't *not* have her, and he'd never felt anything like this pull. She said something else, and he swung his face toward her, trying to refocus, trying to find some way to make her understand.

"You—there's something about you," he gritted out. "I can't...trust myself. Can't touch you. Will...hurt you."

"You won't hurt me," Cressida countered. Then she took another step forward, the reduction of the space between them causing Stefan's cock to twitch hard. A cock he should be in control of because, hello, he was a *demon*. There was nothing about this situation that made any sense.

"I will," he insisted. "There's something different about you. Something I don't—understand."

"Touch me, Stefan," the witch breathed, and Stefan lifted his hand almost without conscious will. He stared at it, then at Cressida, feeling a strange hysteria welling up inside him.

"No," he murmured, though at the word a firestorm of fury erupted in his blood. His hand dropped.

"I'm not forcing you," she murmured, her words awed. "Which means this attraction you have to me... It isn't forced. Which makes no sense. It's not as if I'd ordinarily catch the attention of a demon. Unless he was trapped in my pentagram, that is."

"You do have a very nice pentagram." Stefan shuddered again as desire pounded through his veins, his knees nearly buckling under the strain. His hands itched to take her, his every muscle quivering with the restraint not to take her to the floor. She took another step forward, sidling toward him, and every one of his nerve endings twitched—particularly those in his cock. What was wrong with him? Cressida wasn't compelling him—which meant he was reacting to her all on his own. But that didn't make sense. Her body wasn't lush the way he liked mortal women. Her breasts weren't full enough, her curves not exaggerated. But when she lifted a small, smooth hand to his face, the skin of her palm maddeningly cool against his cheek, he nearly choked.

"Do you...do you want to make love to me, Stefan?" she barely whispered.

His gaze leapt to hers as fury erupted inside him. "You don't know what you're asking."

"I don't. I know I don't." She lifted another hand, her fingers trembling so hard, she clearly had to work to keep them steady on his face. "I want so badly to do this right, to —to make you want me. I don't know if I can, though. I...I don't know if I can make anyone do that."

"Angels above, Cressida," Stefan moaned, closing his eyes as fire leapt in his blood. *This powerful witch before me, surrendering, begging, wanting...* The very idea made his head spin, and he couldn't focus on anything but the need pounding through his blood. Host on high, help him for what he was about to say, but he couldn't keep himself from the truth a moment more. "I want it. I want you."

"*Yes—*"

There were more words, but Stefan could no longer hear them. Need exploded within him, and he lunged for Cressida like a drowning man thrown a too-short rope. He lifted her bodily off the floor and carried her forward, out of the room with its stench of demons and death, and down the hallway. The first room he came to was a bedroom. Not her bedroom, he thought, but it hardly mattered. He'd have thrown her against a wall if there wasn't another option.

As it was, he stretched her out on the bed, then pulled back, the haze in his mind lessening just enough for him to haul in an agonized breath. She was—so perfect, lying there. Fresh and brimming with life and energy, looking up at him with a need that seemed the perfect echo to his own. Need and curiosity and hope and fear and doubt and—

Once again, the truth assaulted his senses, nearly driving him to his knees.

Whoa, whoa, whoa.

The demand clamored more loudly in his mind, but Stefan had to ask the question, had to know. "Um, Cressida—"

"Oh sweet Goddess," Cressida groaned, covering her eyes with her hands as she spoke in a strangled, mortified voice. "Please tell me the Syx doesn't have any rules about virgins. I swear, I will never, ever, ever get laid at this rate. Ever—"

Stefan pulled her hands away from her face, and, laughing, cut off her words with a kiss. It was as if he couldn't restrain himself around this woman, couldn't keep his hands, his mouth, his tongue to himself. Cressida's confirmation of what his own senses were telling him didn't change anything about his destination. It simply changed the route.

If she was going to let him be her first, he was going to make sure it was an experience she never forgot.

"We don't have any rules about virgins, princess," he murmured, brushing his lips over hers. "Especially not for virgin princesses."

"Oh, thank the Goddess." Cressida sank back, letting him come down with her. His kiss deepened to a soft, rhythmic pulse against her lips. She tasted like honey and cinnamon, a recipe no human had ever perfected before, but a combination that called to him like everything else about this woman, a bewitching concoction he couldn't get enough of.

"A virgin," he purred against her mouth, reveling as she shivered in his arms. He traced a line of kisses up her jaw to her ear, playing with the tender lobe as she arched beneath him, as if trying to get her body closer to his. He tugged on the lobe with his teeth but didn't say anything else, instead rolling back slightly to take in the beauty of her body once again. She was strong, firm, and her psychic ability radiated around her like a rose-hued corona. He drew his hand down her breast, her waist, and she moaned in appreciation, arching herself against his palm as he traced the flare of her hips. "That opens up all sorts of possibilities."

Her lids lifted again, the eyes beneath focusing on him suspiciously. "Don't toy with me, demon." Her words were part plea, part demand, and a new spike of need thrilled through Stefan.

"I wouldn't think of it." His hand kept moving, however, edging over the curve of her thigh until he reached the vee between her legs. Once again, he nudged her legs apart, and once again, they fell easily, setting fire to his blood. Heat and promise coiled around him, making his already stiff shaft twitch.

She gave every indication she was wet and ready for him, but a demon couldn't be too sure.

Stefan drew his fingers up the delicate folds that hid her channel, and Cressida dropped her head back on the bed, her lips parting on a groan. Her reaction told him without him having to ask that she'd not only never had sex before —she'd never been touched. If her only experience with men had been Marcus, he could understand why there was no urgency, but still, it seemed a crime.

One he was happy to rectify.

He drifted his fingers along her quivering skin, up, then back again, up then back, always circling but never quite touching the tight nub of nerves that swelled eagerly every time he ventured close. Cressida might not know exactly what she was missing out on, but she did know she was missing out on something, and her hands fisted into the sheets, her body writhing in anticipation.

"Stefan," she whimpered, the word an entreaty he had no intention of denying.

"I've got you," he murmured, then slipped his finger into her entrance, causing her to seize up, her ass clenching as she lifted off the bed.

"Shhh," he said, pulsing gently as she collapsed back to the bed, barely inside her channel and already surrounded with her wet heat. He set his jaw, wanting to move slowly— until Cressida gasped with incoherent need. Without fully meaning to, he inserted a second finger alongside the first, gently stretching her wider. She groaned, her breathing going decidedly shallow, and he risked a glance at her face.

Her eyes were closed, her brows drawn together as if she was focused on a problem of vexing proportions, her expression so intent that Stefan's heart gave an ungainly lurch. And, because he was a depraved son of a bitch, he withdrew his slickened fingers and returned his soft touch to her body, only this time he didn't merely circle her clit, he centered on it, swirling his fingers with practiced experience as she gasped.

"OH!" Cressida's eyes flew open, and her gaze pinned on Stefan's as he grinned—grinned! As if she wasn't completely ready to explode. "What are you *doing*? And where are your clothes?"

"You close your eyes, you miss a lot." He shifted on the bed, his body gloriously naked. Sleek muscles moved easily under his fair, perfect skin, interrupted only by the soft brush of hair over his chest and extending down his belly and—

"Oh," Cressida murmured again.

"I'll take that as a compliment. "Stefan bent one of her legs until he positioned himself between them, then leaned down to place a kiss on the inside of her knee. Cressida couldn't keep herself from jumping again. Then she froze for a long moment, transfixed as he kissed a slow trail up her thigh.

"Stefan," she whispered as he moved still higher, drifting his lips over her hip bone.

"Do you trust me?" he whispered, the vibration of his voice over the sensitive point nearly making her eyes cross.

"Not at all," she moaned. She didn't trust any of this. She didn't know what she was feeling, or why, or how it had become such a burning fire within her to have Stefan do— whatever he wanted to her. To her and with her and through her, over and over again.

He grinned and moved back over the slight swell of her

belly, his breath cool and intimate on her overheated skin. He didn't make her wait anymore. He leaned down and followed the trail his fingers had mapped out, but now with his lips, his tongue. At the first touch of his tongue, her entire body convulsed, and a sudden fire erupted to life around them, translucent bursts of purple-and-red flame dancing in unrestrained delight.

But Stefan didn't stop there. He continued to tease her with his tongue, his fingers, his lips, until Cressida gripped the sides of his head, her fingers tangling in his hair, wanting him to stop, to let her breathe, let her process—yet she could no sooner speak than she could fly in that moment, her body and mind completely consumed with the intensity of the way he was making her feel. And just when she thought she was getting used to the rhythm, he shifted again, this time sliding up to the point where it seemed like every one of her nerve endings was clustered in a tight ball of—

"Stefan!" Cressida gasped, and she suddenly exploded into a starburst of sensations that felt like her entire body was coming apart. She jerked in Stefan's arms, her back arching, the purple and red fire lighting his skin leapt and roared with energy.

"I've got you, I've got you, princess."

Cressida blinked hard, willing herself to focus again as Stefan leaned away, not even trying to wipe the self-satisfied grin from his face.

He lost that grin when Cressida lunged for him, clearly unprepared for her to follow him up, or push him backward with a force that was part primal, part magic. Stefan dropped onto the bed, his eyes wide, then jolted in shock as she climbed on top of him.

"No," he started, but the word seemed to get stuck in his

throat as Cressida slid up his legs and positioned herself above him, straddling his hips.

"Please don't deny me, demon," she said, staring at him with a combination of need, want, and exultation. The eyes that stared back at her glowed a fiery red, and when the demon spoke, it was little more than a growl.

"Cressida," he began, but she didn't want to hear the warning in his voice, didn't want to hear his excuses about why this wasn't a good idea, why they should wait, why she should reconsider.

She sank down over him. Stefan's body went rigid as she stretched around his shaft, and a surge of deliciously wet heat swamped her body. This was nothing like what she'd expected—there was no pain, no tearing, no doubt. There was only Stefan, filling her so full, she couldn't imagine how she could ever be complete again without him. Only Stefan.

She sighed low and deep, her exhalation almost more of a feral groan even to her own ears. She planted her hands on his shoulders, her fingernails digging into his flesh, but Stefan didn't seem to mind, while she was lost in the sweet slide of her body over his, the pulsing rhythm of their movements growing deeper, longer, with each thrust. Stefan reached up and clasped his hands on her hips as she braced herself on him, and she was dimly aware of the fire dancing along her knuckles. She would be seeing purple and red flames in her dreams for the rest of her life, she was sure, and she'd welcome it every time.

"Yes..." Cressida murmured, or she thought that was her voice, though it was soft and ethereal and seemed to take on a life of its own, swelling to fill the whole room. Stefan's gaze snapped to her face, and she didn't miss the change in his intensity. He began moving faster, pulsing up into her, his red-hot eyes glittering with a need so bright and clear, it had to be reflecting her own. Where she felt he ordinarily would have asked her to slow, to wait, to draw the moment out, he seemed to move with redoubled energy, his mouth stretching into a fierce and possessive grin.

"Yes, Stefan," she whispered, and he stared at her more wildly, the sound of his glamoured name driving him to a harder, pounding rhythm. "Yes .."

"Ahh!" Stefan's shout cut her off, and suddenly, a wave of mind-shattering energy seemed to explode out from the center of them, bursting all the way to the heavens for a split second, then rushing back into her heart, her core, the marrow of her bones.

Beneath her, Stefan bucked in instinctive response, and he howled something in a language she didn't know as she threw back her own head and cried out, fiercely, wildly exultant.

They collapsed together on the bed, utterly spent.

13

Stefan stared at the far wall, his lungs heaving, while Cressida pulled herself to her feet and stepped away from the bed, wrapping the sheets around her. "No one's here," she muttered.

"Were you planning on an audience?" She turned back to look at him, wide-eyed and hopelessly disheveled, and he caught his breath. She looked impossibly gorgeous wrapped in the sheets the way she was, and he grinned as she bit her lip.

"No. It's just that—no one's bothered us. At all." She frowned, looking at the door to the bedroom, as if she expected the troops to come rolling in at any moment.

"And that's weird because...? Other than you having a demon in your bedroom?"

She laughed, her anxiety dialing down a notch. "Other than that, yeah. The fact that no guards have been dispatched to my apartment surprises me. Because your torque failed and there was the attack..." She scowled. "Oh my god. Those dead demon bugs. They're all over my living room."

"Not anymore," Stefan said, laughing at her startled expression. "All part of the service, ma'am. We in the Syx aim to please. But why do you think Marcus will be down here? Isn't he supposed to lay off while you're on your little dates?"

"Well, yes, but..." She blew out a long breath. "Honestly, none of this is going the way it was supposed to."

Stefan patted the bed beside him. "Maybe this would be a good time for you to explain how it was supposed to go, and we can see where you screwed things up. Oh, never mind, we know that—it's when you chose a dill weed as your head study buddy. But we'll get to that."

Cressida crossed back to the bed and sat on it, her attention snagging on Stefan's skin as if she was seeing something that wasn't really there.

He glanced down sharply, but no—his glamour remained intact. "What?"

"There was fire," Cressida said. "Floating around my fingers, over your skin, there—" She reached out and didn't quite caress his arm. "It didn't burn me, but it was there."

He nodded. He'd seen it too, and it mostly looked a bad pyrotechnics effect, but what if—

Cressida seemed to hit on the same realization as he did. "What if *that's* what happens when a witch partners with a demon?" she asked, her eyes going wide. "What if that fire, or whatever it is, is what will take out Ahriman?"

Stefan considered that. "Could be. I haven't seen that particular type of fire in anything I do. We tend to go for the old-fashioned kind. But I have seen flame like that. Sort of."

"You have? Where?"

"Oh, just a part-time Tarot card reader I know. She's started throwing fireballs around like it's her job. But if you can throw it too..." He tilted his head. "Well, that'd be cool."

Cressida breathed out a stuttering sigh. "I can't tell anyone—maybe Dahlia. But no one else."

Stefan kept his face as neutral as possible. "No? Why's that?"

"Because I..." She cast her gaze down, regarding her hands as if they no longer belonged to her. "I need an advantage against those in the coven who wish to do me harm. Something I can use that no one else expects. Some strength they're not aware I have."

Stefan stared at her. "You know, not to get all up in your business, but your little coven sounds more like a nest of vipers than the Sisterhood of the Traveling Pants. Where's the camaraderie? The joy? Where's all the moon hugging?"

Cressida frowned at him. "What are you talking about?"

"I'm just saying, most covens seem a little more, I don't know, *chummy* than you guys. What happened to the Scepter Coven that made you all suck?"

"We don't suck," Cressida protested, but her mouth tugged down at the corners, and her tone was dismayed. Stefan decided to leave it at that. The truth was, he didn't know much about covens, but there was something decidedly...off about this one. Something important.

"Okay, well...anyway," Cressida continued. "Since I don't know how much time left we have together, would you mind if I tried to compel you? Not sexually, I promise. I wouldn't do that. But it's just—you're so strong..."

Everything on Stefan went stiff again as she moved toward him. He tried to ascribe his interest in her body—his continued, pronounced, and very evident interest—to the fact that she was simply an attractive female, with her tumble of dark red hair, her vivid green eyes, her full mouth that snagged his attention as she bit down on her lower lip in concentration.

Surely that would be enough to tempt any demon, especially one as depraved as him. She also was a jumble of conflicting emotions—her stern, stoic demeanor masking a roil of fear, vulnerability, and a drive for success that had more to do with not letting anyone down than a true taste for leadership. She was a messy, fallible, glorious human—and yet none of that explained Stefan's hissed-out breath as Cressida dropped her hand to his chest. Her fingers were cool and soft, but her touch burned him so much, he had to fight not to flinch.

Stefan swallowed as she pushed him back, then drew the sheet down his body. He self-consciously twitched for the trailing edge. "I'm cold," he muttered.

"You're not cold. You're burning up with heat."

Her almost clinical survey of his body should have helped convince him her gaze wasn't intimate, and certainly not sensual, but it didn't. Cressida breathed out with appreciation as she flattened her hands on his chest. "I couldn't focus on anything specific before," she murmured. "You were too overwhelming."

"I get that a lot." Still, as she pressed both hands to his chest, Stefan's eyes nearly crossed. He would be okay with them going back to where she was overwhelmed. The full attention of the witch beside him on the bed was affecting him in a way he wasn't prepared for. And his cock was already throbbing, barely covered by one corner of the sheets. Given how fascinated she seemed to be with his collarbone, he didn't hold out much hope that she'd ignore his full and straining shaft. He wasn't sure how he was going to handle that.

"Your glamour is impervious to my view. I can test that, see if I'm stronger now that we—I mean since we—"

He narrowed his eyes at her. "I feel so used," he declared,

and was rewarded by the blush of embarrassment that stained her cheeks.

"I'm sorry," she said, continuing to draw her hands along his body, curving them over his shoulders. She darted him a quick glance. "Did you mind very much?"

"I'll get over it."

"Good." She blew out a shaky breath, and he realized— her hands were shaking too. "But your glamour is as good a test as I can think of. I'd like to see you—"

"No, you wouldn't," he said with absolute authority, grateful to be back in familiar territory. "I don't look like other demons, who are horrible enough. Most demons are self-made creatures, usually based on whatever they think will scare humans the most."

"Really?" She seemed to be listening to him, but that didn't slow down her sensual exploration of his body.

Stefan swallowed. "Yeah. So you'll find demons with prongs, with haunches instead of legs, claws and wings instead of arms, animal heads, multiple heads, inverted or upside-down heads—whatever is a mortal's worst night-mare, chances are a demon has stumbled upon it. There are a lot of us, and...um, what are you doing?"

Cressida drew her fingers up and down the arch of his neck, as if she'd never seen a throat before. The movement was impossibly gentle, again almost clinical...and unbear-ably erotic.

"Your skin is so warm."

"A steady diet of brimstone will do that to you." He would have broken off and simply focused on breathing through his nose as she moved her questing fingers to his jaw, but she didn't give him the out.

"Continue explaining about your glamour," she urged.

"Ahh..." Stefan could feel his lips tremble, but it wasn't

really his fault. "That's a little difficult to do with your fingers in my mouth."

"They're not in your mouth. They're *on* your mouth." If anything, she stared harder as she traced the outline of his lips, and Stefan's cock responded with such a powerful spasm, it nearly lifted him off the bed. Cressida muttered a frustrated curse and leaned forward, her face only inches from his. "I don't understand why I can't pierce this veil. Continue. How are you different?"

Stefan could feel the instinctual spell of compulsion radiating from Cressida, but he didn't know if that was what drove him to continue speaking or if it was the aroma of jasmine and vanilla wafting up from her hair, the scent of human heat and sexual interest that filled his every breath. While, ordinarily, talking about his demonic form would be the last thing he'd want to do with a beautiful woman leaning over him, her naked breasts swaying toward his chest, now he reached for the conversational gambit as if it was a lifeline.

"Like I said, I didn't get the option of choose-your-own-horror. By the time I realized I'd been transformed into a demon, the damage that'd been done to me was already set. In some ways, it was far less shocking than you'd expect for any self-respecting demon. No animal parts, no extra limbs, no bright shiny things sticking out from me in all directions, dripping with poison."

That caught her attention, and he breathed a sigh of relief as her hands stilled on his mouth, and her gaze met his. Hers were no longer filled with the sleepy kind of haze that dogged most humans who were on the verge of abandoning themselves to sexual impulses. He didn't know if that was a good thing or bad thing anymore.

"You saw Boltar?" she asked. "His true form?"

"I can see everything," Stefan said without hubris. "Demons can recognize other demons, generally speaking, unless they're spelled otherwise. But the Syx sees all."

"But Boltar couldn't see you."

"He couldn't. He's kind of a self-centered guy, though. He wasn't trying very hard."

"Okay." Once again, she jogged left when he would have been far more content with her remaining on the straight and narrow. She reached up, her touch leaving his mouth to trail up the side of his face, tracing the delicate contour of his ear. This, in particular, he shouldn't feel, given what had happened to him, but a demon's life didn't work that way. The touch of her light fingers on his glamoured ear was exquisite torture, going straight to his groin. Then again, everything was going straight to his groin. It was like an express lane to insanity.

Before she could prompt him again, he plunged on, his eyes drifting shut to try to focus on his words. Mistake. It merely meant every unexpected drift of her finger, every soft exhalation, was that much more in focus in his mind. But he conjured up an image of his current demonic appearance and—that definitely helped.

"I pretty much look like I've been dipped in acid. Like Voldemort on a really bad day. My body is bleached white, I have no features—no nose, no ears. My eyes are sunken into craters. I look just enough like my regular self, however, that there's no mistaking who I am. It's not like you could walk by me and not think—oh, that's Stefan of the Syx after he got his face sliced off."

Cressida murmured a soft objection, sounding genuinely dismayed, and Stefan resolutely kept his eyes shut. He didn't want to see either horror or pity in her eyes, for all that he was deliberately trying to incite them.

"If you can tell me all this, why don't you simply show me?" she asked.

Stefan tightened his jaw. "Because I don't want to. It doesn't matter why." Technically not true, but she didn't need to know that. The rules guarding witches and demons were ancient and absolute, even if he was a Syx. But some of those rules had been deliberately scrubbed from the books before the covens had gotten wise to their demon-summoning ability. As far as Stefan was concerned, witch ignorance was definitely bliss.

"And what about your body? What does it look like?"

"It's less problematic, which has its good and bad points as well. Again, there are the acid burns, some bits of skin bleached white, others black. The bones broken and reset at almost the right angles, but not quite, causes a permanent lurching limp. The damage to my feet doesn't help that. My arms are relatively intact, but my hands were broken and put back together by a monkey on fentanyl, I'm pretty sure. Not a good look. All of it is encased in skin that's more scars than dermis, and you've pretty much got a sack of pain. The fact that it looks almost like my original form if you squint really hard and turn your head to the side is a trick I've never seen replicated in another demon."

"Why did it happen to you, then?" she asked. Her pressure shifted on the bed, as if she was sitting up, and Stefan breathed a tight sigh of relief. He was so deep in his story that he could almost keep from imagining her deep red hair tumbling over her pale shoulders, her flashing green eyes fixing on him, her soft, full lips, bruised from his kisses, parting and—

Okay, this wasn't helping. Back to the tale of the crypt.

"It happened because it was the nature of my sin," he said, with a frankness that was somehow made easier because his eyes were closed. In his mind's eye, he could see the cause for all his troubles, well—not the true cause, not really. He was the cause, and he'd long since come to terms with that.

"You started to tell me about that," she murmured, and he nodded, though he didn't open his eyes. He wanted to tell her, he decided, wanted her to know. It was water under the bridge...but water he'd been treading for a very long time.

"I was one of God's most beautiful Fallen, if I do say so myself. A wonder to behold. While everyone had their claim to beauty, though, mine took it a step further. I was not only spectacular, I was desirable. Particularly to mortal females. It wasn't something I set out to be, it simply was. And I— didn't handle it well."

"You fell in love?"

He snorted, his mouth twisting with derision. Her fingers were winding through his hair, which was making it difficult to focus. "I didn't fall in love. Demons or angels—that's not how we're built, even when we understand the capacity for the pure and profound feeling of love itself. But I wasn't equipped to manage the kind of human love that was presented to me. Lust I understood. Reveled in, in fact. Desire was something that had form and meaning and function. And love—the resolute, stoic, unmitigated devotion of one form for another, I understood that as well. But the darker side of love, where devotion and need and want all mix together, *that* I didn't understand. Didn't understand the desperation it could drive someone to, the almost manic energy, the—"

He broke off as Cressida's weight suddenly shifted, and his eyes snapped open. "What are you doing?" He gasped as he stared up at her—up, because she was perched above him, her hands on his chest once more, bracing herself. Her ass rested on his abdomen, mere inches away from his full and ready cock. Now her hair was fully tumbled over her shoulders, and her lips had somehow darkened since the last time he'd seen them. Even as he stared, her small pink tongue emerged from her plump mouth and licked the surface of those beautiful lips, and heat swelled through Stefan, making him sweat.

"This is easier," she murmured. "You're too big otherwise for me to reach everything I want to reach."

She leaned forward then, her hands lifting to his temples to feather back his hair, and Stefan momentarily lost his ability to breathe as her breasts swayed in front of his face. "What's your plan here, princess? You've fulfilled what you set out to do already. I've already checked that box, in all manners of speaking."

"I'm not so sure," she said, and she moved up on her knees as she steadied herself on the bed, her hands to either side of his head. The movement separated their bodies— which should have been a good thing, but it forced him to look up into her eyes—which was a very bad thing. "I was compelling you."

"Maybe you were, maybe you weren't. Trust me, I was made for sex." In his mind, the sentence changed somewhat, dangerous but no less honest for all that danger. *I was made for sex with you.*

But Stefan didn't give that subversive thought voice, and Cressida didn't let him focus on it anyway.

"Then, given the full choice, would you have sex with me again?" she asked. She widened her stance and walked her knees back, her eyes locked on his. Then she settled her hips flush against him, his shaft compressed against her belly. The combination of heat and softness was almost

Stefan's undoing. "Would I know if you were doing it because you wanted to versus because you had to?"

He narrowed his eyes at her, willing himself to imprint her beautiful image in his mind, assuming he still had his mind after all this. "Would it matter?"

She rocked against him, almost experimentally, and he hissed out a sharp breath. "I think it would," she said. "I'm trying very hard not to compel you in any way."

"I'd say you were doing a good job of not compelling me right now."

"But you don't want me to touch you. You're letting me, but you don't want me to."

"Want is maybe not the best..." Stefan's words trailed off as Cressida lifted off him again. Despite himself, he instantly missed the contact. Before he could have time to process that loss, however, she slid down his legs, lifting one knee, then replacing it between his legs so that she was straddling his right thigh. Then she stroked her long, delicate fingers down the length of his shaft and took it into her hand.

"You want me to do this?" she asked, and he could feel the conflicting energies rising up from her, the natural compulsion due her as high priestess warring with an unnatural dampening force she was trying to effect on her own abilities. "How would I know?" she whispered.

She dropped her face to his shaft, and he felt the warm, raspy wetness of her tongue slide along his skin, his traitorous cock jerking in her hand. When she opened her mouth and slid it over the tip of his cock, he groaned, driving his head back into the pillows. She slid it back out, making a wet, sucking pop with her lips, and he nearly lost control right there.

He felt compelled, all right, but in point of fact... "I don't think you're forcing me to feel what I feel, princess," he managed, but that was the best he could do. Because the truth of the matter was, she *might* be compelling him. Whether she wanted to or not, she might not be in control of how much she was forcing him to submit to her. "I'd like to believe that my body is reacting the way it is because there's a beautiful naked woman on top of me, her hands all over me. But when that beautiful, naked woman is a witch and I'm a demon—that changes things. How much, I don't know."

"I agree." She sighed, weighing his shaft in her hand, her other fingers reaching down to cup his ball sac. Stefan didn't even try to stop his whimper. "I would want this to be of your choice, but I don't know how to ensure that. There must be something in the sacred grimoire."

Stefan snorted, trying to put together the last two brain cells he had left in the face of her untutored stroking. "I doubt quite seriously there is a prescription for ending a witch's compulsion on a demon while he remains in her presence. That would be a one-way ticket to disaster."

"Oh!" Cressida froze, her right hand still clasping his cock, her left mercifully dropping away from his balls before she fisted them too. Her eyes were wide, her face rapt, and her grip—ah, distracting.

"You're wrong!" she said, completely oblivious to his reaction. "There's something exactly like that—an old story dealing with an exorcism, no less. Or..." Her face blanked for a second, then darkened with renewed emotion. "Or at least there used to be. But *if* it's there, we need to read it."

And she scrambled off the bed, pulling the sheets with her.

14

"Wake up, wake up, wake up," Cressida hissed into the phone, striding quickly down the hallway of Dahlia's floor. Her captain wasn't picking up her phone, however, and that was unusual. Not the most unusual thing about this night, but unusual.

Behind her, Stefan stalked with an almost lethal grace, letting her mutter without butting in. He hadn't said much of anything, in fact, since they'd left her apartment. When she'd returned from the bathroom fully dressed, she'd been surprised to see him also dressed and waiting for her, his body apparently completely recovered from her touch, his manner once again easy, almost arrogant in its nonchalance.

Everything that he'd said to her was burned into her brain, however—especially the nature of his sin. She hadn't missed the fact that his information on that score hadn't been completely fleshed out. He'd apparently seduced a human, but from what she'd seen, he'd seduced a lot of humans. He could probably seduce a mannequin right out of a store window and not think twice about it. So what made his interaction with this particular human horrific enough that he must spend an eternity as a demon in punishment? Surely unrequited love wasn't that unexpected among the angelic pantheon?

Unfortunately, she had other problems to solve at the moment. "What is the deal?" she growled into her phone as her call once more went nowhere, simply ending in the ether.

Finally, Stefan spoke. "Do you have a signal?" he offered up, and she turned around to snap at him—then checked her phone. She frowned.

"Why wouldn't there be a signal?"

"Could be any number of reasons," Stefan replied, shrugging. "Could be something completely unrelated to the coven, or it could be a security measure to jam all communications other than sanctioned lines."

"I'm the high priestess. I'd like to think I'd have a sanctioned line."

"Yeah, well, you're dating a dickhead who's the head of security. So, on balance..."

"I'm not dating—"

"Oh, my bad. You're married to a dickhead. I'm pretty sure that makes things worse."

"I'm also married to you," Cressida couldn't help but point out, her heart giving a little flip at the words, and Stefan grinned at her, positively wolfish.

"And we haven't had anyone show up yet to cancel the honeymoon. So yeah, there's probably jammed communications in the mix here somewhere. Heck, you could be the one doing it."

"That's insane." Cressida turned back before she got drawn into a shouting match. There was something about Stefan that made her throw all her reserve out the window and react on sheer instinct. Worse, when it came to him, her instincts were completely ridiculous. All she wanted to do was explore the way he made her feel, the energy that seemed to flow from him directly into her, igniting a power she'd always striven for but never quite reached.

Had she truly changed, and so quickly? Barely an hour had passed since the hellspawn had struck and Stefan had fried his tracking device, but Marcus should have been knocking down her door by now. If her own energy surge had blown up his communications console somehow...

Surely that was impossible.

But something else that Stefan had said remained in her mind, driving her forward to her captain's quarters. He'd mentioned the danger of information about demons being shared in the grimoire, specifically a spell that could break the compulsion between a witch and her charge. And Cressida had read something about a demon possessing a witch in the grimoire and needing to be exorcised...she was almost certain. It'd been ages ago, so she could be wrong. But if she was right, they could have the information they needed right at their fingertips.

Fortunately, she was by no means the only demon scholar in this building. Dahlia had also pored through the grimoire as part of her duties to Cressida. In part to bolster Cressida's own knowledge of the rules and history of their coven, but also in part, Cressida suspected, to ensure that Dahlia was never surprised by any turn of events that might bring Cressida to harm. Dahlia believed she needed to know twice as much as Cressida did to protect Cressida half as well as Dahlia felt she should.

Only now, Dahlia was ignoring her. Or Cressida was being blocked, which irritated her far more.

She stalked up to Dahlia's door, lifting her hand to pound.

"It's late," Stefan said, his words barely a murmur in the hushed hallway. "Even if she isn't asleep and can hear you raise the alarm, she isn't the only witch on this floor. Do you really want to wake up—"

The door swung open before them, and her captain stood there, fully dressed, her eyes alert, her expression concerned. She flicked a glance briefly to Stefan, then stared at Cressida. "What is it?" Dahlia asked. "What's wrong?"

Not waiting for Cressida to respond, Dahlia stood back and ushered them both inside. Cressida glanced around her captain's apartment. It was similar in layout to hers, though not as lushly decorated. It was also empty.

"Where's the exorcist?" she demanded.

"Freelance exorcist, technically," Stefan drawled. "That's an important distinction."

"The exorcist?" Dahlia repeated, her tone only slightly startled. "Safe in his rooms. I was checking the feeds as you approached, which is how I saw you on this floor."

"So you had no interruption in your feeds?"

Dahlia frowned. "There was a blip about, oh, I don't know, an hour ago, but then nothing. But I'm on my own network." She gestured to the console station set up on the dining room table, another difference between their two apartments.

Stefan blew out a long whistle as he looked at all the screens that showed various consorts in their rooms. "This is totally illegal, I have to think. If you ever decide to stream *Bachelor: Witchgrooms*, though, you are going to make *bank*."

"It's for their protection," Dahlia informed him crisply. "They know they're being watched."

"Even Jim?"

"Especially Jim," Dahlia said, with a dark edge that made Cressida glance at her. Her captain's energy regarding the exorcist had been off from the beginning, and she didn't fully know why. Dahlia had never so much as glanced in the direction of any man before—or woman, for that matter. What was it about the human that was rattling her so much?

Either way, this was no time to be delicate. "Show Jim Granger to me," she said crisply, and Dahlia obligingly turned to the screens. She gestured to the one at the top corner.

"He's there. Sitting in prayer—or standing in prayer, or kneeling in prayer, the way he's been since we first ushered him into the room. He's not eaten, and he's barely drunk anything but the bottled water we provided after thoroughly checking the seals."

"It's always the seventh seal that'll get you," Stefan cracked.

Cressida narrowed her eyes. "He knows he's being watched, as you said."

"He does. He checked the phone, his cell phone, all the drawers. He identified the location of the bugs and devices. He carried his cross around from room to room like he either planned to bless the space or bludgeon anyone standing behind the doors. Then he started praying."

"And that bothers you?" Cressida asked. "Why?"

"It bothers me because he is no longer a priest, and the psychic energy we're charting in his room is pegging the meter." She gestured to another screen filled with jittering waves of color. "I suspect his prayer is actually a deep psychic meditation, but I don't know for what. We're picking up psychic energy for the demons too, but that's to be expected. Granger's isn't."

"Well, he's got to do something besides sharpen his spike," Stefan put in. Both women ignored him.

"Where are the records of the Scepter Coven, including the grimoire?" Cressida asked. "You have the files locally?"

"Of course," Dahlia said without hesitation. She moved to another laptop and swiped it on. "Saved to my personal drive. And, huh. It looks like you're right. This whole section of the complex has gone dark, communicationswise. Marcus must be losing his mind."

"Told you," Stefan observed mildly as Cressida scowled at Dahlia.

"He didn't send up an alarm?"

"If he did, I haven't gotten it. But I'm on a closed network, and like I said, nothing's been damaged here. The world could have blown up and I wouldn't know it. I can ping him?"

"No," Cressida said hurriedly, her mind racing. The hellspawn had shown up after she and Stefan had been left alone long enough for him to wind her up, but before his torque had apparently shorted out. Marcus should have heard the commotion, should have investigated. That he hadn't...

She thought about the purple-red flame that had flowed across her skin. Could Stefan be right? Was she capable of frying circuits without realizing it?

"Is Marcus monitoring your apartments too?"

Dahlia hesitated. "After a fashion. Marcus is within his bounds to keep tabs on anyone in the coven but you, but that doesn't mean I have to give him everything he wants simply because he wants it."

"Words to live by, I always say," Stefan said drolly.

Cressida literally felt her temper fray, and Dahlia clearly sensed it as well, because she hurried to explain. "I created a loop as soon as I arrived, and set it into the security camera. Whenever I consider it reasonable for me to not be in the meeting rooms, I'm not. Whenever it's reasonable for me to be asleep in my bed, I'm asleep in my bed. Marcus could discover the insertion of the video easily enough, but I'm not his focus. He's merely trying to do his job. And I'm willing to let him do that job, as long as I can maintain my own level of privacy."

"So he can't see us?" Cressida asked.

"No. Right now, to all appearances, I'm in my bed, and no one is in the main room."

"But we were on candid camera in the hallway," Stefan pointed out. "Surely you don't have that one rigged too— you do!" he answered his own question with a gleeful chuckle as Dahlia glanced at him. "I like you more and more, El Capitan."

Cressida tapped her lips. "I need us to speak with Jim Granger, privately, if possible, and to allow him to review a section of the sacred grimoire to get his take on the information from an exorcist's perspective. Is that something you can arrange?"

Dahlia hesitated. "I can't countenance that. The grimoire is—"

"Dahlia," Cressida snapped. "I was taught the same lessons you were. I wouldn't ask if it wasn't important."

Her captain sighed, then checked her cameras. "No," she said at last. "The exorcist is awake, but Marcus has eyes on him, and you can bet he's watching those feeds—if he's awake. Which, even if he's not, there's the playback. He'll see."

Stefan snorted. "Good thing you trust this guy. He's got an awful lot of authority."

"Marcus will do whatever it takes to protect the coven— and to protect Cressida." Dahlia's voice was absolute, almost startling in its certainty, and Cressida wondered if she sounded that way as well when she spoke of the man. Probably. "He's always been committed to both."

"What a champ," Stefan put in, narrowing his eyes at the man on Dahlia's screen. As she'd described, he looked absolutely like a man lost in his prayers, bent over his sacred, lethal cross. "What story did the exorcist give you about why he was rocking out at Storm Court?"

Cressida watched him too. "He said he was in the neighborhood and heard the call to adventure, and couldn't resist it. How much does he know about demons, do you wonder?"

She directed the question to Dahlia, but it was Stefan who answered. "Well, gee, I don't know," he said. "He specializes in how to get demons out of humans. It seems likely he would've done a fair amount of study on the nature of *being* a demon along the way. He strikes me as being thorough like that."

"Can you transport yourself into his room?" Cressida turned and asked him. "The way you showed up outside my doors? I know you didn't take the elevator."

"I'm hurt," Stefan said, laying a hand on his chest. "How dare you accuse me of such a thing?"

"What's your plan?" Dahlia asked Cressida.

"We have to believe Marcus is watching us. We need to get inside Granger's room, but if he suddenly gets access to his feed again, we need it to look like it's reasonable for us to be there and that we have it under control. If Stefan suddenly appeared in the center of the exorcist's sitting room and we entered a few minutes later, it's possible that Marcus won't interrupt us at all. It would also be reasonable for us to be tracking them both. He has to know that you have a setup in here as well."

"Of course," Dahlia said. "He's the head of security."

"Another important side note to all this," Stefan said, holding up a hand. "Cressida's not the only one with spiffy new superpowers here—"

"What spiffy new superpowers?" Dahlia interjected, but Cressida waved her off.

"I can be a one-man, on-demand jamming session too. If that's the kind of party you need." He winked. "And I can actually do it on purpose, not just out of instinct."

Cressida's cheeks heated as Dahlia spluttered, "What are you talking about?"

"Meaning if I want to, and especially since you guys aren't going all demon-block on me, I can interrupt all of Marcus's electronic surveillance. This isn't my first rodeo, and it's not my first interaction with human ingenuity. For the record, Marcus is about a C+ on that scale. His tech just isn't that great."

Dahlia turned to him. "You're wrong. We have access to the best tech in the world the instant it's available."

"Well, the best tech you're aware of, maybe. That's a far cry from the actual best. But I digress. I'll go do my poof thing, you do your showing-up-aghast thing, and we'll see what intel the exorcist can offer. Deal?"

A moment later, he vanished from the room.

Dahlia went instantly to her screens. "I'm replaying the last time you came to my rooms," she said quickly. "Fortunately, you tend to wear the same outfit most of the time. I appreciate that."

Cressida frowned down at her tunic and leggings. She'd worn similar clothing since she was a young girl. There were a lot of things she'd done since she was a young girl, come to think of it, patterns so ingrained, the thought of striking out with her own choices had never occurred to her.

Was that...had that been done on purpose?

She shook off the rogue thought. "It's comfortable." The moment she said the word, however, she winced. *Comfortable*. Comfortable for her, or for those who watched over her and guided her steps?

"It also makes my life easy," Dahlia agreed, missing Cressida's scowl as she stared at her monitor. "Okay. We're spliced in. There was a blip in the feed, but now we're recording live. And there's Stefan."

On the screen in Granger's room, Stefan stood in the center of his sitting area, looking around as if admiring the view. The exorcist emerged from his bedroom, a broad grin on his face. Then he spoke.

Static erupted from the speakers.

"What the hell?"

"He's jamming the feed," Cressida said. "Like he told us he would. If we want to know what they're talking about, we should probably get over there before Marcus does."

"First, a moment," Dahlia said, laying a hand on her arm. "I need to ask you something."

"Of course. What is it?"

Her captain's face colored as she searched Cressida's eyes. "Did you do it? Him, I mean? Did you, ah..." She flapped her hands. "Consummate the marriage?"

"I wish everyone would stop calling it that," Cressida said irritably. "It's not technically a marriage."

"Well, technicalities or not, did you do it?"

"I..." Cressida hesitated, the blood rushing to her cheeks. But there was no reason to lie. She didn't want to lie, actually. She wanted to own what she'd done, revel in it. It had been her choice, and she'd made it. "Yes. I did it. We did it. And I have to tell you, I'd do it again and again and again, if I could. It was an experience unlike anything I'd prepared for. Definitely unlike anything I'd read about."

"Excellent." Dahlia grinned. "And you *didn't* catch on fire, apparently."

Cressida stiffened. "You mean metaphorically?" she asked, her words careful, cautious. No use worrying her captain unnecessarily.

"No. I mean in real life." Dahlia flapped her hand. "Like, actual flames running over your skin."

"Well, yeah. I sort of did." Cressida narrowed her eyes as Dahlia flinched. "Why? Is that important? And more to the point, how could you have known to ask?"

Dahlia pointed to the monitor. "Because the exorcist said you probably would. We need to get to him and the demon, right now. Before Marcus shows up."

15

"You're looking good, exorcist."

"Not nearly as good as you are, demon." Granger grinned, eyeing Stefan with clear speculation. "You realize that a demon having sex with a witch changes the playing field significantly?"

Stefan laid an innocent hand on his chest. "I was being compelled."

Granger chuckled. "Yeah, you keep telling yourself that." He looked around the room. "When do you suppose they're going to show up?"

"Any minute. You know this room is wired for sound."

He nodded. "Sound and sight, yep. I happen to have been an expert in surveillance in a former life."

"Former life. Would that be the life before becoming a priest, or after?"

"The good Lord grants us but one life to explore to the fullest before calling us back to His embrace and setting our feet on a new, unimagined path," Granger said. "Who are we to limit the possibilities that His creation affords us?"

Stefan regarded the man steadily. Granger was right, of course, but the man stood too easily with him, too relaxed, especially considering that Stefan was a demon.

The older man smiled. "I know what you're thinking."

"I sincerely hope that's not true."

"I suspect a small company of witches will be breaking down my door quickly, so all I can really say is this: we're all part of the divine plan, Stefan. Our choices are our own, but they're choices we mapped out long before this moment. One million different pathways, one million different steps, one million different yeses and nos—all of them within the realm of possibility, all of them blessed by the Father."

Stefan snorted. "I can guarantee you there have been some choices in my life that have not been blessed by the Father."

"Then you don't give Him the credit you should," Granger said simply. "All the joy, the suffering, all the intensity of a single human lifetime is the swiftest intake of breath before an exhalation of stunning and powerful love. And we are all loved, Nur-ayya Dadanum, until we cease existing entirely, which only the barest few souls ever do. Yours will not be one of those souls."

"How did you know—" Stefan's barked question was cut off as someone pounded at the door, however, which was pushed open a second later.

He pivoted as Cressida and Dahlia entered. He didn't miss the fact that Cressida's eyes leapt to him, while Dahlia focused solely on Granger. She shuttered her gaze quickly enough, but not quickly enough to miss a demon's careful focus. *Interesting.* The exorcist might think he knew a thing or two about Stefan, but Granger wasn't the only smart guy in the room.

"Why did you guys even bother to knock if you were just going to break the door down?" he asked, to give Dahlia a chance to collect herself.

Cressida scowled at him. "Sound?"

"Jammed. I could keep blocking visual as well, but you seem to get off on Marcus taking a peek."

"No, keep jamming it," Cressida said, surprising him. "I'm here with my captain at arms, and I've locked down the floor as a precaution. No one gets in, no one gets out."

"You've been busy."

"Keep jamming it," she said again. "It will take him a good twenty minutes to break through the seals. After twenty minutes of no contact, he's well within his rights to do so. And we've got work to do."

"Fair enough." Stefan shrugged. "Consider them jammed."

He watched as Cressida and Dahlia moved forward, Dahlia leaning over the spotlessly clear dining room table. She hauled around a messenger bag he hadn't at first noticed and placed it on the table, then slid out a laptop.

"Mr. Granger, we haven't had a chance to get to know each other, and I regret that we still won't have much time here," Cressida said while Dahlia was setting up. Stefan nearly bit his own tongue in two trying to keep himself from making a joke.

"I'm the one who owes you an apology." The sincere dismay in Granger's voice had them all stopping and turning, especially Dahlia at her computer station.

The exorcist sighed. "There are calls that are meant for young men to answer and those that are meant for older ones. I shouldn't have interfered in your challenge, Ms. Frain. I was drawn here for a reason, I thought, but I didn't realize the reason was my own hubris. I'm sorry if I've been a difficult addition to your retinue to explain to your council. I don't know why I felt so strongly I should be called to step forward, but I did."

Stefan stifled his snort, but it wasn't because of Granger's earnest apology. It was due to Dahlia's darkly flushed cheeks. The witch ducked her head and kept typing as Cressida stepped forward smoothly.

"Not at all," she said. "I'm more grateful than ever that you're here. I think you can help us."

Granger's brows lifted. "How?"

"You know demons—specifically the exorcism of demons from their human hosts."

"I haven't officially done that work for a long time."

"Yet you still carry around a spiked holy cross that looks like more of a weapon than an artifact of the faithful. So how long have you been *un*officially performing exorcisms?"

Granger's beatific smile faltered somewhat. "You shouldn't be able to put me under a compulsion. I have no demon within me."

"Don't get too uptight about that, padre," Stefan drawled. "You can't walk with my kind for as long as you have and not have some of it rub off on you." Still, as Granger sputtered beneath the weight of Cressida's compulsion spell, Stefan performed some recon of his own. He blew out a quick sigh of relief as he confirmed that Granger was not, in fact, possessed. He wouldn't be the first exorcist to have suffered that fate. Not every demon could be a Syx, but that didn't mean they wouldn't enjoy blasting their own kind to the other side of the veil if given the opportunity.

Still, Jim Granger was one hundred percent human—if a human who was also ex-priest, ex-military, and, Stefan was sure, a few other exes that he allowed the man to keep to himself for the moment. As a demon, he could read Granger's thoughts instantly, but, unlike many of his fellow Svx, he preferred to use that ability only when absolutely necessary. Starting with the human he'd ignored all those millennia ago to his own everlasting damnation, he felt the trauma of human emotion at a soul-deep level. He preferred to leave mortals to their own crazy-making thoughts.

"I do have you under a compulsion spell, Mr. Granger, but only to ensure your honesty. I apologize, but please understand. I don't know you. I can't trust you. And I need you. Dahlia and I both do."

Stefan glanced back at Cressida, surprised that she'd tacked on that last, but it seemed to have the desired effect. Granger focused on Dahlia, and this time, Stefan happily and delightedly pilfered the man's thoughts. There was some extremely suspicious energy going on between those two, and they only barely realized it. What Dahlia might have suspected was a mild flirtation and Granger thought was merely his acknowledgment of the young woman's beauty and strength, was something far more primal. Something Stefan was pretty sure would explode seven ways to Sunday if they ever got close enough to strike sparks.

"Very well. How can I help?' Granger asked at last.

Cressida exhaled, and Dahlia turned the laptop around to what looked like a search page. Stefan wasn't a fan of most new technology, but he couldn't help being interested here. "That's the sacred grimoire?"

"Digitized," Dahlia said. "Held locally on my laptop, which is encrypted. I'm not saying it couldn't get stolen, decrypted, and disseminated...that's always a concern. But the program has to be reloaded once a week and self-deletes at the end of that week. We have taken whatever precautions we can to ensure its safety while still maintaining access to it."

A faint beep sounded from Dahlia's wrist, and she glanced down at her technical watch. "Marcus just pinged me. I'll respond that all's well and you're with me in Granger's rooms, but you know he'll be coming here. We need to move this along."

"Right," Cressida said sharply. She refocused on Granger. "What do you know about breaking the bond between human and demon?"

He frowned. "I specialized in extracting demons from humans. The bonds that tied them together were unilateral, one way. The demon reached out and gradually snagged a human through a variety of means, then wound his control around that human more insidiously. The first step is always to get the mortal to doubt themselves—their beliefs, their truths, what they know of their universe and the people around them. The second step is to cut the human off from those who love him. A demon cannot operate in the face of pure love."

"Not technically true," Stefan pointed out, but Granger waved him off.

"A Fallen who has still kept the essence of his soul is not the same as a demon," he informed him. "You're attempting to be redeemed. You don't count."

Stefan opened his mouth, then shut it again. He'd never considered it from that perspective, but now that Granger had presented it so baldly, it was an obvious distinction. The Syx had become the Syx because of their own mortification at what they'd done. They'd leapt at the chance to make right what they'd made wrong, their transgressions against God's children. In return for their immortal service, they were given a strength to level against the worst of their own kind. It took a demon to take out a demon, of course, but the Syx weren't your ordinary demons. They went after their own kind with a focus and a fervor. There was never any question of an attack being met with love, because they were only going up against other demons. There wasn't a lot of love to go around.

But a human, fresh off the apple cart, confronted by a demon... Could they turn him back with pure love? Surely not.

As if hearing Stefan's internal argument, Granger continued. "Most humans don't have the ability to maintain a state of pure love. It takes a very deep meditation, or a very strong and present emotion. Most of the time, if you've been targeted by a demon, you've already begun to break down your connections with other people. You're already at risk, in other words, because you don't hold love within your heart as a strong and present light. It's more a memory, a hope, or even a cause for despair because you think, for whatever reason, you don't deserve it or that it'll never reach you in the first place." He sighed. "No matter how much love is out there in the world, there are those who can't see it. That's who a savvy demon will target. They only go after stronger targets when they're incensed."

Stefan weighed that, nodding. The man wasn't wrong.

"Once the hold has been established, it goes very quickly. The human withdraws, turns inward, stops taking care of himself. Then, in some cases, begins to actively harm himself—sometimes others too, but mostly it's more internal than that. The demon doesn't need to act out as much as it needs to act in."

"So how do you break that hold?" Cressida pressed. 'From everything I've read, it's more a question of going in and forcibly removing the demon from the human or place, literally casting it out. No matter the ritual or specific method, that's the end goal."

"That's the end goal," Granger agreed.

"So let's turn it around," she said. "You have a human who has deliberately summoned the demon and has a demon in her thrall. She's in control. The demon is subordinate to her. He hasn't taken all the steps to ensure that she's alone, afraid, cut off from her society. In fact, in some cases, she's surrounded by her supporters. But even if not, even if she simply summons the demon in a solo act, she's the one with power. How does she break that bond of compulsion while not sending the demon back into the hellfire from whence she summoned him?"

"Not to interrupt," Stefan said drily, "but there's hella demons out there right now who you aren't actually summoning from hell. You can pretty much find them at your local Walmart."

Granger ignored him, focusing on Cressida. "Why would you want to do such a thing?"

"I—" She stumbled, blushing, and Stefan's gaze snapped to her as well, noting the exact time she seized on a socially acceptable reason for her question. He couldn't read her thoughts, but she was still a woman, and a woman he'd slept with. He could tell when she was lying—or, if not lying, not sharing the whole truth. This would be one of those times.

Still, she pressed on. "I keep turning around the requirements of the sacred grimoire in my mind. On the surface, it appears to require a demon and witch to act in concert against Ahriman. But that's not the letter of the law. The letter of the law states that the demon is wedded to the witch, and that she draws her power from that bond. But that doesn't make sense. Every compulsion spell allows the witch to draw power from the demon. So why is marriage necessary? The inference is that this act of marriage propels the demon into a different relationship with the witch, and *that* is what's important in the attack on Ahriman. Otherwise, the stipulation of wedding a demon is simply a redirect —something so abhorrent, it was designed to forestall any attempt to go up against Ahriman. Which makes no sense."

"It's our sacred duty to overthrow Ahriman," Dahlia said automatically, as if it were a mantra pressed upon her from birth. Which, of course, it had been.

"It is. And yet no member of the Scepter Coven has attempted to overthrow him in all these long years, in part because of the requirement to secure a demon stronger than me. No witch would dare be so foolish, so instead, I've assembled three demons who separately, the coven can manage."

"As far as you know," Stefan observed drolly.

Cressida rolled her eyes. "But it's important to note— these demons remain in the coven's thrall. The only way they could be truly stronger than me is if I release them, and that's simply not to be done. Not in the midst of such a dangerous moment as attacking a far stronger demon."

"What was your original plan, then?" Stefan asked.

"My *original* plan was to satisfy the letter of the law by wedding the demons, wait until they annihilated each other —or, if they didn't do that, leave them cooling their heels in their cells under heavy coven spells—and, together with Marcus and possibly the human, if there was any benefit to be had there, confront Ahriman on my own, no demon assistance involved. But now I feel like I'm missing something."

"We don't have much time," Dahlia prompted. "You

mentioned something about an exorcist in the grimoire?" Dahlia prompted.

"Yes." Cressida turned toward Granger again. "In one of the more celebrated battles of our history, a witch summoned a demon—who then possessed her."

"Ouch," observed Stefan.

Cressida ignored him. "An exorcist was called in to extract him from the witch, but the thrall in which she held the demon made it nearly impossible. Dahlia, can you find the passage?"

"Searching for it," Dahlia murmured, and Cressida glanced to Granger. "Have you ever worked with a coven?"

"That would be no," he said, shaking his head. "In the situation you describe, I'd first have the witch end her spell, though. She'd have to trust me to handle the demon without her magic."

"It's...that's weird," Dahlia muttered. "It's not coming up."

"Let me think..." Granger tilted his head. "Look for *promissio infernalis* in your grimoire. It should be in the same section as your requirement to wed a demon."

"Do it," Cressida said.

"Infernal promise." Dahlia nodded. "That sounds familiar."

She sat back a moment later. "Nothing. And nothing with the modifier Infernal that speaks to our issue here." She shook her head. "That's so strange, though. I feel certain I've read something about an infernal promise pertaining to a demon spell before. But this search function is inviolate. If it was there, we'd find it."

Granger frowned. "Very well. Look up *contractus daemonium* instead. There should be several instances."

Dahlia bent forward, only to jerk back a second later.

"It's there, but it's listed only once." She bit her lip. "In the section describing the termination of the coven, how it will be destroyed at the end of days."

A loud knock crashed at the door to the suite, making them all jump.

"High Priestess Cressida!" demanded Marcus Frost. "Are you hurt? Captain Dahlia!"

16

"This has been a mistake from the beginning."

Cressida regarded Marcus across the table, startled at the change in the man. After he'd dispatched Dahlia and his guards to return Stefan to his cell —and keep him there—he and Cressida had returned to Cressida's apartment. Now they were sitting together, almost touching but not. It was their most comfortable position, and had been for almost the past ten years, since they'd evolved from childhood friends into a strange awareness of each other. An awareness that, at least for her, had always hovered somewhere between attraction and affection, without ever quite moving forward to love.

Marcus, clearly, had never even reached the point of attraction.

And even her own attraction to her fated consort was something she needed to rethink, given the way her body had responded to Stefan the night before. She should be ashamed, she knew. Though there'd been no formal decla-ration between her and Marcus, he'd been her staunch supporter since she'd first entered the coven. Looked after by the lawgiver who'd found her and bonded to one of the youngest male witches ever accepted into the coven—a foundling, like herself—she'd formed the unit of security with Marcus she'd desperately needed as a child. Never once had Marcus been presented to her as a brother, so their relationship had never taken on that level of familiarity...but when they'd hit puberty and had grown in awareness of each other, they hadn't naturally paired off either. There was simply a comforting *knowing* between them, an understanding that everything would work out the way it was meant to work out when the time came.

That time was now, yet everything was going wrong.

"You were attacked by hellspawn. We're still trying to track down how they even got past our barriers, let alone who summoned them. No one in the coven would dare, but outside..." His voice trailed off. He seemed fixated on the attack portion of the previous evening, though she hadn't kept anything from him other than the most intimate moments of her time with Stefan. It was enough that the coven knew she'd welcomed the demon into her apartments. No one needed to know anything more.

Marcus, for his part, hadn't asked about Stefan at all, other than quizzing her on the Syx's ability to take out the insect horde. He'd not seen the mesh shift she'd worn before Stefan. There'd been so little left of it after the attack, she'd happily incinerated the remainder. She told herself it was to ensure that no poison left from the biting creatures remained on the fabric to harm her, but that wasn't the only reason, if she was being truthful. She also didn't want anyone to know about that shift or the way Stefan had touched her when she'd worn it, or especially about her physical and emotional reactions when she'd accepted that touch.

But the hellspawn attack seemed to fascinate and horrify Marcus by turns.

"Those creatures are so ancient," he said, sagging forward in his chair, his elbows on the table. His silver-blond hair was tousled and his normally young-looking face creased with a worry she'd never seen him express before. He prided himself on presenting a mask of benign indifference, no matter the trouble or the odds they faced. There had been threats to the coven before Cressida had ascended to high priestess. Marcus had served as chief of security for years by then, shepherded into the position by their lawgiver mentor, Fraya, despite his young age. He'd kept them strong; he'd kept them safe.

He'd never encountered hellspawn, though. She had, and with Stefan's help, she'd taken them *out*.

"We have nothing in place to deal with such creatures without drawing on the services of a demon. And we can't rely on that. Not now, with the horde so undependable. We would need to amplify our own strengths to be able to summon them at such short notice and put them to work destroying the creatures." He glanced back up at her. "You say the demon did so willingly?"

"He did," she said smoothly. "Of course, he was under my compulsion. I don't know how much that affected his decision-making ability." It was a lie, of course, but she was getting better at lying, it seemed, even to Marcus.

He made a face. "The best thing to do is to test the same process out on one of the other demons, but they are tainted stock as well. They're operating under the compulsion of the marriage ceremony. So it would need to be an external demon."

"We don't need to bring another demon into the mix,"

Cressida countered sharply. "I think we've got more than enough to deal with as it is."

"And you weren't hurt?" he asked her again. He seemed unable to move past that point either, but Cressida couldn't give him the satisfaction of the full answer. She'd been chewed up and spit out like a dog toy, but Stefan had healed her, inch by glorious inch. That simply wasn't something she was prepared to explain to Marcus.

"I wasn't injured," she assured him. "Any slight bites or scratches were gone by the time I cleaned up. I think the magic I was wielding to deflect them helped with that process as well."

"It makes sense." Marcus blew out a breath, then glanced at her with a lopsided smile. "You know, I half expected to feel your compulsion on *me* after the cup ceremony. I haven't at all, not even echoes from when you directed the demons to do your bidding. I would have thought there would be more connection between the six of us because of the ceremony."

Cressida chuckled. "I would think the last thing you would want would be to access the thoughts and emotions of another human in my thrall, let alone the demons."

"Purely as a point of curiosity. There's nothing in the sacred grimoire about how the members of the retinue should interact with each other, merely that they're all expected to support the high priestess. One way or another, I'll assure you that support. I'm just sorry I wasn't there to protect you when the hellspawn struck. We can't trust the demon to react like that again, to protect you so completely, without the proper compulsion spell. Those creatures should never have come through the veil."

She nodded, but she had bigger worries. Before them rested her computer, with its own copy of the grimoire.

Cressida's was set to go poof later tonight, a situation she didn't worry so much about given that Dahlia had a backup. But now it seemed like the grimoire was incomplete.

She gestured to the screen. "What do you know about this demon contract language?" she asked. "If I'm reading it correctly, the breaking of the contract between witch and demon pretty much ushers in the Apocalypse for our coven. But I feel certain I've read other sections of the grimoire that stated how it could be done."

Marcus grimaced. "You're mistaken, I'm sure. A witch must always stay in control of her demon. Always. There's no precedent for her giving up that control because the demon would kill her. Period."

"And if that happens?" Cressida pushed. "Would the coven truly be at risk?"

"Well...no," Marcus allowed. "I've asked the lawgiver before about this point. In the event that one of the demons turns on the high priestess and kills her or incapacitates her, Goddess forbid, an auxiliary fail-safe spell is triggered to contain the demon—freeze it in place. Then coven leadership would go to the next strongest witch in the room, who would immediately assume control of the demon."

"So there can be no true partnership between witch and demon," Cressida said thoughtfully. It was a lesson she'd learned as a very young girl, one of the first lessons, in fact. Yet now, it seemed...flawed. Incomplete.

Marcus's response was absolute. "No, there cannot. A witch controls a demon and then either sends it to the Goddess or returns it to whatever hole it crawled out of. That's it. Demons and witches cannot work together any other way."

"And the exorcist passage?" Cressida prompted.

He blinked at her. "The what?"

"There was an old story of one of the coven being possessed by a demon she'd summoned. And—"

"Oh—that." Marcus grinned, startling her with his sudden change in demeanor, as if he'd suddenly remembered an old joke. "That's a straight-up error, but we're on it. We're retranslating sections of the grimoire at the lawgivers' request. You wouldn't know because you've only just become high priestess. Elysium Gray was overseeing it."

"Retranslating," Cressida echoed. "Why?"

"Apparently, it's fairly routine. The ancient verbiage has gone through several translations over the centuries, and the lawgivers want it to better reflect the original Sumerian. Along the way, certain stories are turning out to be later additions, not part of the original codex. We're archiving those as we find them."

It sounded reasonable, and yet Cressida couldn't help a natural resistance to Marcus's offhand manner. But she didn't have time to quibble over the ancient book anymore.

"You have to be right," she said. "I thought we were on to something, something that would explain the need for the demon-witch connection. It just doesn't make any sense otherwise. The spells required to take down Ahriman require the strength of the coven, nothing more. And if simple demon energy was required to make this spell stronger, then so be it—we could have summoned a demon. There was no need to wed one."

"It seemed like a simple thing to do," Marcus said ruefully. "Setting it up the way we did, obeying the letter of the law without truly dirtying your hands. It seemed the easiest way to follow the ancient edicts without you being debased by a demon."

Cressida kept her expression perfectly neutral. What she'd done with Stefan had been about as far away from debasement as she could possibly have imagined. "Well, it's done. The coven seems completely mollified, and they're preparing for the attack on Ahriman. The grimoire says only that the consort must be present. Once again, there's absolutely no specific indication as to what he does other than stand there and look pretty."

Marcus smiled. "Well, you can rest assured I'm going to be doing more than that. We've summoned the best spell casters of our order to New York. They're assembling at the full moon in the sacred grove as the grimoire requires."

"Sacred grove," Cressida muttered. "Yet another foolish detail. We should have consecrated ground at headquarters long ago. It's far too dangerous meeting the way we are in Central Park. It is not as if the land is given over to primeval forest the way it once was."

"The location has the weight of centuries behind it, and our confrontation with Ahriman will take place on the night of the full moon," Marcus said, shrugging. "There's some magic that even the march of technology and science cannot overthrow."

"Fair enough." He was right, Cressida knew. The gathering of the Scepter Coven's strongest spell casters, fresh from their strengthening ceremonies in the hearts of their ancient community, would bolster Cressida's efforts significantly. All she had to do was call the magic that they willingly offered up and direct it like a spear directly toward Ahriman's heart. Though the creature was an ancient demon and probably didn't even have a heart, the center of his power remained the same. With the heart destroyed, the creature's power would be dramatically diminished. If he lived at all, he would be a husk of his former self. The covens would be safe. "We'll do what we have to do and then take our place as leaders in the fight against the demon horde. Once Ahriman is destroyed, we can start expanding our efforts from securing the covens to protecting the world at large."

"What about us, then?"

The question was so soft, Cressida almost thought she hadn't heard it, and she glanced sharply back to Marcus. He watched her, his eyes steady, his hands flat on the table, the way he did when he had an important point he wanted to make to the coven leadership or when he was concentrating hard on a spell.

"What about us?" she ventured.

"With the death of Ahriman, there will be no need to maintain the retinue. We'll send the demons back beyond the veil and release the human. The joint marriage will be annulled."

Cressida twisted her lips. "I never wanted to call it a marriage. That was the wording the lawgiver kept insisting was appropriate, but this is no marriage."

"Should it be?"

Cressida blinked at him. "What are you talking about? I'm not truly going to marry a demon." The very thought made her blood rush in her veins, and without wanting to, she summoned a picture of Stefan in her mind. Beautiful and vulnerable, lying on her bed, his eyes pressed shut in concentration, his body quivering with need. She'd never felt more powerful than she did with him beneath her, and it was a power that scared her. Scared her and drew her at the same time.

"What? No." Marcus's voice was sharper, irritated, and she blinked back to the present, refocusing on him. "Of course you're not going to marry a demon. Even thinking such a thing is tantamount to heresy, grimoire or not. I'm not asking about a demon, and before you deliberately confuse the issue further, I'm not asking about the exorcist either. I'm asking about *us*. What we've talked about for all these years. What we've dreamt of. There must be a ceremony we can undergo immediately after severing your royal retinue, binding us together."

"Oh." Cressida's eyes flared wide, and she would never have predicted the flurry of emotions roiling through her at Marcus's words. Because of course he was right. They had discussed this so many times in their plans for the future. Plans that included defeating Ahriman once and for all. After the demon had fallen, all that would be left would be for them to take the coven into a bold new chapter of its power, the malevolent force of Ahriman transferred to the positive, life-giving creed of the Scepter Coven.

No other company was strong enough to bend Ahriman's energy to its will. No other company was strong enough to force it through the prism of their spell craft and then direct it to the service of witches everywhere. The horde that now ran rampant across the earth would feel the power of their magic and would know they had destroyed Ahriman. They would cower and scatter, but they would eventually be rooted out, never to defile the Goddess with their presence again.

It would happen, and Cressida would be the tip of that arrow, her spell casting the cleaving edge that sliced through the filth of the horde. But that wasn't what Marcus was asking about specifically. And she knew it.

Had the attack of hellspawn triggered this? Was he truly worried about her...or, even more than worried, was he coming to recognize that he had feelings for her?

And why wasn't she happier about that?

She turned to him and smiled, forcing her words not to sound hollow. "Of course I want us to move forward, the moment that everything is settled with the coven and we're free to pursue our own lives again. Lives that we'll share as we lead and protect the witches of all the covens, not only Scepter. There will be much work to do, and I can think of no other person I'd rather be doing it with than you."

"Truly?" he asked, and there was the first sign of vulnerability in his eyes that Cressida had ever seen. She stuffed her own unruly emotions back into their box and took his outstretched hands.

"Truly, Marcus," she said. "The Scepter Coven needs strength, and we will be that strength. Again, there's no other person I've ever imagined standing beside me to complete this journey that we began so long ago. We'll go forward together and take the world by storm."

"The cycle will be unbroken," he breathed, and squeezed her hands hard, then turned away in time for Cressida to blink away the first beginnings of a tear.

17

S tefan pushed himself from his position against the wall as Marcus left. He could tell the moment Cressida realized he was there. The stiffening of her spine until the point it was about to crack seemed a good indication.

"How long have you been listening?" she asked, her voice completely neutral. He didn't know the woman all that well, but he suspected she was annoyed. That made two of them.

"Long enough. You really think this douche nozzle is your ticket to eternal power in the coven? Because I gotta tell you, I don't like your odds."

She pushed her hands through her hair. "Fortunately, I don't have to pay attention to your opinions. You're here as a battery, Stefan. The sooner you realize that, the better."

He raised one sardonic eyebrow. "Well, that's good, since it seems to me you didn't mind me going—and going—and going."

"Stop it," she snapped, her voice breaking a little, and she suddenly seemed on the verge of tears.

"Whoa, whoa, whoa." He lifted his hands. "I come in peace. Well, I came in peace. I hung around because your little powwow with the magic midget proved too interesting to leave."

"And I can send you back to your room this instant should I so choose. I may not be enough to send you myself —" She broke off, her lips twisting in a wry grimace. "Then again, now, maybe I am."

He shrugged, lowering his hands again. He liked the spark he was seeing in Cressida, but it seemed blocked by a heaviness he couldn't understand. So he pushed more. "You could, and then I could find a way around it, like I did with Mighty Mouse's attempt. Again. It's become my second-favorite pastime."

"And why do I get the feeling you're dying to tell me what your first-favorite pastime is? Please don't make me regret asking."

"Not at all, princess." Stefan grinned, watching her closely. She was trying to keep up her edge, even her anger, but there was something vulnerable underneath that façade, something important. Something he wanted to let blossom in his protective embrace. "I'd like to show you that, actually—assuming you don't have a hot date with Boltar or Zeneschiah?"

"I—" It was clear she was about to snarl something cutting at him, but Cressida abruptly stopped. Her shoulders slumped, and Stefan knew he'd won.

So why did he feel like he'd lost?

She sighed. "There will be no Boltar or Zeneschiah."

Cressida's words were so soft, Stefan didn't know if he'd heard them correctly. "And that means exactly what?"

She gestured with a weariness completely out of place on a human so young and full of potential. "They're loathsome beasts, and they've killed or tormented more humans than I can count. I make no apologies for using them for the coven's aims, for our crusade against demon kind. They deserve to be judged, and they will be judged. By the Goddess, not me. But I won't continue to keep them trapped in my retinue, slowly drained of their power, the way the lawgivers want me to do. The lawgivers and Marcus too."

"Okay," Stefan said in the ensuing silence. *This* was why humans were so complicated. Cressida was happy to blast any demons off the map who were a direct threat, but faced with torturing one to advance her cause...she couldn't. Or she wouldn't. "Seems like a shame to waste all that demon mojo, though, now that you've got it trapped."

Cressida's mouth lifted in a half smile. "Perhaps you had the way of it from the beginning. Perhaps I'm not a good fit —for the coven or for the role of high priestess."

"Wrong." Stefan's response was immediate and visceral, and the sharp rebuke vibrated between them, causing Cressida to shoot her gaze at him in surprise. "I appreciate your decision not to hook up with Z and B, more than you know. I even appreciate your noble reasoning, though, let's face it, princess, you're not doing it because of some misplaced appreciation for their deeply buried and fucked-up souls."

Stefan's pulse jacked as he spoke, the underlying truth in his words turning on him in scathing rebuke, but he too had a job to do here. Rout Ahriman and protect the coven. He couldn't do either if Cressida faltered, yet what had he done since the moment he'd shown up on her doorstep? Challenge her. Test her. Make her doubt herself.

He was getting the impression she'd been dealing with that her whole life. There probably wasn't a single person in the Scepter Coven she could call her friend except Dahlia—

and Dahlia wasn't enough to stand against the strength of all those allied against her.

It was time Cressida understood exactly what she faced —inside and outside the coven. He'd begun worrying about it with the onset of the hellspawn attack, but he'd not known the extent of the powers arraying against the high priestess until he'd been left alone in his rooms by Marcus and his goons. Then, he'd promptly left on a scouting mission outside this little witch fortress...a scouting mission he needed to take Cressida on too.

"Tell me something, Cressida. Other than this latest attack by the demons on your Serbian sisters, how much do the various covens keep track of the activities of demons?"

She frowned, seeming genuinely surprised by his question. That didn't surprise him, given what he'd seen building on the streets of the Big Apple. "You mean, demons all over the world?"

"Aa-yup."

"We don't keep track of them. We keep to ourselves— each coven its own force, separate and distinct. We don't meddle in the affairs of demons except to pull one or two into our midst, as needed."

"And they've left you alone."

"By and large..." Cressida's eyes were sharp on him as Stefan began walking around the room. This apartment. This building. This city. Layers of protection that kept the witches removed from the outside world... Why hadn't he seen this before?

Probably for the same reason Cressida hadn't. He hadn't wanted to.

"What are you getting at, demon?" she pressed him.

"Because you're pretty cut off in here, wouldn't you say? No one knows you're in the city, human or demon. That's always the plan, isn't it? Get in, get out, sneak a few demons into your pentagrams, then poof. You're back in the wind."

"Well..." Cressida paused, considering. "We've maintained secrecy for a reason. Witches are easy to persecute. Staying hidden has allowed us to survive."

"And when you hit demons, it's always in ones and twos, you say. Not whole swaths of the horde."

"Of course not," she said firmly. That tracked too. Despite their strength, the witches of the Scepter Coven knew they needed to be careful around the horde. "That would draw too much attention."

"Aa-yup. Sort of like what you're doing now. Drawing attention, I mean."

"What are you *talking* about?" Cressida snapped. "No one knows we're here, no one knows we're gearing up to confront Ahriman."

"No one," Stefan drawled, "except the dozen or so witches of East Side who are gathering in Central Park for your throw down under the full moon. Except the hundred or so demons you pulled in for a danceathon a couple of days ago, which resulted in a fair number of them getting sent to their great reward, while the others wondered what the hell'd happened."

She stiffened. "You did that. Not us."

"Well, sure. But you provided the barrel, the fish, and the big flashing arrow. Something like that...it could be noticed."

"Noticed? You're saying we're in danger. How?"

He held out a hand. "Much easier to show you than to bore you with the details, princess. Trust me."

Squaring her shoulders, Cressida strode the few steps needed to reach him, then put her delicate hand into his. As always, Stefan felt the jolt of her touch all the way to his toes, and as always, it disturbed him. He'd been no stranger to female companionship since he'd become a demon, and certainly not in the time before, when his role as a Fallen angel had given him the means and opportunity to become intimately familiar with women from every walk of life without any fear marring their enjoyment of his touch. Never once had a woman affected him the way Cressida did. She wasn't trying to seduce him. Far from it. She wasn't even trying to control him, not anymore. He'd probably made a mistake letting her see how ineffective that compulsion spell was unless she threw everything behind it, but he didn't care. There was something she needed to see. Something the entire coven seemed to be missing—or deliberately ignoring. He didn't know which was worse.

He dissolved them both into smoke.

A moment later, they reappeared on a New York City sidewalk, Cressida gasping by his side. It was early evening, and the weather was brisk and windy, but Stefan barely felt the breeze, and he suspected Cressida didn't either. One of the advantages of traveling demon class, you had a ready-made heat source whenever you needed it.

Instead, he curled her arm into his and started up the brightly lit street. They were in the shopping district of Manhattan, the tony shops of this area catering to the super-rich as well as to the ogling tourists who swarmed the window displays hoping for a glimpse of the superrich. As it turned out, they were bound to be disappointed. The wealthiest of these shops' clients either sent their minions to do their buying for them or shopped in exclusive appointments after hours. They couldn't be bothered to deal with the madding horde.

The horde itself, however, was a different issue altogether.

"Do you see what I see?" Stefan asked conversationally as they strolled up the wide boulevard.

"I'd first like to know how you were able to escape the bonds of the coven so easily," Cressida said tartly. "There's no way you should be outside the compound. The pentagram has been drawn."

"The pentagram has been broken, princess," Stefan said. "In three places, only two of which were my doing. The first break looked like it'd been scuffed out by somebody who knew what he was doing too. It wasn't a mistake. That little bug problem we had last night? Not a mistake, and not the horde getting lucky. It was planned. I don't know why yet, but it was planned."

She glanced at him hard. "Who would do that?"

"Most likely? A witch or witches who wanted to use the power of the pentagram for themselves. You take the existing pentagram with its highly specific containment spells, break it, and you can still use those spells to augment a larger pentagram for your own purposes. Whoever set up a secondary pentagram probably did so after you set up your little wedding party, or you would've noticed. I couldn't find any trace of a wider pentagram, but the fact that the smaller one hadn't been quite shattered I found...troubling. Someone went to some effort not to be caught."

"That's why you were able to move about freely."

"Well, I wouldn't go that far, but it certainly didn't help keep me in my place. Sooner or later, somebody else would've discovered it. You got enough juice to keep Zeneschiah and Boltar tied down, but that has more to do with the drugs you're pumping into their systems than any true magic you've got rocking. You really want to keep us under your collective wings, you're going to have to do a better job with housekeeping."

Cressida nodded. "Fair enough. But why did you bring me outside the compound? They'll know immediately that I'm gone."

"They will," he agreed, "and they'll also know that you're with me. In fact, it can be easily spun as you taking me out for a stroll to deal with the newest problem that's confronting your coven. A problem no one seems to be paying attention to, I might add."

"And that is?"

"Look around, princess. Tell me what you see."

Her nerves showing a little more obviously, Cressida did as he asked. She took in the crowded street with all its tourists mixed in with some of the businesspeople of the area. It was past the end of the workday, and traffic was thick and slow. The crush of people did nothing to diminish the energy buzzing along the streets of the city, however. It jumped and rattled and spun, seeming to gain in frenetic leaps by the moment.

"I see—sense—the energy, if that's what you mean," she said. "It's like an electric current snaking through the city."

"Not the whole city, not exactly," Stefan said. "In fact, it's a very narrow circuit surrounding a select few buildings on the west side of the city as well as a fair portion of Central Park. Not a closed circuit, but an open, spiraling one. If you were feeling a little cynical, you might call it a beacon. Or a target."

"What are you—"

"You're a witch of the Scepter Coven," Stefan said, cutting her off. "Demons are your playthings. You mean to tell me you don't feel them here, right now?"

Stefan watched as Cressida stiffened, then glanced around sharply. He could tell the moment she saw the truth about the people around them Holding her tight the way he was, his glamour provided an impenetrable psychic barrier surrounding her. They couldn't see her, not who she really was, and they certainly couldn't tell he was a Syx. To the demons crowding the sidewalk, they were just two additional New York pedestrians, out enjoying a lovely evening stroll.

"There are so many of them," she murmured. "That can't be normal."

"It isn't normal, even for New York, and believe me, this place is a hotspot for freaks. Half the publishing professionals in the city are possessed by demons. But this? No. This is all about the Scepter Coven's little field trip to the big city."

"The summons to Storm Court?"

"Maybe to start, but that doesn't explain the continued pull," Stefan said. "There's a pretty big disturbance in the Force, and it's centering here. It's strong enough to serve as a beacon to a pretty high level of demon too. That's what's surprising me. This isn't your usual riffraff sniffing around for trouble. These demons are players, the kind who go where the action is. Apparently, the action is here. I find that very interesting."

"I find that borderline terrifying," Cressida replied drily. "We don't have the numbers to combat this number of demons, not with our strongest spell casters needed for Ahriman. And I wouldn't trust bringing new ones in."

"Agreed," Stefan said. "They'd have to cross the demon moat, and that wouldn't make anyone comfortable. So maybe now's a good time for you to tell me a little bit about the enemies you've built up over the years."

She slanted him a startled look. "Enemies? The Scepter Coven doesn't have enemies."

"Annnnd I'm thinking that's bullshit, based on the

number of demons we see here. Because either you've got trouble in the ranks or an ineptitude that goes beyond a broken pentagram or two, or you've got an outside force who's deliberately stirring up the horde."

Suddenly, she got it. "Because of the mass summons," she said. "That's never been done before. And demons died."

"Bingo. It's one thing for demons to run riot on a coven. Boys will be boys, and all. But a coven suddenly blasting a big chunk of the horde into goop? That's different. That's new. And that's dangerous. Add to that even a single ripple that the coven's thinking about taking out Ahriman, the closest thing we've got to a superhero? Well, there's a lot of hands in the horde looking for a crank to turn. You just gave them one."

She twisted her hands, once more betraying her nerves. "I need to prove my worthiness for the role of high priestess. I can't fail in my attempt to overcome Ahriman—or be attacked by the horde before I even get the chance. I've worked my whole life to claim this position. I owe them my life and all my strength."

"Yeah, about that." Stefan pounced on the opening she gave him. "You sure you're remembering your time here with the coven correctly? Because no offense, but they don't seem to have your back."

"They've *always* had my back."

"Except for the hellspawn attack. And the dynamic duo of demons who are hella stronger than you guys needed to score, if your plan was to have three weak demons to satisfy the demands of your grimoire. And, oh yeah, except for Marcus dicking you over by not dicking you over. You're right. They seem like a great group, and I just met them. I can't imagine they've only recently started their shit."

"They've *always* protected me, and I can prove it." She glared at him. "As well you know. You can read my thoughts, my memories with a single touch, were I to let you. Shall I let you? Do you dare see what I can show you?"

Stefan didn't hesitate. He felt Cressida's guard slipping even as she rolled the idea around in her mind. He knew once she considered the full ramifications of what she was offering—letting a demon plumb her memories—she'd withdraw from his touch immediately. So he didn't give her the chance.

They were walking past a narrow alley fronted by two ornate statues, relics of a bygone era. By some miracle of recent street cleaning, the alley was pristine and untouched. Stefan turned sharply into the shadows and pressed Cressida up against the wall. A heartbeat later, his lips covered hers. Her mind burst open to him, and he plundered it.

And immediately saw that Cressida hadn't been lying— or being dramatic. He raced back through her memories as far as he could go, memories she herself didn't fully understand, he suspected, as she'd been barely more than a toddler when they were formed. She'd been found in what looked like a small-town hospital waiting room, though there were no specters of Child Services adults lurking in the background that he could see, nobody at all paying much attention to Cressida in the rush and screaming of a waiting room overcome with some kind of terrible accident. There was only a toddler girl dressed in a pink dress and black shoes, sitting quietly on the bench. The shoes took up most of her attention. They were black and shiny and they pinched her feet, but she already knew enough not to cry. Knew enough not to make a sound. When she looked up and saw an old woman standing in front of her, gray haired and gray eyed, she didn't cry either. The woman reached out, and Cressida lifted her arms, and no one paid them any attention.

Something about the scene nagged at Stefan's mind, something that seemed wrong, out of place, but Cressida's thoughts were unspooling too quickly for him to linger.

The lawgiver was the one Cressida called Fraya. She became a constant fixture in Cressida's mind, and shortly after, a young boy joined their small makeshift family. Marcus, Stefan assumed. All well and good—and then came the promises.

Stefan hissed as the picture unfolded in his mind. Turn after turn, the lawgiver secured advanced training, spell casting, gifts, money, for Cressida and, to a lesser extent, Marcus, by putting forth a single vow that both her young charges heard, over and over again. The young, gifted witch would defeat Ahriman. It was simple and clear, and the coven took it as a proclamation. Fraya was either intensely confident or staggeringly foolish, so caught up in her blind ambition that she believed more of what her young charge was capable of than was reasonable. Stefan was betting she was merely a fool, but even the rashest fool could gain a following, and the lawgiver definitely had that following. So did Marcus. But Cressida...

Alone. Cut off. A solo practitioner in the midst of what was supposed to be a sisterhood, with no one but Fraya, Marcus, and Dahlia to support her...why?

Anger simmered through Stefan's body. Cressida was being set up for brilliant success or soul-crushing failure. And the horde, who were not known for their sentimentality, had evidently picked up on the energies brewing here. Or, more likely, someone inside the coven had tipped them off. Neither Marcus or Fraya would put the coven at such outright risk, but did Cressida have enemies she wasn't aware of?

Either way, an entire delegation of them was currently waiting outside Cressida's door, slavering to keep the witches in their place. It wouldn't do for the covens to start controlling demons outright, after all. They could band together. They could enlist the aid of the Syx or humans like Jim Granger or the Dawn Children and present a serious threat against demon kind, the likes of which the horde had never seen. After six thousand years of an accepted world order...Cressida was changing the rules.

He was totally down with that. But there was a hesitation, a clear and present self-doubt that had been deeply instilled in Cressida, wrapped up in her misguided sense of deep subjugation to the woman who'd saved her as a child, to the coven that she'd been set up to save from her earliest days. Once again, the trauma of being a human nearly staggered Stefan. Cressida's entire life had been justified by beliefs, emotions, betrayals, and associations too twisted for his demon soul to unravel. He couldn't heal anyone from the inside out...so he'd start from the outside in.

Rightly or wrongly, the coven had set up Cressida as a demon-killing witch queen ready to take out the biggest, baddest demon of them all.

It was time she started looking the part.

18

Cressida blinked in a daze as Stefan lifted his mouth away from hers. She'd never revealed so much of herself in a single kiss, and she wasn't at all sure how she felt about it. She struggled to remember why she'd given that gift in the first place.

Stefan didn't take long to remind her. "Your memories suck," he said, grinning down at her.

"So you—wait. What are we *doing* back here?" He'd reached for her hand and was pulling her farther down the narrow alley between two posh buildings. There was no trash lining the narrow roadway, and it didn't reek of urine —much—but it seemed one dumpster away from being a rendezvous point for a drug deal.

"I'm a demon and you're a witch," Stefan scoffed. "You're really that worried about what New York can put up against us? At least the normal side of New York?"

When they reached the back of the building, the space opened up into a sort of box canyon for delivery trucks, with enough space that a moderate-size vehicle could back up to the various docks to unload its wares. One such truck was tucked into what looked like an abandoned loading bay. The rest were empty and locked tight.

Stefan stood back, scanning the buildings, and Cressida narrowed her eyes, trying to see what he saw. Jewelers, clothiers, perfumeries—all the best for New York's finest. Some of these vendors had been in these buildings for decades, some were barely staking their first claim to the prized territory. This far away from the thumping energy of the horde, the more effervescent electricity of the city swept to the fore again, humming and buzzing. It was no accident that so many of the world's richest and most famous gathered in New York City, no surprise that it was the home of irrepressible audacity in the creative arts and of relentless innovation in the financial sectors. The city was filled to the brim with Connecteds, or with people who fed off the energy of the Connecteds, and it had been since its founding.

"Here, I think," Stefan said, making his choice. He tugged her forward again, toward a small dock at the end of the row. It would take a reasonable-sized truck some maneuvering to get into place here—and the store probably wouldn't take deliveries at all unless they came in the dead of night. It'd be too difficult to get in and out otherwise.

The bay was currently locked tight, but not completely abandoned.

"Cameras," Cressida warned as Stefan stopped in front of the bay. The lip of it was about five feet off the ground. Great for backing a truck into, less useful for a human hopping up to the platform. A narrow door was fixed into the side of the wall beside the larger bay, with a set of plain concrete steps leading up to it. The door looked rarely used, the space around the stairs spotless. Wherever the good workers of this establishment took their smoke breaks, it wasn't here. Probably because of all the neighbors nearby. This was New York. There were always appearances to be maintained.

Stefan peered at the tiny official-looking camera at the dock. It was clearly activated, swiveling as it followed them across the front of the bay to the stairs. Stefan seemed to think so too, as he gave the fish-eye lens a cheerful wave. "Shouldn't be too long now."

He was right. The door at the top of the stairs opened less than two minutes later, and a slender young man of about twenty-five gazed solemnly down at them with an air of...what? Cressida had expected bemusement, even resignation, if not outright annoyance. She was surprised that anyone came to the door in the first place. But the young man's manner was too amped, too excited. He was trying to maintain his air of decorum, but beneath...

She glanced at Stefan. He grinned up at the man, and for a long moment, no one spoke. Or at least they didn't speak out loud. Who understood the ways of a demon?

"Of course," the young man said, though Stefan hadn't said a word. "Do the others know?"

"They will when they see me. Probably best for that to be in person. Not everyone is as sensitive as you."

"Then come with me." The man seemed to warm up further with the flattery, then he stepped back and motioned Stefan and Cressida inside. The door opened onto a sizable loading bay that held dozens of empty racks pushed up against the wall, but no merchandise. The racks tipped Cressida off to the idea that this was probably a clothier of some sort, but clearly not one that would leave its precious wares out in the open to get sullied by delivery truck exhaust.

The young man moved forward, quickly leading them

out of the delivery area and into another small corridor, this one much more nicely detailed. It seemed to be a row of offices, and he hesitated briefly at one of them. Stefan shook his head.

"We'll do our business in the front of the store. We'll need room to move around."

"Of course," the young man murmured, as if this were the most normal request in the world for a demon to make, and Cressida pursed her lips. She didn't get the feeling that Stefan frequented the tonier shops of New York City, even if, as a demon, he wouldn't be turned away anywhere. Demons who walked the earth never lacked for resources, each according to their unique vices. But though Stefan walked with the air of a man used to wearing the finest clothes, those clothes were glamour. They didn't cost anything because they were made of magic.

She wasn't made of magic, however, and when she walked into the main showroom of the couture clothier, she struggled not to gasp.

There were no customers in the shop, only a half-dozen shopkeepers, who gazed at her and Stefan, transfixed. The clothes on display were attractive in an elegant, understated way, gracing mannequins whose elegant poses seemed eerily serene. Jewels gleamed from one case, watches from another, and—inscrutably—small tables were set up around the room, creating almost an intimate bistro feel. What was this place?

"Welcome, welcome." A new man moved smoothly up to them, first shaking Stefan's hand, then Cressida's. He lingered over her, his penetrating gaze sweeping her from head to foot, making her feel self-conscious. She was dressed in her usual utilitarian clothes, of course, and she hadn't paid any attention to her hair. Plus, the New York wind had been especially stiff outside. What must she look like?

The man smiled at her warmly, as if he could read her thoughts. "We are delighted to be of service to you, High Priestess Cressida," he said, transferring his attention to Stefan. "How can we help?"

"You work with Connecteds," Stefan stated baldly. The man merely raised his brows.

"Every shop worth its salt along this row works with Connecteds, and several more in the area," he informed them calmly. "Of course, not every Connected can afford our unique mix of accoutrements, but we pride ourselves on catering to a specialized clientele." His gaze shifted back to Cressida. "I will say, we were unaware that the new high priestess of the Scepter Coven had returned to New York City. If we had known, we would have extended an invitation to visit us earlier."

Cressida frowned, shooting a quick glance to Stefan. None of the proprietors of the shops along this avenue had ever extended so much as a hand wave in her general direction. Why would they?

She thought back to Elysium Gray and her unfailingly elegant attire. "Did you work with the former high priestess?" she asked, unable to quell her curiosity.

"Alas, no," the man said without rancor. "Mistress Gray was rather fond of Chanel, and we found the brand had become far too diluted to be of interest to us anymore. She also was older and preferred a classic silhouette. I suspect for your needs, you would do well with a slightly more contemporary look."

"Well, thank you. Perhaps I'll have the opportunity to check out your offerings some other time. Right now, we're a little busy."

"Not too busy for this." Stefan pulled out a chair at one of the tiny tables and poured himself into it. Immediately, a staffer appeared at his side with a glass of champagne on a salver. The young man placed the flute on the table in front of Stefan, then whisked away as quickly and quietly as he had come.

She quirked a glance at Stefan. "You just pointed out that there's an entire mosh pit of demons at my doorstep. Do I really have time to go shopping?"

"You definitely don't," Stefan agreed. "Which is why you buy from this shop going forward. It will save you all kinds of time." He turned to the shopkeeper. "She needs everything, and she hates to try things on. You have a seamstress?"

"Of course," the shopkeeper said.

Cressida didn't miss the way the shopkeeper's brows arched, the only indication he was apparently willing to give at the news that he now clothed the high priestess of the Scepter Coven. He lifted a hand, and a young woman came forward, as neat and trim as if she'd come from central casting, complete with a small cloth measuring tape clutched between two carefully manicured fingers.

Cressida scowled first at the woman, then back to Stefan. "Seriously, I don't think I have time for this," she said again.

"You have time to change the way you think about yourself, and more importantly, to change the way others think about you. You have the capability in almost every environment to do this simply with your mind, but you choose not to. Whether it's a conscious choice or the results of conditioning that you're not even aware of, I don't know, and frankly, I don't care."

"The coven didn't choose me to lead them because of my fashion sense."

"And thank the Almighty for that," Stefan said drily. "But more to the point, they didn't choose you at all. You chose yourself, or your lawgiver did."

Irritation knifed through her. "It was my choice to ascend. It was my place. No other witch is willing to take this challenge. I am."

"A conversation for another time." He shrugged.

But Cressida wasn't having any of that. They were outside the walls of the coven. There was no Marcus here, no cameras, no surveillance. "If you've got something to say, demon, you'd best say it now."

"Fair enough." Stefan leaned back in his chair, sipping his champagne. The shopkeeper and the seamstress stared at them both, absolutely mute. Cressida was relatively sure that Stefan would wipe their memories when all this was done, but that wasn't her primary concern right now. Her concern was the look of utter speculation on Stefan's face.

"I see in front of me a woman of modest accomplishment."

"Don't flatter me," Cressida cracked, but Stefan kept going.

"Perhaps above-average ambition, moderate charisma, probably more grit than most. Where you're really rolling a twenty, though, is in potential. Untapped potential. By its very nature, untapped potential means potential that nobody has yet seen. So explain to me more clearly how a woman who's done nothing special except gain the seal of approval of a coven lawgiver is now in the position to take on the biggest bad of all time?"

Cressida stiffened in indignation. "I accepted the challenge."

"And again, you mean to tell me that no other witch in this generation or, hell, any generation before you in recent history has had the sac to take on your mythical nemesis? Because I call bullshit on that."

"I..." Cressida hesitated, confronting for the first time the reality of what Stefan was saying. Though the answers bubbling to her lips were real and absolute, she caught the inherent illusion in them. No one *had* stepped forward, as far as she knew, but she'd never thought to ask why. Maybe there had been no need, with Ahriman remaining in the shadows. A dire threat that had only materialized now. Or maybe...

It didn't matter. None of it mattered. "Well, I'm what you've got now, like it or not."

"And believe me, I like it," Stefan said. "Deep inside, you've got what it takes to lead, no doubt about it. But the woman who walks out of this shop tonight needs to be fundamentally different from the woman who walked in here. Especially with so many demons hanging around, waiting for your autograph. Because if there's one thing you need to know about the horde, we place a lot of stock in appearances. So if you look the part of a baller, we're going to treat you like a baller. If you don't, we'll just as soon walk all over you to get to whoever's really in charge. "

"Are you kidding me?" Cressida stared at him. "You think I can just put on a pretty pair of shoes and all my problems will be solved?"

"Dude, it's not like you're the first one. Hello, Cinderella? Dorothy? Puss in Boots?"

"You're insane," she said, shaking her head. "Out of all the demons in the world, I had to find the one who was insane."

"Go get measured for superhero boots. You're going to need them. We'll have everything ready for you when you get back."

Bemused, Cressida followed the young woman to a discreet door tucked in behind elegant clothing displays. That door opened onto a corridor, which led to several dressing rooms off to either side. The last one was the largest, with mirrors along one wall, tufted couches, and standing racks for clothing.

Cressida stared, completely at a loss. "I have no idea where to begin here," she finally admitted. "I don't pay any attention to clothes."

Another voice sounded at the doorway. "Music to my ears. But you gotta wear something, I guess."

Cressida turned abruptly. The woman who joined them was someone Cressida had never seen before—and she certainly didn't look all that impressive at first glance. Slender and compact, her hair pulled back into a functional ponytail, she was pretty enough, in a streetwise sort of way. Her gray eyes swept the room as Cressida stared at her, lingering on all the dresses and hooks, and she drove her fists deeper into the pockets of her battered hoodie. She wore black pants and boots as well, and...well, she looked like a criminal.

She also smelled faintly of charred skin...and a second later, Cressida was nearly flattened by the wave of power that flowed in her wake. She staggered back a step, gasping.

"Who are you?" Cressida demanded. The woman looked familiar—but she definitely hadn't met her before. Which meant she must have seen her face in one of the security reports that Dahlia faithfully provided her each week. She wasn't another witch, though the power within her was strong enough to set all of Cressida's chakras spinning. "What are you doing here?"

"Well, the long answer to that we probably don't have time for, but the short answer is—Stefan asked me to stop by. We go back a bit." She grinned, looking around the room, rocking back on the heels of her scuffed boots. "You don't want me on clothing detail, though. I totally suck at that, and you guys caught me at the office, where nobody generally sees me if I don't want them to. But the name's Sara Wilde, and—"

"Sara *Wilde*?" It all came together in a jolt for Cressida with a stomach-roiling jolt. Sara Wilde—or Justice Wilde, as she was now more formally known, was one of the most powerful Connecteds currently walking the earth, and she'd recently ascended to the council of a mysterious group of demigods who were amassing untold power. After the horde problem was fixed...the covens were eventually going to need to address the Council. But they were years away from that. "What are you doing here?"

"Relax, I'm not paying a house call as Justice." Justice Wilde shook her head. "Like I said, I was working late. When Stefan sent up a call about you playing with fire, I got curious. So I thought I'd drop in."

Cressida's hands began to tingle with heat, and she hurriedly put them behind her back, even as Justice Wilde regarded her with keen interest. She didn't know much about this woman or her abilities, but...there had been something about her wielding fire in one of the reports. "Stefan brought you?"

A new voice rang out behind them, rich with satisfaction. "Well, that's maybe overstating it. No one brings Justice upon them. She goes wherever she wants."

Cressida spun again to take in the demon lounging against the opening to the dressing room. "You know, it sort of defeats the purpose of having a private dressing room if you're going to throw a party in here."

Sara snorted beside her. "Get used to it. Demons are the worst at respecting personal space."

"It's one of our charms," Stefan allowed. Still, he looked happier than Cressida had ever seen him, and she took a moment just to stare. He'd known she was about to face a challenge she'd never expected, and he was doing all he could to prepare her—from the outside in, and from the inside out. What had she ever done to deserve his help? She'd kidnapped him, insulted him, compelled him against his will—and then practically thrown herself at him. Why was he helping her?

It didn't seem to matter why, though. Not to Stefan. He practically glowed with pleasure as he took in the Justice of the Arcana Council, the two of them squaring off like gunslingers of the Wild West. Or Wilde West, maybe...

"Justice," Stefan said, his grave expression ruined by the tug of his smile.

"Demon." Sara Wilde nodded back. "You owe me, by the way."

He shrugged. "I owe you for a lot of things."

"Truer words were never spoken." Then the Justice of the Arcana Council shook out her hands—and they burst into blue-white flame.

Cressida jerked her own hands up, staring at the sudden flare of reddish-purple flame that twisted and roiled around her fingers. "What's happening?" she whispered.

"More than anyone around you might be expecting, High Priestess, but that's their problem, not yours," Sara answered. "For the time being, let me teach you how to throw some fire."

19

S tefan eased into position next to Jim Granger, unsure of whether to feel cocky, vindicated, or scared out of his mind. He suspected he wasn't going to like the answer.

It'd been a full day since he and Cressida had completed their field trip outside the coven walls, and he hadn't seen her once. She'd absorbed every lesson Sara Wilde had thrown at her, managed to craft a few credible fireballs of her own, and by the end of it, she'd walked out of the tony Fifth Avenue shop with an entirely new wardrobe and a clothier for life...at least, after they'd cleaned up all the fire damage.

But the future remained a little murky. Cressida now understood what she could technically pull off as a witch with a demon consort. But would she—could she—do it in front of her coven? Would she be willing to step out from the shadow of her own screwed-up beliefs regarding these people?

Stefan surveyed the chamber. They were in some sort of conference room for the damned, complete with a pentagram etched into the floor and walls with decoration that echoed early Medieval torture chamber—pikes, swords, whips, and even a few well-oiled chains. None of the pieces looked used, so they had to all be for effect. Clearly, Marcus must have been doing the decorating.

The exorcist glanced his way. "Wondered when you'd make an appearance," Granger murmured. "You missed Marcus's speech to the coven. He's making Cressida out to be some kind of virgin sacrifice for the good of the people."

Stefan smirked. "Well, close enough. I thought she'd be here by now."

"Patience is a virtue. For a being more than six thousand years old, I would have thought you'd have learned that by now."

"Funny how that works." At that moment, however, the crowd at the far end of the chamber began to stir and then actively start chattering. Stefan perked up, straining to see, but caught himself in time as Marcus turned sharply on the dais, his eyes seeking him out. It wouldn't do to let wonderboy know he had anything to do with Cressida's new look.

So he kept his face studiously neutral as the high priestess of the Scepter Coven swept into the room.

She was—incredible.

Cressida's rich auburn hair still tumbled over her shoulders, but instead of her usual tunic and pants, she wore a gorgeous black cape lined in green silk, which flowed out around her shoulders to reveal a perfectly tailored black silk suit topping high-heeled leather boots. A choker of fiery emeralds graced her neck, the perfect match to her bright, alert eyes. Stefan wasn't sure exactly what Marcus had told the crowd, but Cressida wasn't looking like any virgin sacrifice.

What she did next, though, made his teeth grind.

After sweeping the room with an insolent, confident gaze, not hesitating a moment on him or Granger, she caught sight of Marcus. Her smile flashed wide, her hands went up, and she moved toward him, allowing him to sweep her into a full embrace.

The coven burst into heartfelt and sustained applause.

"What is *that* all about?" Stefan growled.

Granger hummed a short breath beside him. "Most likely, it's about her putting up the appearances she must in order to convince the coven she's going to be the leader they expect her to be."

"She should find another way to do it, then. I don't trust that asshat."

"You don't get a vote," Jim Granger pointed out, less than helpfully.

"Yeah? Well, I should. This is bullshit, this little game she's playing with this retinue. She's not going to bang every one of us, I don't care what fairy story she's fed to her coven."

Granger chuckled beneath his breath. "What makes you think she hasn't already banged all of us, as you so colorfully put it, and merely spelled you into not knowing?"

Stefan wasn't fully conscious of moving. He only knew that one moment he was sitting next to Granger at the edge of the chamber, waiting for foot soldiers to show up with the other two demons from their holding tank—and the next moment, he had Granger pinned to the back of his chair, his hand gripping the mortal's throat and clamping down—

He flung himself backward before the instant could be completed, sprawling into his own seat once more. A few of the witches on the far side of the room glanced over, then went back to their own conversations.

"Dammit—dammit, I'm sorry, man. I didn't mean to—are you okay? Are you—*dammit!*"

Stefan snarled as the wave of pain struck him. He grabbed his own head with his hands, his fingers tight on his temples. There was so much screaming in his mind that he could barely breathe. He'd lifted his hand against a child of God! Not merely lifted it, he'd attacked a human with the intention to do severe bodily harm, and had only brought himself back from the brink in the barest nick of time.

Beside him, Granger straightened in his chair, but Stefan couldn't focus on him at first. The rules of being a Syx were inviolate and not all that dissimilar to the rules of being a Fallen. The first and most important being: you do not —*ever*—harm a child of God. Under no circumstances. They could be the vilest piece of filth that walked the planet; as a demon, it was not his place to send them to God's judgment. Only they could make that decision—say, by attacking Stefan or one of his brothers outright. The Syx were allowed to defend themselves, but even in that defense, the likelihood was next to nothing that they would ever be *forced* to take a life.

And here he'd nearly choked the breath out of Granger because the man had made a joke?

Stefan went still, then pulled his hands away from his face, his gaze pinned on Granger again. The bastard was smiling. Grinning, actually. "That *was* a joke, right?"

Granger's grin morphed into a darkly amused chuckle. "That was a joke."

"You realize how close you came to dying just now?"

"About as close as I would any day walking down the street," Granger countered. Stefan scowled, and Granger shook his head. "You are a dangerous being, Stefan, the iron fist of God, set against the damned. But you're no danger to a human. Which is a pity, because humans were your undoing all those years ago, weren't they?"

Stefan looked away, his heart still racing. "I don't talk about that."

"You don't, but perhaps you should," Granger said mildly. "I didn't only serve as an exorcist, you know, when I wore the collar. I had my share of learning the worst that humankind had to offer, and finding ways for those who came to me to forgive themselves their sin."

Stefan snorted. "I don't think the problem is me forgiving myself."

"Don't you? Do you really believe that your beloved Father—"

"He's not *my* beloved Father. Not anymore."

Granger shrugged. "Fair enough. Then do you really believe the..." Granger broke off, his eyes going wide. "What am I asking? It's not a question of belief for you, is it? It's a knowing. You were there. You stood beside the Father as one of his most precious creations, perhaps listening to his very words as he spoke of the children he had set upon the earth below. Is that so?"

Stefan made a face. He avoided conversations with priests for exactly this reason. Sooner or later, they would ask some version of this question, and he never had a good answer for them. "Unfortunately, I can't help you, padre. When I committed my sin, my memory of everything before that sin was wiped out, at least in terms of my time as an angel, Fallen or otherwise. I know the circumstances leading up to my sin so that I may never forget the acts that laid me low, and I know everything that happened after that sin. The passage of six millennia hasn't dulled the memory of how I took my demonic form. But being an angel? Existing in the brightness of God's glory? No. I don't recall anything like that. I certainly don't recall standing around chatting with God about how He did or didn't forgive His children their transgressions."

Granger took this information in stride. "So then call it a matter of belief, as I began. Do you really believe that the Father would keep a ledger of the sins of his creations? At least one more exacting than their own?"

"I..." Stefan frowned. It was never his place to question the decisions of the Father, though he certainly had seen the worst of what humanity had to offer. The atrocity that humans were capable of committing against one another, whether pitting the strong against the strong or, far more often, the strong against the weak and unprotected, had shaken all the members of the Syx at one time or another, perhaps none so much as Grigori. He didn't know the big man's sin, but with each new act of human depravity he was forced to witness, the giant seemed to withdraw more deeply into himself.

As for Stefan, he merely tried to avoid thinking about it. And fortunately, with the demands on the Syx, he didn't have time to reflect too often.

Granger was still waiting for an answer, however, and Stefan tried to give him one. It was the least he could do after attempting to choke the man to death.

"The Father and His child together created their plan, long before that soul takes its place on the earth," Stefan said, the words coming to him as if from a long-ago catechism he'd forgotten he'd ever learned. "Only the beginning is charted, and perhaps a few key points. The rest is up to the child to discern. Each would learn, each would do their best, each would, one day, return for an accounting."

"An accounting," mused Granger. "So a judgment."

"Not...judgment, not the way you're thinking of it."

Stefan winced as a searing pain skated across his brain. "I think I need to stop talking about this. I don't think I'm supposed to remember."

"And yet you do remember," Granger prodded. "You can."

"Sure, I guess," Stefan said, gritting his teeth now. The pain was building again in his mind, taking his breath away.

"That's important," Granger said, then clapped Stefan on his shoulder, the move so unexpected that Stefan once more focused fully on the ex-priest. The headache fled as quickly as it came, leaving him gasping in relief.

He stared at Granger. "Did you just do some mojo on me, old man? Because that is seriously not cool. And I didn't think you could do that."

"Demons," snorted Granger. "Always so filled with hubris they can't see the truth in front of their faces."

"You know, you aren't a consecrated exorcist anymore, and more to the point, I'm not inhabiting a human. You have no power over me."

"Clearly untrue," Granger mocked, though his tone remained light. "I nearly incited you to choke me to death, and that was with one tossed-off line. I'm not the only exorcist in existence either. There are some servants dedicated to the Father who don't have the slightest bit of Connected ability beyond their own faith who could take you to your knees."

"Doubtful."

"And then there are the Dawn Children, descendants of the Fallen."

"You know about those?"

"Any exorcist worth their salt knows about them, for all that they're nearly impossible to find," Granger said. "Their ways have been written down often enough, surviving in myth and legend. And let's not forget where we find ourselves at this moment, as a witch brings up two bound demons and you, a Syx, allow the indignity of being at least somewhat bound within her compulsion spell. A demon may be the first and best offense against another demon, but humans are not without their own tools."

"Yeah, well, tell that to the humans who beg to be saved from demon kind. I think they're more than happy for the help of the Syx."

"As they should be. As I said, the first offense is always the best, and you and your team are certainly that. And demons must always be acknowledged for their strength. It's why I'm curious about the charade that's about to go on here."

Stefan looked around, frowning. "What do you mean?"

"This coven isn't ready to go after Ahriman. They haven't completed the required rituals. The grimoire was no longer complete, but the section on Ahriman remained intact, from what I could tell. There's much Cressida and her Marcus have yet to do."

"You don't need to refer to him as 'her Marcus.' Marcus by itself is fine. Or better yet, dickhead. It suits him."

Granger eyed him. "You do know that Marcus will make his play for Cressida before all this is done, and she no doubt believes she owes him her fealty. It will prove a difficult choice for her."

Stefan's mind shot instantly to the scene in Cressida's apartment with Marcus, where she quite clearly demonstrated how difficult that choice would be for her. Only she was choosing the wrong guy. "I still can choke you to death, you know."

"I'll keep that under advisement. But the gathering of witches here is not of the coven's strongest. Dahlia has shared enough of their customs to make that clear. What-ever is happening today, it isn't the attack on Ahriman. So what is it?"

"Uh-huh. More to the point, what else, exactly, has Dahlia shared with you?"

To Stefan's immense delight, Granger colored. "She serves the high priestess, to whom I am officially affianced."

"You're more than that, buddy," Stefan observed drily. "Seems kind of a dumb move for Dahlia to...unless...wait a minute. She's not allowed to consort with ordinary Muggles, is she?"

Granger sent him a questioning look. "With who?"

"Never mind. It's all becoming clear to me."

"Well, it's not what you should be focusing on." Granger pointed to the far group. "Those witches are warriors. They serve Dahlia and Marcus, both of whom are escorting the trapped demons here. Which will leave us with a major part of the coven's security force in this room, yet no lawgivers or spell casters. Why?"

"Ummm...training?" Stefan hazarded.

"Training, or a test of Cressida of some sort," Granger agreed. "A test they wanted to conduct out of view of the greater coven. I don't like it."

Stefan didn't like it either. But at that moment, five figures emerged from the far corridor, and Stefan winced at the two in the center. The demons Boltar and Zeneschiah had been enjoying themselves way too much on the coven's dime. In the few short days since they'd arrived in Storm Court, their glamours had begun to wane, and glimpses of the creatures beneath showed through.

"That's...interesting," Granger murmured. "Is that supposed to happen?"

"That would be negative. Demons prefer to hold on to

their glamours. It's what we do." Stefan narrowed his eyes as he took in the two demons, but neither Cressida, Marcus, nor Dahlia appeared to notice that anything was wrong with them. If anything, the three witches treated the demons as if they were about to spontaneously explode into a killing fury. These two didn't look like they could explode into much more than a couple of cheese puffs. What had happened to them?

"Stefan of the Syx, Jim Granger." Cressida's voice carried over the open space, sort of an unofficial call to action. Stefan and Granger stood as the security force of the Scepter Coven spread out around them in a full circle, the two guards nearest to them reaching out their hands, clearly expecting Stefan and Granger to take them. A quick glance back at Marcus and Dahlia confirmed that their hands were firmly locked with the other two demons' as well, while Cressida remained in the center. Stefan wasn't sure he liked that setup.

"Are we going to play dodgeball?" he asked, his voice as loud as Cressida's had been. What the chamber might be lacking in décor, it made up for in acoustics.

Cressida met his gaze, her eyes wide and intense as if she was desperately—and unsuccessfully—trying to mind-meld with him, but it was Marcus who spoke. "We need to know if we can channel your strength as the sacred grimoire demands. The strength of the demon combining with the strength of the witch."

Stefan looked around the circle. "I'm pretty sure this isn't what the grimoire had in mind."

"We will drop the wards on this room. Per information provided by High Priestess Cressida and confirmed by my own troops, our enemies remain outside, circling. They'll have their shot at us."

Stefan's jaw dropped. "Their *shot*? Are you nuts? You can't seriously be thinking of bringing those guys in here—"

"It is done," Dahlia intoned.

Stefan flinched, but for a long moment, nothing happened. There was a high whistling, the rush of underground trains as the subway system rolled and raced by, but no one came racing into the room from the varied and many tunnels. No one attacked from the sewers. No one—

Then the entire chamber exploded with blinding light.

"*Hold.*" The order came high and clear from the mouths of many at once, and Stefan braced himself, unable to tear his hands from the compelled hold of the witches. Roiling in the center of the space were more demons than he'd seen in any one place since he'd gotten back from spring break in Cancun. They burst forth and battered against the hold of their little witch circle, a circle that wasn't going to survive with so few master spell casters, Stefan didn't care how strong the Scepter Coven secret handshake was or how powerful their pentagram.

"Hold!" demanded the joined voices once more. Cressida's voice carried clearly this time but there was something wrong. A different entity was coming through the energy of the demons as if they'd been a mask, a beard for something worse. Sort of like the three ancient lieutenants of Ahriman had been in Storm Court. Stefan shot a glare at Zeneschiah across the floor. The minion of Ahriman stood with his face alight in half horror, half ecstasy, his body caught up in a burst of energy that he clearly was not directing. He was as much a puppet in this as all of them, which made it all the worse when the cluster of demons split in two and out stepped a creature of so much power that Stefan blinked in surprise. Not Ahriman, he thought, but still...impressive.

Even more intriguingly, this was a female demon, a fearsome gold-plated dragon straight out of a thirteen-year-old human's most fervent high-fantasy fantasy, complete with flaring nostrils, flapping wings, and fiery breath. The demoness turned, then turned again, her scream loud and long, as if she was as startled as the rest of them at her summons.

This—was going to be bad.

Stefan lurched forward, turning as quickly as he could to release himself from the circle and lock it down once more, protecting the coven from their own foolishness.

But by the time he turned again, it was too late.

Cressida was gone.

20

This demon *wasn't* Ahriman, Cressida was certain. Which was good. Ahriman shouldn't be able to be summoned without Cressida being involved. The sacred grimoire was clear on that point.

Unfortunately, however, other than it not being Ahriman, Cressida didn't know who in the seven hells this demon was.

That was bad.

As outlined by Marcus and totally approved by Cressida and the lawgivers, tonight's summons of the Scepter Coven was supposed to call only those demons in the immediate vicinity that had begun amassing because of Ahriman's impending arrival—then order them back to wherever they came from. No death, no sending them to the other side of the veil, merely a quick return-to-sender to clear the city of unnecessary distractions. Simple. Easy.

This demon's appearance was anything but simple and easy.

She was a dragon of almost mythical perfection, large and coiled and scaled in gold, her wings arched tight over her body. Cressida stepped into the center of the pentagram, pulling from the strength of the witches' circle—a circle that had significantly weakened at exactly the same time that the ancient demon had taken form. But the demon wasn't looking at her—she was looking at Stefan.

"*You*," she ground out, with such fury that Cressida found herself glancing back to Stefan—who couldn't see either one of them. The demon might be a Syx, but he couldn't reach her in this circle while she invoked the highest level of protections that she and Marcus had spelled into existence. The circle was holding in part because of Stefan's strength, but the witches of the Scepter Coven still held the power. And, as head of the Scepter Coven, Cressida knew their powers were hers.

She lifted her chin along with her voice. "You were not summoned here," she announced, and the demon whirled to face her. "You will go."

The demon sneered. "A baby witch. You don't even know enough to fear me, do you?"

"I fear no demon."

"Well, you should," the creature hissed, edging closer. "You've attracted far too much attention for one so small and weak. With one command, I could call upon the demons surrounding this hovel to attack your entire coven. You really want me to do that?"

"You brought those demons?"

"Not brought them. They came of their own volition, tipped off by the Scepter Coven's summons of so many demons in one place. I was bored, so I decided to tag along. You don't know the powers you're dealing with, do you, in your pathetic attack on Ahriman?"

Cressida narrowed her eyes. "How do you know anything about that?"

The demon laughed, a low, scornful sound. "You witches are all alike. You think that the universe was created on your watch, that no one stronger has ever come before you, and surely no one stronger will ever come after. Do you truly believe that your precious coven has never attempted what you are attempting now?"

Cressida stiffened. Stefan had said much the same thing, in only a slightly less scathing voice. "What are you talking about?"

"I'm talking about your history, baby witch. The old saying never does go out of style. Those who control the present, control the past. Those who control the future..."

"You're saying that others have attempted to overthrow Ahriman before me. And that records of their attempts have been erased?" She'd feared as much when she'd learned of the missing passages in the sacred grimoire. What else was being systematically hidden from her—from her, and from the entire coven?

"Well, it's not such an unlikely scenario, is it?" the demon mocked. "Think about it. Your attack on Ahriman was motivated by what? Power? Did they promise you control of the coven if you're able to succeed? Because that's the usual gambit. But it's not the only reason that's made a witch step up and be counted. Sometimes it's as simple as life or death. That always makes for a vigorous attempt. Other times, it's money. On the rare occasion, it's love. But by far, power and control of the coven is the easiest carrot to dangle in front of a baby witch too stupid to realize she's being duped."

"You're lying," Cressida said, squaring her shoulders. She could feel the strength of the demon before her, but she had strength too. "You're a *demon*. Your entire purpose in life is to confuse and manipulate and deceive. Why should I listen to you?"

The demon hissed a low, challenging chuckle. "Ordinarily? You shouldn't. Especially now that I know you have a Syx in your midst, particularly that one. That means I was lied to...and I don't like being lied to." The demon swung her gaze to regard Stefan, who remained staring at the pentagram as if he could explode its secrets with the sheer intensity of his gaze. "But I've been watching you, baby witch. I can feel your hunger and your flaws. You seek to strike, but you don't know what you're doing. With the shift in magic that's taken place over the last several weeks...it's a dangerous time to be a witch."

Cressida narrowed her eyes. "No more dangerous than it's ever been. And certainly no more dangerous than it is to be a demon, no matter the era."

"You see, that's where you're wrong," clucked the demon. "This new influx of magic hasn't just upgraded you puny humans, and it hasn't merely added more of the horde to our numbers. It's *reinvigorated* the horde. We didn't need any amplification to our magical abilities, our strength. But you could say that we needed a little boost of confidence. Mortals have grown so much stronger over the millennia, especially those who follow the witch's path. Your circles have improved, your techniques of control have grown more complex. While the horde? We don't change. We are as God first made us all those millennia ago. There are no new demons, did you realize that? I mean, yes, there are an *awful* lot more of the horde walking the earth than there used to be, but they weren't created out of dust. They're merely breathing different air now. Much more pleasant air for many of them, though not for all, it should be noted. Not for all."

. . .

CRESSIDA FROWNED, trying to follow the path of logic the female demon was taking. In some respects, she reminded her of the lawgiver, presenting a circuitous pass to her ultimate destination, drawing Cressida along with her. As if she didn't want to outright say what she was getting at. For the lawgiver, this was because she wanted to develop Cressida's abilities to discern and solve problems. But what was the demon's goal here?

Something else didn't add up. Demons didn't work with witches of their own volition. They were *summoned*. They were coerced.

Almost without realizing it, Cressida tapped into her newfound well of power and reached out to the ancient being, rifling through her thoughts. This demoness, for all her ancient might, had breached the pentagram of a Scepter Coven witch. In this pentagram, Cressida held more power than the demon perhaps fully understood. So she reached out, and she rifled, and she learned the piece she most needed to know. The demon's name.

"Who summoned you here, Belessunu?" she murmured. She didn't have to speak loudly. The sound of the demon's name could reach it across any length of land or water, any patch of sky, even all the way to the other side of the veil. The sound traversing the mere feet between them was barely more than a whisper, but it served the purpose.

Belessunu curved her supple neck until her dark gaze once more rested on Cressida's face. Her smile turned into an approving grin. "There you go, baby witch, reaching beyond your grasp. But I like it, I like it. What you need to understand is that *nobody* summoned me here today. I came of my own volition, by the rights accorded me through your own sacred grimoire. Your defenses are nowhere near as strong as you think, not when it comes to the coven. Your strength does not lie in their strength, no matter what you tell yourself, no matter what others would like you to believe. I come because to all things there are seasons, even for demons. And I would warn you, since you have set upon the path to attack Ahriman, that you should choose your friends more carefully. The Syx is no ally to you. He is a force unto himself, not to be trusted."

Cressida lifted her brows as she watched the ancient demoness. The beast's attention had returned to Stefan, but she wasn't watching him with anger so much as interest. As if she'd been told something she'd always believed but now wasn't quite so sure.

"What do you know about the Syx?" Cressida asked.

The demon answered without hesitation. She was compelled to do so. "Probably the same as what they told you. I do not lie, not in the traditional sense. They were told a fantasy shortly after they committed their sin, a fantasy they held on to with such fervor that their unit was born. A fantasy that was carefully cultivated and maintained and enhanced by the Archangel Michael." The demon's lips twisted. "The sword of God himself."

"How do you know it's a fantasy?" Cressida demanded. "What is it they believe?"

"I know because the very nature of what they want is a flawed premise," the demon retorted. "Redemption. And the archangel holds it out like a carrot on a string. They've become his enforcing hand, yet in all the years of their service, they have come no closer to their precious redemption. They're being used, as you're being used. That in and of itself would not be so much a problem, except that they refused to acknowledge it. They refuse to see the lies they're telling themselves."

"Or it could be you who are telling lies."

"To you? No. I don't need to tell you lies. You've been fed a steady diet of lies since you were very small. I'm here to tell you a singular truth. You are stronger than you know, Cressida Frain. Not because you're special, and not because you've learned more and better than anyone around you. You're quite depressingly average, now that I've met you."

Cressida rolled her eyes. "That means a lot, coming from you."

"But what sets you apart is not who you are, but what you've done. This earth was created in the service of God's children, and all they have to do is ask and receive. But they do not ask. They remember the mud from which they were formed far more than the stardust. I'm told it's human nature."

Her glance shifted to Cressida. "But it's not your nature. You were born to shine. For the first two years of your life, years you can no longer remember, you were told that every day. It was only *after* that you forgot it."

"After what?" Cressida asked sharply. "After I was abandoned?"

The demon's lips curled back from her fangs. "That's not mine to say, baby witch. But you are right, in the end. I *was* asked to come here."

Cressida frowned. "I thought you said you came at your own volition."

"I said I was *asked*, not summoned. I was asked to come here and rip you limb from limb."

"Asked by who?"

"Ah...but that would be no fun to share. Know that I wasn't the first, however. The hell spawn visited upon you were also a special request." Before Cressida could interrupt the demoness continued. "It was a sudden invitation, an unexpected one, but one I couldn't resist. Still, I would've rather enjoyed seeing you confront Ahriman. There's an energy to you that almost makes me believe you could have pulled it off."

"You speak as if I won't," Cressida said. "I'm here to tell you that I will."

"You won't, baby witch. You can't. You'll be dead."

Then she stepped back, and chaos filled the room.

The flurry of demons that poured into the coven's circle was unlike anything Cressida had ever experienced before. Even the influx of summoned demons in the Storm Court club was nothing like this. Those demons had come in with an express purpose, culled from the pack by their strength and sophistication, all part of Cressida and the coven's spell. This was different. These demons were wild, untamed, practically feral, and she realized in a heartbeat this was what had been visited upon the earth with the recent opening of the veil to allow in more members of the horde. This primal hatred of all things human, of all things born in and blessed by God. These demons hadn't acclimated to the point of the understanding that marked demons that had walked upon the earth for thousands of years. Though they'd been hatched at the dawn of time, they'd not truly taken their first steps until now. It was as if they'd been held in stasis, an experiment gone wrong, frozen in place until such time as they could be released into the natural environment.

And now they were.

For all that they were chaos, however, they weren't strong, Cressida realized. Once again because of their inexperience among mortals. They were raw and terrifying, particularly to the uninitiated. But they weren't powerful.

There was something here she should be understanding, she thought. Something important. Belessunu was nowhere to be found, however, and as Cressida moved forward, her hands up, spells falling from her lips like a spray of gunfire, she lost that understanding. It slipped away as swiftly as it had almost come to her. She didn't have time to mourn its loss either.

Because the circle of power was broken.

The screams of the witches around her suddenly penetrated Cressida's fog. She turned, realizing that her own coven was staring at her with horror-struck eyes, and she was no longer alone. A ring of defenders stood around her, facing out, hands up and weapons at the ready—the three demons and the human. Marcus, however, was gone.

"Attack!" She commanded her own cadre of demons without hesitation, and Boltar reacted first. He launched into the melee and started hurling demons right and left. Zeneschiah was right there with him, his glamour slipping away to allow his fire drake persona to rush the floor. Every demon he struck burst into flames and then bubbling goop as they returned back beyond the veil. Stefan and Jim Granger worked side by side, the Syx teeing up demons for the sole purpose of helping the exorcist to strike them with his mighty cross, like a baseball bat over the top of the plate. Over and over again, the demons struck, and over and over again, Cressida and the others fought back, each time gaining ground, but not without paying a price. As she had with the demon spawn, she suffered more injuries than she expected she would—fire scorched her hands and blackened her skin, huge gashes were torn in her thighs, her arms, instantly cauterized by the heat radiating from the battling demons. Small blessings, she supposed, but blessings nonetheless.

And then, so suddenly that it took her breath away, it was done.

She gaped around her, swaying. As the smoke cleared, no other figures remained upright in the circle, other than herself, Stefan, Zeneschiah, and Boltar. Jim Granger was out cold on the floor, Marcus leaning over him, and Cressida blinked. When had he joined the battle? She honestly couldn't remember.

The witches of the Scepter Coven stood at the fringes and stared at her with wide eyes—too wide. She risked a glance down at herself in dismay. Her beautiful clothes! She'd had them all of a few hours, and they'd been ripped to tatters, the luxurious silk stained red with the blood of demons...

Wait.

Demons didn't bleed red.

She stumbled forward, her sight dimming as a roar reached her across the open space.

"Cressida!" Stefan howled.

21

S tefan blew forward in such a rush of panic that he was already half-vaporized by the time he connected with Cressida. She was injured—mortally injured— he could tell immediately. These weren't like the simple cuts and burns from the hellspawn. The demons that'd been drawn into the Scepter Coven's stronghold tonight had meant business. Their job had been to weaken the high priestess, if not kill her outright, and they'd clearly cared a lot about doing their job well.

"I've got you," he murmured into Cressida's ear, but she was well past hearing him. He winked back into existence in the place she held strongest in her mind, an almost austerely decorated bedroom. These weren't her opulent high-priestess quarters in New York City, Stefan realized immediately. In its duress, Cressida's mind had retreated to the last place she'd felt safe. To where she considered home.

He looked around, his lip curling at the simple furniture, the rough sheets of the bed on which he laid the high priestess. Cressida needed to redefine what a decent home was. Once she was his...

The pain that cut across his mind was almost blinding, and it knocked Stefan completely off the bed, sending him sprawling to the stone floor. He roared with irritation as he came to, then leapt up.

"I didn't *mean* it," he spat, stalking back to the bed as Cressida stirred.

"Mean what?" she managed.

But Stefan was burning with an unholy rage now. That Cressida had been injured was infuriating enough. But he was a demon of the Syx, and before that... Before that, he suspected—no, he *knew*—that he'd wielded more power than any of the Fallen angels before him. Yes, his sin was pride, but it had been well earned. He would not be healing the high priestess of the Scepter Coven in a mean and small apartment, no better than a monk's quarters. His glamour was not merely for his own purposes.

With every step that he took approaching Cressida, the room around him changed. First the floor was covered with rich carpet. A fire was laid in the cold grate that had not been there before, and now it sprang to life. The walls were no longer bare brick but paneled over with inlaid rosewood and hung with gilded paintings, the oil paint thick and lush on the canvas.

Around Cressida, the simple cot with its cotton blankets and thin coverlet was replaced with a king-sized bed piled high with pillows and fitted with silken sheets, Cressida nearly lost in the center of them. Enough of her wounds were still bleeding that she squeaked in alarm, apparently horrified at staining the sheets.

"Don't worry about that," Stefan ordered, for in this place, at this moment, he could deliver such an order. She was a mortal, a broken child of God, and before he was consigned to the depths of infamy, it had been his task not only to heal, not only to raise up the children of God, but to inspire and delight them, to remind mortal souls of everything that awaited them, both above and below, if only they dared to believe.

Now he brought his hands up as Cressida stared. "What are you doing?" she demanded, but she didn't attempt to stop him or throw up any resistance as he stretched his palms over her.

"You are a beloved creation of God," Stefan said, his fury still raging within him at how much damage she'd suffered at the hands of his brethren. His brethren! He was as much to blame for her injuries as the meanest of demons that had slipped inside the coven's circle. He was as much responsible for her care and healing. He would make her whole, not by his power alone, but by that which had been granted him millennia ago, that which he still could use by the grace of the Creator.

He dropped his hands to Cressida's burned and bloodied skin.

The scream that tore from her barely registered in the maelstrom of his mind. Because it was working. From his hands extended a light so intense that Cressida's remaining tattered clothes vanished in a puff of smoke, while her injured body was swiftly and gloriously transformed. First her skin was healed of the deep gashes from demon claws, then the burn marks were brushed away, then the bruises and scrapes were healed. She shuddered beneath his hands, surrendering to him, and he couldn't keep his body from responding to that trust, either his glamour or his physical form. He gritted his teeth as temptation twisted and writhed within him. Now that she was healing, his fury was dissipating, but what was replacing it was a desire so maddening, he could hardly breathe.

"Stefan," Cressida whispered, and he stretched his hands farther, moving up her legs, her torso, skating the high swells of her breasts, until he paused, breathing heavily, his hands suspended above her face. She hadn't sustained any wounds here, at least not the physical kind. But her eyes still held the haunted fear of any mortal when faced with the desecration of a demon.

Stefan's lips twisted, his own disgust surging once more to the fore. She was probably afraid of him. She should be.

Distracted as he was by the stricken look in Cressida's eyes, Stefan barely registered the movement of her hands until it was too late. She reached for him, closing her hands around his.

"No!" he cried, but not before both of them were thrown into the maelstrom.

—⊷—

FOR A LONG MOMENT, Cressida couldn't see, couldn't feel anything but waves of agony pouring through her body. She stared, trying to pierce through to what lay beyond the fire, but her eyes were blinded with a light so bright, she might as well be standing on the surface of the sun. Stefan remained in front of her, his hands caught tight in her grasp, but his form was shaking uncontrollably, his head thrown back, his body racked in a paroxysm of pain.

His head and body were shifting too. In one moment, Stefan was his glorious, beautiful self, the Stefan she'd now known for days, the powerful member of the Syx. In the next, he transformed into a hideous version of himself—the abomination of his original beauty that she'd seen once before. His ears and nose ripped clean away, his eyes scorched into dark and staring holes, his body riddled with a million scars. If anyone had ever met the beautiful demon before in his full glamour, they would know that this was the same creature. They would know and they would be horrified to the core. But that wasn't the last transformation of the demon that she saw. There was a third evolution of his being, also linked to the first two. A new entity so magnificent, she couldn't quite grasp it with her ordinary senses. He was a creature of light and magic and beauty—endless beauty. The gilding of the sunlight on the leaves in a sylvan forest. The trembling of a single drop of dew on the edge of a budding rose. The glow of distant magic surrounding a shooting star, everything he touched became more beautiful and stayed that way for an eternity after his passage.

But that being didn't last, just as the horrifyingly debased creature didn't last. In the end, it was the glamour of the demon that took hold of Stefan's body once more, his rage and pain and need coalescing beneath the surface of his beautiful face and gorgeous form.

Cressida drew in a long, racking breath. "You're not kidding around when it comes to this healing stuff, are you?"

"Let...go," Stefan managed, and she could tell by the strain in his voice that he was still battling a force unleashed within him. "Slowly."

She nodded, but his request wasn't as easy as she wanted it to be. A strange, depraved part of her soul wanted to keep holding on to him, to claim him for her own, and never let him go. Was this the reaction he inspired in every human he touched, she wondered? The thought inspired both heart-wrenching compassion and a deep and twisted jealousy, twin flames raging on the same quivering wick.

"Let go," Stefan said again, his tone more pleading this

time. "You must, Cressida. I don't have the strength to leave you."

She felt the base and terrible urge within her flare up once more. The demand, the *need* to keep him for herself. Shocked at her own depravity, she opened her fingers wide and let go of Stefan's hands.

The burning fire within her winked out, and she flopped back on the bed. A bed that was surprisingly lusher than it really should be.

"What's up with—" She gestured to the sheets, then froze.

Stefan hadn't moved either. "Cressida," he whispered.

Her name on his lips was part warning, part entreaty, but Cressida didn't know how to respond. Her fingers...were glowing, still heavy with the fire of his touch. She rotated her fingers, staring at them as red-and-purple fire jumped and sparked around them, her hands a blur of energy.

"What's happening?" she whispered.

"I don't know." But the panic in Stefan's voice made his words a lie. She turned her focus to his face and met his gaze—though not because he wanted her to, she knew immediately. Stefan was bathed in sweat, his jaw set, his eyes fierce. His entire body, in fact, was rigid, and...naked. How did he *do* that so quickly? She looked down the glorious length of him, her eyes going wide as she noticed something else. He was fully and completely ready for her.

"Stefan?"

"I'm not trying to seduce you," he gritted out. "That wasn't the point of this."

She chuckled. "Well, that's a pity. Because I'm more than happy for you to seduce me."

With a touch of her glowing hand on his shoulder, she pushed him back, and he toppled to the side of the bed, breathing heavily. As she'd done before, she followed him over, straddling him as his eyes flared wide.

"What are you doing?"

"What does it look like?" She paused, the effort costing her more than she'd like. "Unless...you don't want me to do anything with you? Are you hurt?"

"Not—hurt," Stefan gasped. He also didn't respond directly to her question, though, so she hesitated above him, then placed her hands on his shoulders.

Stefan convulsed, but the way his shaft leapt against her body, it didn't seem like it was a bad thing. "What's this?" she breathed.

"A myth," Stefan managed, his eyes going wide. "A lie, you could say. The Fallen who found human love spoke of it, but one by one, it was discounted. More likely, I'm being tested, reminded of my failures."

"Then I want it to be gone," Cressida ordered. Instantly, the fire in her hands died away, and Stefan sagged against the bed. Relieved, yes, but also...something else. She wasn't sure what, and a moment later, she didn't have time to worry about it. Stefan opened his eyes and pinned her with his gaze.

Gone was the doubt and confusion. Gone also was any hint of pain in his expression. Replacing it was a look of pure, unadulterated *want*, a desire so intense, it fairly radiated off him.

Then he smiled.

"You seem to be in a very precarious position, princess," he said, and he settled his hands on her hips, edging her back until she could feel the touch of his shaft against her. Her body clenched, and his grin only widened. "But I think you like putting yourself in precarious positions."

"You..." Cressida gaped down at him. His change of

mood was so immediate, she almost didn't trust it, but every time he slid up against her body, almost to the point of entering her before retreating again, she found she really couldn't focus on anything else but that. "Ah, are you feeling okay?"

Stefan blinked, his smile faltering slightly. "What do you mean?"

She didn't like losing his smile. She wanted it back. She ground against his shaft, guiding it inside her, and Stefan's expression eased. "What's the last thing you remember before me climbing on top of you?" she asked.

His grin returned. "I'd rather just focus on that," he said, seating her more firmly on him. She hissed out a long breath as he filled her, and gave herself over to the sensation. He stroked her once, twice—long, mind-blowing passes that filled her up and made her feel like she could fly. Her fingers seemed to spark against his shoulders, and she quickly moved them away, curling her hands into fists that she ground into the sheets. She'd had only the barest lessons in working with the spectral fire that Stefan's touch had awakened within her, and she didn't want to hurt him with it. Then again, could you hurt a demon with fire?

She sighed, allowing her own smile to tug at her lips. There was so much she didn't know about Stefan yet...and so very much she wanted to learn.

She shifted her body up, positioning her breasts higher, and Stefan took immediate advantage. He leaned up and drew a nipple into his mouth, making her gasp with the sudden circuit of energy that went from his mouth to her groin and back again.

He growled as she ground into him, his hand snaking behind her back, positioning her against him. Then he pressed deep inside her.

"Yesss," he moaned against her breast.

He reached up with his other hand and captured the back of her head. He bent her toward him, now moving his hips in a deep rhythmic movement that somehow seemed to touch her everywhere at once, inside and out, until she could feel her own reaction building. She managed a soft whimper, which he seemed to instantly understand, and she felt him swell within her, making everything more immediate, more intense, more—right.

"Stefan," she pleaded, but when she tried to pull her face away from him, to truly see him, he resisted. He held her in place, and the growl in his throat grew to a sharper, harsher tone. With her arms tight around him, her hands flat on his back, what her eyes couldn't show her, her fingers truly felt. Stefan was changing beneath her, his glamour shimmering and writhing, straining to release the demon within. A demon who, in this case, retained the form of the man whose glamour she had become so accustomed to. A demon who, in this case, was not so far removed from the Fallen angel he had once been that his body didn't still bear the remnants of that glorious raiment, no matter how burned and scarred it had become.

"Stefan," she begged again, and something shifted in her own voice, deepened. Not the compulsion of a witch bent on controlling her demon, but the cry of a woman whose heart could no longer bear *not* to see the truth of the demon who'd somehow claimed her.

In her arms, Stefan went nearly still, barely continuing to rock into her, holding the tide of their shared passion at an ebb, all the energy around his body snapping and crackling, and Cressida drew in a shocked breath. Because she knew—she knew. She had pulled this demon to her in her hubris and fear, desperate to find a solution against Ahriman. She had thought she could rule him, force him to help her, tempt him into helping her reach the next level of her powers through the release of her virginity. He'd been part of a hastily contrived plan the moment she realized she had a demon of true power in their midst—a Syx. Surely, of all the demons in the world, a Syx would draw Ahriman out.

But in this moment, all Cressida's plans, all her preparations, all her ideas fell away, and there was nothing but this being whose arms were wrapped around her, his breath harsh against her skin, his heart pounding wildly beneath her own. His glamour, his skin and muscles and bone— whether smooth and perfect or warped and deformed, it didn't matter anymore. Nothing mattered except that she was able to look him in his eyes, see him—truly see him.

"Stefan," she whispered for a third time.

It was as if she'd spoken some fell incantation. Stefan pulled back from her shoulder, slowly, trembling, as if he was making every effort to keep himself hidden from her— and yet failing. When she could see him, her heart momentarily quailed in her chest.

This was not the most beautiful demon of the Syx, the demon who had made six thousand years and more of human females swoon. This was the face of the damned, exactly as he'd described it—yet infinitely worse. Broken, scarred, burned, and mutilated, his mouth a bare gash of pain, his eyes nearly lost in sunken pits. Nearly, but not completely.

"Stefan," Cressida whispered, laying her hands on either side of Stefan's face as she stared into those fathomless, fiery eyes, coal-black orbs shimmering with roiling red. It was almost as if she could see all the way to Stefan's heart—and even to his soul—the fear, the self-loathing, the doubt...

And something else.

Stefan looked back at her desperately, mutely, unable to speak through the pain that clearly racked his mind and held his body in a vise of agony, but he couldn't hide the truth from Cressida, not now that her eyes were open enough to see.

He loved her.

A demon condemned to eternal servitude, a demon whose sin had left him broken and discarded, good for nothing other than blasting into nothingness creatures of the horde more twisted and heinous than himself —loved her.

And what was more shocking, and frightening, and impossibly real...

She loved him back.

The climax of their intertwined bodies struck Cressida with the suddenness of a thunderclap, quick and hard enough to make her gasp even as Stefan surged forward as well, both of them caught up in a tide of release that made her sight go blank for a long, perfect, precious moment, her mind letting go of everything she thought, everything she feared, everything she hoped for and simply, gloriously, *was*.

Spectral fire erupted around them in an intense, purplish-red inferno.

22

S tefan collapsed beneath Cressida, her body slick on top of his, her hair tumbling over her shoulders, surrounding them both in a sea of deep red curls. She laughed, and the sound could as easily have been the crash of the ocean or the peal of bells, as loud as his heart was pounding. Once again, he was reacting in ways he'd never experienced before with a human woman, and, now that the haze of sex had left him, there was something she'd mentioned that he wanted to follow up on, some memory she'd triggered...

"I really *do* like the way you heal a girl," Cressida sighed, her body a warm, liquid weight on his, and he lost his entire train of thought. Instead, he circled her with his arms, holding her tight to him. She smelled of starlight, he realized dimly, though that couldn't be right. It'd been so long that he shouldn't even remember the scent.

With Cressida sprawled against him, boneless and content, they drifted in and out of sleep for another few minutes, and he thought he could possibly stay in exactly that position for the rest of his immortal life. Cressida couldn't, but he was a demon, and she was—

He frowned. There it was again, that strange aroma wafting up from her hair. *Starlight*. Which couldn't be possible, of course, and yet...

"What are you thinking about?" she murmured, and he found himself considering the question as if he'd never heard it before. Arguably, not too many people wanted to know the thoughts of a demon, but what few humans understood was that a demon was bound to answer the questions that you put to it. It was simply that usually, you weren't going to be happy with the answer. In this case, though, it seemed positive enough.

"I was thinking you have a scent in your hair that shouldn't be possible. One I haven't experienced in...a long time," Stefan murmured. There was no point in making a fuss over it.

"Because you healed me?" she asked.

He pursed his lips, rolling that idea around in his mind. It was as good a reason as any. "Probably."

"Is it a good scent?"

He chuckled. "It's a fantastic scent. It takes me back a bit."

She lifted her head and regarded him curiously. "I thought you couldn't remember anything from before that time—and don't try to," she added hastily. "I don't want that to cause you pain."

"It..." He frowned. Cressida was right, it should have hurt him to even consider the scent of starlight. "It doesn't cause me pain, so it's not from the, ah, time before. It must still have been around me during the change." He didn't push too hard, though his reticence had as much to do with his own self-preservation as with her entreaty. But there was no pain as he mentally poked at the edges of the lingering aroma. "It's clean, and cold, and something else. The scent of possibility. As if the heavens have drawn in a breath and are holding it before whispering a new creation into being."

"I like that," she sighed, snuggling closer to him.

He did too. About as much as he liked the feel of Cressida Frain in his arms. He didn't want to explore that truth too closely. He knew where those paths all led—to a brief and absolute goodbye, before anyone did anything—or said anything—they couldn't take back.

He decided to move the conversation into safer territory. "What will you do once you defeat Ahriman?"

She glanced up at him again. "What do you mean?"

"What's next after that? For the coven, for Earth. Surely you've turned the page after you've read 'Ahriman is blasted back across the veil' to see how the story ends."

She was quiet such a long moment that he thought she'd fallen asleep. He'd had that effect on human women before, but only for the best of possible reasons. Then Cressida shifted, her head resting on his chest as she stared up toward the ceiling. She frowned, suddenly distracted. "You changed the lighting fixtures too?"

"You had terrible lighting in here," Stefan said. "I don't know how you could see well enough not to run into the furniture, except for oh, yeah, you had hardly any furniture."

She snorted but didn't allow herself to divert from the topic. "Ahriman has served as the focus for the Scepter Coven since our inception. He was the strongest demon to terrorize humankind, the endless adversary, the reminder that we're not as powerful as we think we are, hidden in the shadows. Defeating Ahriman will remind all witches that we weren't meant to stay in the shadows. We were meant to work together in the light, in a spirit of cooperation and lasting goodwill."

"You can't rely on that. I've lived among humans six thousand years. Goodwill that lasts beyond a few months is about as rare as a Fae sighting."

"You've seen the Fae? I thought that was a myth."

He snorted. "Live anywhere long enough and you'll find that most myths prove out, one way or another."

"Well, the goodwill of the covens isn't a myth. It's a blood oath, and it would be sworn to us were we to remove the threat of Ahriman. More to the point, however, it would shift the balance of power between the witches and the demons. We've always had control, but it's been a control hard-won, fraught with danger and confined to sacred circles. With such a defeat, we could join together to find ways to hold back the horde that's been dumped across our world."

"Hold them back?"

She shrugged, the move a study in Stefan's sensual awareness as her sleekly muscled shoulders shifted against his belly. "We no longer have the luxury to hide in our covens, picking and choosing which demons we wish to control. Ordinary humans are being affected with the resurgence of the horde, and Connected humans are at the greatest risk of all."

Stefan's brows lifted, though Cressida couldn't see that. If she could, she'd be very impressed with his focus, he was certain. "How so?" he asked casually. It was one thing for witches to assert themselves against the demon horde. They had skills in that regard, and a certain birthright to their efforts. But they weren't always the most sophisticated of Connecteds, he found. They tended to rely on their potions and ancient books, while many of the strongest Connecteds relied on drugs and nanotechnology, both enhanced by magic. It made for an uneven playing field, to say the least.

Her next words sent a stab of concern deep into his belly. "They believe they know enough through their science and technoceutical development to combat not only the most modern of assaults against their magic, but the most ancient," she said simply. "They're wrong. Demons don't care how sophisticated a human is or how finely attuned their psychic skills. They care only to kill or to possess or to control. There's no other option for them."

"That's certainly true," Stefan said, his voice carefully neutral, though his heart spasmed with unnatural pain at her innocence. Demons didn't have much use for humans other than as food, one way or another. Either they used them as mules to procure drugs or to feed other vices, or the humans themselves were the vice. Harming a child of God was an addiction all its own. Not all demons actively pursued it, but those that did couldn't stop—wouldn't stop, really, until they were blasted to the other side of the veil.

Which was why an influx of the horde was such a dangerous thing. Up until now, the number of demons roaming the earth was fairly constrained. There was a pile of them, but it wasn't like there were new ones immigrating in every day. Those that had slipped into this world at the dawn of humankind remained until they were routed out and only a scant handful found their way here to stay through the summons of the unwary. Witches weren't counted among that latter group, not usually. They knew enough about their ancient enemies to keep their guard up.

But now, things were different. A knot of demons focused in a small area could do real damage, particularly to sensitive Connected. No one was prepared for a demon invasion. And, though there were some humans who were able to guard against such an invasion and even, in rare instances, fight back, only witches had the power to both summon demons and reroute them. Most witches called demons from the other side of the veil, so returning them to that location was merely the closure of the circuit. But witches also had the ability to summon demons who were already on this earth. Generally speaking, they returned them back to whatever bolt-hole they found them. But it didn't have to be that way. Technically.

"Do you know how to return a demon to the other side of the veil when they didn't originate there?" Stefan asked.

"Of course," Cressida said. "Most of the demons who answer our summons, however, are from the other side of the veil. The grimoires were created using those names that hadn't ever crossed over."

"Really." Stefan had never thought of it that way, but it did make a certain sort of sense. The ancient books had been written when the knowledge of demon kind was still fresh and the stories that had been handed down were from the dawn of recorded human history. At that point, there were far more demons on the other side of the veil than those roaming the Earth. In addition, the earthly demons weren't in any hurry to reveal themselves. Not only did they not want to be the hired help of a witch, they didn't want to be discovered by anyone, most especially not an angel of the Lord. Or, arguably worse, a member of the Syx.

But again, times had changed.

"Your ancient book may well call upon a demon who's now living above a noodle shop, not in the ninth circle of hell," he contemplated. "Have you made adjustments for that?"

"You may not have realized this, but there's been precious little demon summoning going on for the past hundred years or so. It still happens, of course, but more as a pro forma, a learning exercise than true witch-over-demon authority. That's a problem. Even before this influx, demons were losing their place. Forgetting that the role of the witch was to control, not be controlled."

"Well, speaking from personal experience, I can tell you the idea of being controlled by a human is less than palatable, particularly if you're not on board with the whole 'one of God's children' thing. By and large, you guys aren't that smart. It chafes."

Cressida rolled over to face him, weary amusement lighting her eyes. "Hey, now. You're a *demon*. You don't exactly have room to judge."

"Look, we're not the ones who invented Twinkies, is all I'm saying."

"Uh-huh. And what is it you think the purpose of demons is, if not to serve?"

Her teasing words struck him more harshly than he was sure she intended. "There's no reality on this plane or any other where it's a purpose of demons to serve. You've found an avenue to yoke them to your will, and good for you for doing so. But don't ever make the mistake of thinking they're answering some sort of higher calling by doing your bidding. Demons exist to give a black pit of despair a face. That's it. Nothing more." Irritation raced through him, and he flinched away from her, his own self-loathing flaring hot and bright.

Cressida sensed the change in him, though she took its meaning wrong. "I'm sorry, Stefan," she said hurriedly, peeling off him. "I meant you no disrespect—"

The word had barely dropped from her lips when Stefan was yanked out of one plane and into the next, with a speed and urgency that could only mean one thing: a summons from the archangel.

"What in the actual—" The wind was sucked out of him as he took form once more surrounded by mist. The archangel stood before him, pale and waxy in the smoky space. "*Now* what? I've been doing everything you asked of me!"

Michael regarded him with a smile that was little more than sneer. "You've done quite a bit more than I've asked of you, even you would admit."

"Well then, I've been doing my job. What more can you possibly want?"

"You misunderstand my intervention," Michael said. "I come not to reprimand you, but to warn you. I couldn't do so in front of the witch."

There was an edge to the archangel's voice that Stefan hadn't heard before, and he narrowed his eyes. "Before we get to that, what is the angels' take on witches, exactly?" he asked. "It's been too long since I walked among you guys to know, even if I could remember. You can't be fans."

"They're God's children as well, for all that they do not claim Him," Michael said evenly.

"That's maybe true, but it doesn't answer the question."

"And since when do you feel it is within your rights to demand anything of me? Even something as minor as an answer?"

"When *you* are about to demand something of me that isn't technically within the letter of the Father's law," Stefan shot back. He could tell the instant he said it, his words were a direct hit. The Archangel wanted something above and beyond his pay grade, and Stefan was the one he'd chosen to deliver it. "And before you get all uptight, just spill it. No threats or warnings are needed. If I can do it, I'll do it."

The archangel regarded him a long moment. "Ahriman is ready. He won't wait until the full moon to be summoned. He wishes to move now. He can too, with the breach the witches have opened to him. He will come and he will kill Cressida Frain without your help."

Stefan blinked. "What?"

"There's no other possible outcome. The grimoire of the Scepter Coven witches created this illusion that a demon needed to be a minor part of the equation, not the key element of the equation, but make no mistake. Without a demon of sufficient strength and cunning, Ahriman will remain on this earth, when by all rights, he should have been obliterated from it thousands of years ago. He has run strong in the darkness. He has grown more cunning with the turn of each millennia. When he defeats both a witch *and* a demon to maintain his power, he will set himself up as the true father of the demon horde."

"I thought Satan had that position already sewn up."

"Evil takes many faces, whatever is the most expedient," Michael returned stonily. "When one grows too familiar, almost quaint, represented in popular fiction and media as a wily old uncle or rakish player, that face loses its power to inspire fear and horror. Even the Devil of the Arcana Council is no true Devil—he's an archetype, a construct of magic with a specific goal and purpose. Ahriman isn't here to be an archetype. He's here to rend human souls."

"Then why did God create him in the first place?" Stefan demanded. "He had the choice not to do that—humans don't. They only have the choice to be eaten."

Michael's laugh was dark. "It's not your place to question the ways of the Father," he said. "Or to limit the reach of mortals placed in the greatest extremities of challenge."

But Stefan wasn't having any of that. "I've met a lot of

mortals. They could do without the extremities of challenge. Most of them are simply trying to get through this life without coming apart at the seams—they've got enough to manage without the be-all, end-all of evil showing up to crash the party."

"Then it would appear that you have your work cut out for you."

"I'm not the strongest of the Syx—you know that."

"You're not," Michael agreed, with a candor that would have stung Stefan to the quick six thousand years ago, when the world was a picnic blanket of bounty laid out for him to sample. Now it merely made him tired. "What you are is much more important, though. As you'll eventually learn by touch and taste and sight—and pain."

"I have zero time for riddles right now, old man," Stefan snapped. "How do I take out Ahriman?"

"He has already begun his approach, thanks to the Scepter Coven's actions. Belessunu has paved his way, and other demons of great strength are taking note. They know the importance of this summons."

Stefan's eyes flew wide. "Belessunu! That's who that was? She's still *alive*?"

"Despite your puny efforts to destroy her during the revolt of Babylon, yes. And her memory is long. I recommend you return to help Cressida take up the battle before Ahriman catches her completely unawares."

"So all this has been the mother of all setups? You just decided now was the time to take out Ahriman and that Cressida was the one to do it, so you put that whisper in her ear when she was still a kid?"

"Not exactly, though she is better positioned than most to finish the job. However, Cressida isn't the first Scepter Coven witch to take on the challenge, as you yourself have attempted to point out to her—breaking the rules of your incarceration, I might add."

"It was right there, man,' Stefan muttered, waving Michael off. "She would've figured it out eventually. I thought maybe she should do it when it still mattered."

Michael nodded, apparently willing to let this infraction go. "There have been one hundred and twenty-seven witches since the Scepter Coven's inception who have made the attempt, and one hundred and twenty-seven who have failed. She is the one hundred and twenty-eighth. She will be the last, one way or another."

"How do you know that?"

"Because we are running out of time," the archangel said, and Stefan had never heard him sound so weary. "A reckoning is coming for the children of God. There are a million and one potential outcomes of that reckoning, but with Ahriman as part of the equation, the odds for any success at all among the human ranks decrease dramatically. He has remained in the shadows, but that doesn't mean he hasn't watched and learned, much as the witches of the Scepter Coven have watched and learned. When he emerges, as he is emerging now, it's only because he feels his strength and his quarry are sufficient to grant him the glory he needs."

Michael turned more fully to Stefan. "There are many threats to God's children, creatures who have the ability to destroy that which the Father spun to life from His own hand and heart. They've survived by lurking in the darkness. The strongest of them have the sense to stay in that darkness, no matter the temptation presented. This one, we've goaded into the light."

"We, or you?" Stefan narrowed his eyes. "How and why exactly did so many of the horde make landfall all those weeks ago anyway? Did you have anything to do with that?"

Michael stared at him impassively, and Stefan shook his head. "Fine, fine. It doesn't matter. They're here, and Ahriman has decided he wants to party, which means he's officially sticking his head out of his hole far enough that we can lop it off. So you want me to get that job done."

"By any means possible, regardless of the damage to those surrounding you. Even if, especially if, it is Cressida Frain who must fall."

Stefan felt the stab to his gut, but kept his face carefully neutral. He'd been a demon for six thousand years. In the end, no human survived their brief and tumultuous time on Earth. They were always destined to return to the Father... some sooner than others.

He just needed to keep reminding himself of that.

"I'll take care of it," he said.

23

Cressida flinched back as Stefan shuddered hard, his face somehow completely different from the demon she'd been staring at a second before.

"We have to go back," he said abruptly, then lifted a hand when she would have spoken. "You didn't do anything wrong. You didn't offend me, I promise. I just needed a second to regroup and, ah, remember what was important here."

"What's important," Cressida managed, but then hissed in a quick breath as he gathered up her hands. His fingers were practically on fire, and when she stared down at their joined grasp, she could almost see the vestiges of that flame sparking up. "The fire is growing within me every time we touch. I don't know how well I can control it."

He squeezed her fingers lightly. "I've got a feeling you'll do just fine. But we have to get you back to the coven. The summons has begun, and Ahriman is making his move."

"What? What are you talking about?" Cressida scrambled off the bed as Stefan stood, then looked about wildly for any stitch of the suit she'd been wearing. "Um...what'd you do with my clothes?"

"Those are destroyed, and we can't go back for more. Marcus's goons will be all over your apartment. We'll make a pit stop at your new clothier's, then take you back to the coven chambers." Stefan cocked his head as if he were a spaniel testing the wind. "Marcus is...unusually pissed. Or excited. It's difficult to tell which."

Cressida grimaced. "Well, you took me out of the circle at the end of what should have been a triumphant battle of the high priestess and her consorts turning back the demon horde. That probably interrupted his narrative."

"Then as much as I'd like to keep interrupting it, let's get him off his rant. But Cressida..." He stopped and regarded her with an expression she couldn't quite understand. "Know that this test of you and your coven is yours to undergo. I can help protect you from outside forces, but I can't protect you from each other."

She squinted at him. "What are you talking about?"

Instead of answering, he reached out and pulled her close. Instantly, Cressida felt the whoosh of smoke surround her. They were moving too fast for her to draw oxygen, far too fast for her to process the images flashing in front of her eyes. When she tried, she became instantly queasy, and that wasn't helping anyone. Was this how demons traveled naturally? If so, it was no wonder they didn't feel bound to one place.

Focusing on not throwing up, Cressida screwed her eyes shut and held her breath, bursting out in startled exclamation when she staggered forward onto solid ground again. Her eyes popped open, and she recognized the elegant, understated, and quietly lit chamber of the shop where she and Stefan had spent time the previous evening.

"What's this? We don't have time for—"

"Shh..." Stefan turned her once, then again. She felt a quick brush of his hands over her body, and then another blur overtook her, and they were off again. This hop was far briefer, leaving her swaying drunkenly between Stefan and a wall—but back in surroundings she understood. They were outside the chamber that held the coven circle, and the chanting coming from the room beyond was unmistakable.

"I know that prayer," Cressida muttered, her jaw going tight. "By the Goddess...you're right. They're summoning Ahriman—here. They can't do that."

"Hold up there, Sparky," Stefan warned as her fingers twitched with heat. "We need to think this through."

"But they can't summon him here. It's too soon. We're not prepared, and we're inside. They *can't*—"

"Cressida, wait—"

But she wouldn't wait. The summons of Ahriman was a moment she'd been preparing for practically her entire life. She knew how it was supposed to go, Marcus knew how it was supposed to go. But there he was at the head of the circle, his hands lifted in exultant prayer. This was all wrong! Cressida burst into the great hall of the Scepter Coven, fury boiling over within her. They were supposed to be summoning Ahriman in the sacred grove within Central Park, beneath the open sky and with the power of the full moon to sustain them. The energy of the earth below and the stars above was essential to ensure they met the great evil with the highest strength possible.

"Sto—!" she commanded, but a hand slapped over her mouth almost as soon as she'd spoken, a hand she knew too well. It had struck her down and lifted her up more times than she could count since she was a little girl.

"Where did you go?" hissed Fraya, her voice harsh and

demanding in Cressida's ear. "I tried to stop Marcus, but he refused to listen. After you disappeared with the demon, he strode forward, invoking the rule of consort in a time of war. And he has begun the summons! Ahriman is *coming*."

Fraya took her hand off Cressida's mouth, and Cressida turned to her, shaking. She'd never seen her mentor so alight with frantic energy. Her eyes were wild, her skin flushed.

Cressida understood exactly how she felt. "But we're not ready. Our strongest spell casters aren't assembled here. They're waiting to join us in the sacred grove two days from now. We aren't in our rightful place!"

"Marcus decreed there was no time left and—" The lawgiver shuddered. "He's right. Ahriman is stirring. I can feel it in my bones."

"High Priestess Cressida!"

Marcus's accusing voice shouted over the gathering chant, and both Cressida and Fraya froze—the lawgiver's hands clamping down on Cressida's arms in sheer, reflexive fright. Cressida tried to break free, but she was too late, and a moment later, she was roughly pulled from Fraya and hauled forward. She shook off the grasp of Marcus's foot soldiers with a wave of her hand—he wasn't the only witch with power here—and straightened as several of the chanting coven members turned to her with wide eyes, their voices still raising the sacred words. Stefan was nowhere to be seen, but she couldn't think about him—he'd wanted her to get here with all haste, and then he'd wanted her to wait. Where was the sense in that?

There was no time left for waiting. But Marcus was out of his mind if he thought they could face down Ahriman in this closed-in space.

"What are you *doing*?" she demanded. Marcus merely

opened his arms wide, somehow including her in the chant that swelled up to the ceiling, shaking the walls.

"You have returned to the moment of your greatest triumph," he cried, making her blink. Her what? Did he think he was somehow doing this for her?

The chants rose to a more fevered pitch, and Cressida took a few more steps forward, close enough that she could hiss at Marcus with a modicum of privacy, "This is all wrong! Ahriman can't fill this enclosed space. We need the earth and the sky—and the strength of the spell casters, who even now are gathering in the sacred grove. We must go *there*."

"Then take us there," he countered, sweeping his arms out to take in Zeneschiah and Boltar and—Cressida blinked. Stefan now stood with the other demons, surrounded by three witches at the far end of the circle. Though Cressida now understood how easily he could overpower the witches, he didn't make a move. Instead, he watched. Waited. Exactly as he'd attempted to direct her to do.

But everything was confused, and Marcus kept on shouting. "You have before you three demons of great strength, and they can move us to the sacred grove. They await only your command!"

Cressida's eyes snapped wide. He was right, of course. Stefan had just transported her over a great distance in exactly the same way, but instinctively, she could see the flaw in Marcus's plan. Stefan was the mightiest demon present, and he'd only had to move one woman. There were easily fifty witches here. Calling on the demons to use that kind of power... "They'll be drained dry of their energy," she protested. "They'll be of no more service to us."

"That *is* their service. They're your consorts—let them

earn their keep." Marcus reached out, and Cressida saw him mouth a spell that was lost beneath the chanting cry of the coven members. She might hold the power and the rule of the coven, but he was its greatest spell caster. Why had she not recognized the danger in that before now?

A bright surge of energy filled the space as the demons were dragged forward, clearly against their will. Boltar and Zeneschiah stared around with wild, desperate eyes. All traces of their earlier drunkenness were gone, burned off in the heat of the battle against their own kind. They knew what was coming—knew it, and feared it. But they couldn't seem to stop it.

Her gaze swung to Stefan. To her surprise, he allowed himself to be pulled even with the other demons, offering no objection. Instead, he stared at Marcus, his gaze filled with a dark, disgusted rage.

Impotent rage.

Could he also not break Marcus's thrall?

"Marcus, you have to stop," Cressida warned.

"The sacred grove!" Marcus shouted, and he thrust his arms high.

The reaction in the demons was immediate and absolute. They staggered back, their arms flinging wide, and the smoke that had surrounded Cressida when she'd been swept to her childhood room now poured into the coven's chamber. Though they kept reciting the words of the summoning spell, the chants of the witches began sounding more like terrified screams. Marcus had either trained them well, or they were as bound to this moment as she was. She twisted around, seeking any means of escape, then the smoke rushed up and surrounded her. She couldn't see, she couldn't breathe, and a moment later, she found herself moving through space exactly as she had with Stefan.

Well, not exactly. The transporting of the entire coven on the backs of three demons, even three exceptionally strong demons, immediately showed its strain. The trip took longer than the space of one full breath, and Cressida felt the air burning in her lungs to escape, the need to breathe crawling up her throat like a living thing. By the time they reached the clearing of the sacred grove in the thickest stand of trees in Central Park, the effort had taken its toll. The witches sprawled out in ungainly fashion, dropping to their knees and sucking in great lungfuls of oxygen, their chanting all but petered out.

The echoes of their cry hadn't, though, and Cressida drew in her own steadying breath as she straightened, trying to get her bearings. The call was carried high by a new group of spell casters—not *all* the ones she'd summoned, but many of them. Of course, Marcus would have ordered them to their positions, those who'd already arrived in the city. Would it be enough? Her mind raced through the calculations the grimoire had demanded, then her gaze shot to the sky. The moon was not yet full! It wouldn't reach its strongest state for another forty-eight hours. What was Marcus thinking?

There was nothing for it, however. The spell was spoken, the die was cast. The fresh spell casters helped their woozy coven members to their places, and voices both shaky and firm rose in greater strength from the heart of the sacred grove. If there were any vagrants or police officers anywhere close, they'd notice something strange about the space—a coolness to the air beyond even what the blustery late night should bring—but they wouldn't hear the cry of the Scepter Coven. Their magic was far too old for that.

There was another problem, however. Of the three demons, two were now slumped at Marcus's feet, their bodies already becoming more fluid, as if they were sinking into themselves—while the third...

Cressida couldn't stop her startled cry as she saw the chains now binding Stefan. What devilry was this? The thick, clearly spelled restraints draped the demon so heavily, he'd buckled to the ground, and spikes were driven into his feet. Beside him, also on his knees, his mighty cross in his hands and his head bowed as if in prayer, was Jim Granger.

Cressida gaped. The lawgiver stood just behind Marcus and the tableau of demons, but not three feet away, Dahlia was struggling furiously against three of Marcus's foot soldiers. What had he done here? What trap had he laid for all of them?

"What is this?" she demanded. Clearly, this had all been carefully planned. But how...and why?

"Your consorts have completed their service with you. Their work is at an end," Marcus announced, his voice taking on an edge of almost feral joy. He turned to the exorcist. "Release them from this earth, gentle *father*," he fairly spat in his excitement. "Or I'll do it for you."

Granger looked up, and for the first time, Cressida saw fury in the older man's gaze. "It is not for you to direct the will of God, *witch*," he retorted, and though his words were spoken low and tight, they carried easily to Cressida beneath the rising cry of the spell casters' chant.

"Then I will release them back whence they came—broken, battered. They will not go to their maker, but to those who will treat them far less kindly. It makes no difference to me. They're no use to the high priestess in their weakened form."

"You have no right," seethed Cressida, striding up to him.

Marcus turned to her, his face alight. "I have every right," he countered. "I am your wedded husband, consort to the high priestess of the Scepter Coven. It's my right by rule of law."

"They are also—"

"No longer your playthings."

The voice was Stefan's, but it sounded long and labored, and Cressida stared at the mighty warrior of the Syx as he lifted his head. In the space of bare minutes, he'd been bloodied to a pulp, struck through with enough spelled spikes to slow even his colossal strength. Was this how humans would be forced to control demons, she wondered suddenly? Through blood and rage and pain?

But Stefan kept talking. 'Demons of this earth are among the foulest creatures the Lord ever had the forbearance to let draw breath," he growled. "But there are those gentle children of God who would give them a run for their money. No more. They will return to their judgment now."

His hands had been spiked together and driven into the ground, linked by a short chain. But he could move his fingers.

Three feet away, the limp bodies of the demons exploded, coating the witches around them—and Marcus—with steaming black goop.

Marcus leapt back, but with a sweep of one hand, his robes were clean again—pristine white, in potent counterpoint to her fiery red leather warrior's gear. Cressida gaped down at herself for the first time. Red leather?

With an exultant cry, Marcus regained her attention. "And now it is done!" He turned on her. "Complete the spell of Ahriman, High Priestess. Let the new age dawn for this coven and the world."

Cressida swung her wild gaze from Marcus to Stefan, who refused to look at her, and then to the lawgiver, whose face remained bright with energy and purpose. Her mentor nodded resolutely, and Cressida squared her shoulders. This was the task for which she'd been brought into the coven. This was her purpose in this lifetime. After six thousand years of terrorizing the witches of this earth with the threat of his return, Ahriman would now be forced to play his hand. Play, and lose, with the might of the Scepter Coven arrayed against him.

She turned in a tight circle, taking in the faces of her coven sisters and brothers, all of them with their arms outstretched, their throats working, raising their voices to the still-growing moon. The timing wasn't right. The death of the demons at her feet wasn't right. The binding of Stefan and the ridicule of the ex-priest wasn't right. But none of that mattered now. What mattered was that the very stars of heaven seemed poised for battle and the wind itself had stilled, waiting for her to unleash the most unholy of creatures into their sacred circle.

The time had come. And Cressida of the Scepter Coven needed to step into that moment.

She lifted her voice to the heavens and called Ahriman forth.

For a moment, nothing happened.

Then the next moment came, and still nothing happened.

Cressida kept her arms outstretched, her chin up, frozen in the position she'd been taught so carefully throughout the long years of her life in the coven as she repeated the ancient words again and again. It had all come down to this. The endless lessons, the memorization of spells, the strengthening of her mind, her spirit. The sparring with Marcus, her constant companion in listening and recording and learning the chants in all their twisting permutations.

He'd always been right there, bent equally to the task beneath the stern eye of the lawgiver, as dedicated as she was until his own studies of spell casting drew him into other, darker grimoires.

All for the good of her, he would say. All for the good of the coven.

But Marcus wasn't shouting now. As Cressida's eyes strained toward the heavens, she finally came to the awareness that he wasn't standing either. Instead, he knelt on the ground, his head bowed, his hands crossed over his chest in deference, his eyes on the dirt and grass—not on the skies, not on the blessed moon. Not even on Cressida, whose own command shimmered in the air above the wild chanting of the spell casters...casters who were now crying out the timeless words in a somehow different order than she remembered, the words of the spell not at all reflecting the ancient cast and cadence she knew so well that to hear it spoken otherwise awakened a wrongness in her very bones.

And then Marcus started laughing, the sound low, and rich...and insane.

"You have played the role of consort, as you were bound to play it, High Priestess," he declared. "And now the time has come for you to sacrifice yourself to our cause."

In the next breath, the demon Ahriman blanketed the sacred grove with pain.

24

S tefan fought against his restraints like a wild man, shocked at how strong they were. Not as strong as he was pretending, of course, but still, pretty damned strong. When he had burst through the veil into the sacred grove, responsible for so many humans at once it made his head spin, he'd instantly seen the beauty of Marcus's plan. The two weaker demons hadn't merely been drinking themselves into a stupor for their own personal pleasure these past few days, they'd been poisoned. Systematically and thoroughly, since practically the moment of their arrival. Stefan hadn't even noticed because he hadn't been paying attention. Had Marcus known that he would've been so entranced by Cressida that he would have ignored the plight of his fellow demons?

Probably not. More than likely, Marcus had planned on poisoning *three* demons over the space of the last forty-eight hours, not two. He only needed them to live long enough for this last act or something similar. And then, their use at an end, he would discard them as witches had been discarding demons since the dawn of time. Ordinarily, that wouldn't upset Stefan, but in this instance, he made an exception. When he'd sent the demons to their ultimate judgment, he'd done so with the faintest brush of benediction. If it was in the Father's mind to show mercy, then mercy would be shown. He was sure the lists of sins committed by Boltar and Zeneschiah were long and horrific, but as the exorcist had said, they were still God's creations. It had always been the Father's plan to receive them back again.

As Marcus yammered on, Stefan spared a glance at the priest. When they'd first burst through the smoke to the sacred grove, they'd found a small army waiting for them. Stefan had been instantly yoked and spiked to the ground, but the priest had remained unharmed, struck to his knees and held there, but not further abused. He remained on his knees now, and when Stefan glanced at him, the human's eyes were red rimmed with outrage.

"Did you know this was going to happen?" he demanded. "Because a little warning would've been nice."

Stefan coughed, more weakly than he would have liked. "I knew Marcus's energy was off the charts, and I suspected he had another plan. Not this, though. Definitely not this."

"You guys might really want to consider brushing up on your skills in reading witch's minds. Seems to me that would've come in pretty damn handy."

"I'll work on it." Stefan's attention was drawn sharply back to the center of the circle as Marcus began shouting again and Cressida moved forward. It was in the nature of humans to be shouting all the time, but Stefan made a monumental effort to focus as Marcus dropped his voice abruptly—dropped it, but didn't stop with his prayer, a prayer Stefan could barely hear above the wailing spell casters.

"No," he managed, but it was too late. Just as Cressida's cry to summon Ahriman to the grove was also too late.

Ahriman was already here.

When the ancient demon extended his power over the center of New York City's most famous park, he didn't bring fire or pestilence, smoke or death. He could have, Stefan realized with a start. Finally confronted with the essence of Ahriman, he at last understood the ramifications of this demon being so much older than even God's holy choir of angels. It was easy to bandy about phrases like "the dawn of time" when you live six thousand years, but the essence of Ahriman was formed in the crystalline dust of the solar system, a byproduct of the first and wildest acts of the Father's creative fury. Ahriman hadn't existed before God spoke, but he was stirred to life in the exhale of breath after the Father's first words, from the energy that was left to the side when light was formed and darkness made. His was the domain of neither light nor darkness, but the infinite gray space in between. His was the hollow void of emptiness, with no future and no past, no end and no beginning. This was true despair. Not anger, not fury, not fire, not death. But aching, ceaseless *nothingness*, a wandering without end. Here in one being was the anguish that had plagued the darkest corners of the earth since its inception, that drove more of God's children to take their own lives than any rage or fervent cause ever could.

And now Ahriman was here to take corporeal form on Earth, to rule the demon horde in a way not even Stefan could have predicted.

Ahriman wouldn't incite the masses to turn against one another in fury and fire, Stefan suddenly understood. He would get them to turn against themselves.

Cressida's head came down with a snap, and she readied

her next spell, but she had already lost the attention of the spell casters around her. They'd all been prepared for a fight of bloody proportions against a roiling, furious demon they'd read about for probably most of their lives. But the creature before them had no form. He appeared as a gray and haunting mist, a wail of despair so profound, it reverberated through the bones of the trees. The spell casters staggered, their voices growing hushed, then wholly silent, until only Cressida's sharp command rose above them. A few looked up, and some opened their mouths once more, but none seemed capable of uttering another sound. She called out the incantations of the sacred grimoire all alone, her voice growing increasingly desperate.

Then Marcus joined her.

At first, Stefan thought Marcus had come to Cressida's aid, but the moment the male witch started speaking, he knew the truth. Marcus wasn't challenging Ahriman to battle as Cressida was, he was welcoming him with open arms. He was begging him to take his rightful place on this earth with Marcus and the Scepter Coven as his *servants*, not his master or destroyer. They would help guide humanity to their honored place, ruling over the horde. They would put Ahriman into a position of power, for he was nature's force alone. He was not a creature of God or man, but something ancient and powerful and true. He could defy even God himself.

That last bit finally pierced the last of Stefan's fog.

"No," he cried, or tried to cry. The spikes through his body were heavily spelled, rendering his voice almost inaudible to his own ears. But instantly, he knew he was already too late. He had failed; he could see that clearly now. All his thousands of years of service to the Syx were as nothing when he couldn't stand and fight the one time he was asked to by the archangel himself. He was worthless, forever stained—

Beside him, however, Jim Granger suffered no such doubt. He burst out with the roar that Stefan had wanted to claim for himself.

"You *dare!*" the exorcist yelled, struggling to his feet, now using the enormous spike on his cross as a crutch. "You dare to put yourself above the Father. You *dare* to summon a creature you believe to be not even of His making? What kind of fool are you to think that *any* part of the universe is not the result of sure and holy creation? All that is good, all that is bad, all that is right, all that reeks of darkest evil. There is no mistake in this plan, there is neither hole nor flaw, there is only creation in all its grand and glorious chaos. The darkness cannot exist without the light, not in a world of creation. The weak cannot exist without the strong, not in a world that allows for growth. By striking down the hearts of man with this evil darkness, rendering God's children into husks, you spit in the eye of the Lord."

"He is not my Lord!" the witch howled back, and with a wave of Marcus's hand, the priest staggered back, his own hands going to his throat. Stefan once more strained against his bonds, but the magic of the master spell caster had been carefully wrought. As he attempted to rip the spikes out of his skin, it was Cressida who gasped, Cressida whose skin was torn. And as Granger twisted in choked agony, it was another voice that cried out, going from a furious shout to an anguished gargle.

Marcus wheeled around, fixing Dahlia with a stare. "You! Your affection for the exorcist was plain from the beginning, but I allowed it. You know your place as captain of the guard, or I thought you did. But I can't allow your weakness to be your undoing. I certainly won't allow it to be the coven's undoing."

"Hold, Marcus. You have no authority here."

Stefan whipped around and watched a white-faced Cressida approach, her arms bleeding from the wounds he'd caused her. Where her blood touched the ground, it sizzled. Something was wrong about that. Something was wrong about all of this. This attack of Ahriman's was too... static. A haze of gloom was a bummer, to be sure, but it lacked a certain...panache that he simply assumed any battle of primeval forces would require.

Back when the universe was first formed, they didn't call it the big sigh, after all.

What was Ahriman waiting for?

The answer to that happened all at once. Marcus stood fast as Cressida neared, then at the last minute, swept his arm down. Stefan expected the witch's movement to set off a chain reaction of magic, but the reality was much more brutal. The foot soldier standing next to Cressida yanked out a knife and plunged it toward her, even as beside him, Jim Granger shouted a warning. Cressida, clearly aghast, halted in her tracks, her hands going up, her own shout half choked in her throat—and only then did Marcus bring in the magic, and the skies opened to allow a rain of unholy rage to come down.

The bastard had simply needed more time.

Now, Ahriman's army of demons had finally arrived.

Banking that Cressida's distraction at this new horror would keep her from feeling undue pain at what he was about to do her, Stefan acted. He wrenched his body forward, pulling the stakes out of the ground, and separated his hands, lurching forward under the weight of his bespelled chains. As the witches around him woke up to the real and present danger of them being attacked by an entirely new demon horde, Stefan gripped the chains and started swinging. He could no longer see Cressida, or Dahlia and the exorcist, he could only see the shocked and terrified faces of the humans around him.

This was his place in the world, he understood.

This, he knew how to do.

He bent to the task. The army of Ahriman was not made up of weaklings and castoffs, but of the strongest demons that had ever walked the planet. Stefan knew because he recognized some of them for all that they were moving so quickly that he could barely get a fix on any of their faces. But a moment was all that was necessary. As he struck and twisted and lashed out, sending geysers of black goop soaring into the night sky, Stefan called forth the demons that he recognized by name.

A name is a powerful thing. It always had been, since light first swept through the universe. So Stefan called the demons to him, drawing their attention before cleaving their bodies in two. It would've been easier with the other members of the Syx to help, but after their initial shock wore off, the spell casters of the Scepter Coven shook themselves back into battle readiness as well. They were spell casters of no small skill either, and once freed from the enervation of Ahriman's manifestation of mist and anguish, they also bent to their task with growing fervor.

A particularly fast-moving demon with whirling wings blasted into Stefan from the side, looking like hellspawn on steroids. It bit and scratched and tore at him, and somewhere deep in the thick of the battle, Stefan could hear Cressida scream. He blinked down, horrified to realize that he felt no pain. Had Marcus found some way to twist the link that he and Cressida had begun to forge between them into a weapon against the woman? Could that be possible?

The irony wasn't lost on Stefan. He'd spent his entire mortal existence—or the significant part that he could remember—paying for his crime against a woman who had bound herself too tightly to him. A woman who'd gone to her death howling imprecations, vowing that Stefan would never be free of her just as she would never be free of the pain he'd caused her. She was more prescient than she ever realized, he suspected.

But how had Marcus discovered that, and how had he twisted it to his own uses? He was a master spell caster, but he wasn't the sharpest prick in the pack. He couldn't know anything about Stefan's deepest, darkest past.

Another demon struck him in his distraction, the force driving Stefan to one knee, but once again, there was no pain. No pain that *he* felt anyway. He steeled himself against Cressida's howl of agony, then lashed out with greater anger. His momentary restraint, even thoughts of forgiveness for Zeneschiah and Boltar, was now lost in a blur of fury. Nothing mattered to him other than getting to Cressida and destroying anything that stood in his way. Nothing mattered to him more than protecting her—

"Stefan!" Cressida cried out, and it took a second for Stefan to realize his newest injury. Not feeling pain sounded like a good idea, but it was a recipe for getting your legs cut out from under you before you even felt the edge of the blade. Or the rake of a fire drake's tail, in this case.

Before him, a small space in the roiling crowd opened up, more out of respect for the creature he faced than himself, Stefan knew instantly. The fire drake slunk low to the ground, looking so much like Zeneschiah that Stefan had to squint to make sure it wasn't the fiery demon come back to life. But no, this one wasn't drunk, for one thing, and its attention was focused solely on Stefan as words spilled out of its mouth in a rapid-fire spew of vitriol.

"You will *never* get what you seek, never escape what you've done. That is the way of the demon, which you forget at your peril," the creature hissed, darting out to slash its fiery talons at Stefan's chest. The strike missed him but was close enough to singe his glamour, and once again, Stefan didn't miss Cressida's stifled cry.

"You seem to have a lot of attitude for a demon who's about to turn into goop," Stefan rasped back. He lunged toward the drake, hesitating only at the last second, remembering Cressida. He could take this creature apart limb by limb, but he'd be burned in the process, which meant Cressida would feel that pain even if he didn't. He couldn't afford that. The Syx dispatched demons most quickly through hand-to-claw combat, but that wasn't an option here, not anymore. He cast his glance around, but there were no weapons that weren't fully in use, and the humans needed them far more than he did. The crowd split and twisted, and he saw Jim Granger spiking a demon in the throat, then turning to deliver a roundhouse punch to another as Dahlia fought by his side.

Then the drake struck again, scoring Stefan along his arm. He jumped back, returning his attention to the creature and steadfastly trying to ignore Cressida's muted cries.

"The Syx's reputation has been forged in the same pit as the army of Ahriman," the drake lisped. "Its demise will be celebrated there loud and long."

The crowd shifted, and Stefan recognized the silver spike an instant before it nearly struck him, flying at him end over end.

"Demon, stop messing around!" roared the exorcist.

At the last second before the thing brained him, Stefan yanked the holy cross out of the air and plunged it into the fire drake. The demon exploded into a pile of goop—which only served to reveal a new creature that had been standing behind it.

A woman. A human woman.

One he'd let die six thousand years earlier, not realizing her pain and suffering. Pain and suffering that he alone had caused.

"*You!*" she cried, launching toward him.

25

"No!" Cressida flung herself toward Dahlia just as her captain freed herself from her attacker and fought back with redoubled fury—which was good because Cressida had her own troubles.

She whirled around, taking stock. First, there was the swarm of demons Marcus had seemed to deliberately dump on them out of nowhere, straining the reserves of the already exhausted spell casters who'd traveled from inside their stronghold, and confusing the spell casters who were waiting for them in the grove. To add to that, however, every time she moved, another lance of pain sliced through her, though no one got near enough to her to strike. It was as if she was being cut open from the inside—welts and abrasions and outright gashes appeared out of thin air, weeping blood and gore. She could see the edges of some gashes beneath her tight leather clothes and wondered if this was why Stefan had insisted on the ridiculous outfit. It was one way to ensure she would stay physically held together.

Now she pivoted, taking on three coiling demons at once, all of them fire drakes. She hadn't had much time to talk with Zeneschiah, but under her compulsion, he'd explained with great relish how fire drakes assaulted their prey. All but the mightiest of them preferred to hunt in threes for the express purpose of toying with humans, who somehow felt they would attack singly, giving the human time to recover between bouts. They catered to that belief by doing just that—to start.

Cressida didn't have time for demon games, though. She'd felt the weight of Ahriman when he'd entered the grove—the weight, but not the person. She didn't believe that Ahriman was simply a cloud of depressing mist that enervated all he touched. That wouldn't have evoked the fear that stories of the mighty demon had engendered throughout time, a fear strong enough to last some six thousand years without reinforcement. And if what Stefan had said was true and the grimoire had been altered over time to erase the former attempts of witches who went up against the great demon? What would be the point of that if the demon was simply a nameless, faceless ghost? No. The soul-grinding depression wielded by the beast was a mighty weapon, but only a weapon, she was certain. The worst attack of Ahriman was yet to come.

This new barrage of demons proved that. She held her hands out as if to protect herself, and the demons took great delight in her attempt. Though she had clear skills in spell casting and she knew all the ancient enchantments, her power didn't lie in this art like Marcus's did. She was among the strongest in the coven, yes, but not *the* strongest. She'd been supposed to lead, not conjure, and her energies had been scattered because of it, while Marcus's had stayed laser focused.

Now she grimaced, seeing the obvious flaw in her education and training.

The obvious...

Another crack of pain sent Cressida sprawling to the side, fortuitously timed as one of the fire drakes struck. It soared over her, then piled into its fellow, while Cressida curled into a ball of misery, gasping as yellow fire played over her hands. She instantly thought of Stefan and wondered where he was in the fight. Surely he would attempt to help her if he could? Surely he wasn't yet another of her tools who was turning against her in her time of need?

She scrambled to her feet as the crowd parted, and then she did see Stefan, fighting a fire drake four times the size of the ones she'd squared off against. It struck him, lighting his hands up with fire, and a responding crackle burned up the length of Cressida's arm. She screamed and fell to her knees again, shaking her arm viciously. Once again as she staggered upright, fire danced over her fingertips. Not the yellow-white flame of the fire drake, but the red-and-purple conflagration that had erupted with Stefan's intimate touch. That fire had bonded them together, not scorched her in agony...

She stared down at her hands, flexing her fingers wide, and felt more than saw the attack of the drakes—this time all in a mass versus one at a time. Without thinking, she flung her hands out, willing the fire from her hands to create a blast of energy. She'd seen Marcus do something similar, though usually with a wand or other amulet of power to focus the weight of his spell, but she had no such tool. She only had the connection between her and the Syx, and it would have to do.

It did pretty well, as it turned out.

The moment the demons struck the force field she'd sent out, they didn't just fall back, they were incinerated into a wet, smoking heap of black ash. Startled, Cressida pivoted and struck again, and then again. She couldn't force the fire past the reach of her outstretched hands, but anything that she touched, she could destroy. She spun again, trying to find Dahlia in the crowd, desperate to protect her friend. She didn't find the captain, but she did see the lawgiver, and her heart froze solid.

Fraya stood in the midst of easily a dozen demons, her hands up as they advanced, her face hidden in the wild tangle of her hair. Seeing the lawgiver disheveled was almost more alarming than seeing her being attacked, and Cressida rushed forward, thrusting demons out of her way. Around her, spell casters seemed to be gaining on the army, evoking the strength of their ancient bonds, and the outer ring held—no demons were breaking free to terrorize the city beyond their sacred grove. Then again, none seemed to be *attempting* to break free.

Cressida burst from another knot of demons in time to see Fraya lift her hands high, cowering back from her harassers, and Cressida screamed, "No!"

She flew into their midst, her fiery hands driving the closest demons into ash while leaving the rest so she could take up a position in front of the lawgiver. This was the woman who'd always said she'd sacrificed everything to bring her into the coven. This was the woman who'd taught her everything she knew...and who'd also taught Marcus all he knew as well.

This was the woman...who had not forced Cressida to master the skills she needed to be strong, regardless of the abilities of those around her.

This was the woman...who had ordered the sacred grimoire to be erased of the old language Cressida had researched as she prepared to take on Ahriman.

This was the woman who even now placed her hand on Cressida's shoulder, the weight of that hand suddenly and fearsomely strong.

Cressida realized her error too late.

Fraya drove her to her knees as two of Marcus's foot soldiers stepped forward and hauled back her arms, pulling her hands wide and covering them with heavy blankets before the lawgiver grabbed her hair and yanked hard.

"You have done well, High Priestess," she said into her ear, her tone the same voice of the kindly woman who'd lifted her into her embrace more than two decades earlier, the same voice that had patiently and sternly taught her the ways of the sacred grimoire. "Perhaps a little too well. Yours was a place of power in this pageant, but not the place of *highest* power. That belonged to Marcus."

"Marcus," Cressida gritted out, her eyes going wide.

"Of course." Fraya tightened her grip on Cressida's hair as the demons in front of her parted, giving her a clear view to the space before her. While demons and witches still fought on either side, the passage was cleared to reveal Marcus standing alone, his face to the sky, his arms outspread. He was in profile to Cressida, so she could easily see him speaking words, even though she couldn't hear him. "It didn't have to be this way. The grimoire didn't specify whether the witch who confronted Ahriman be male or female, only that he or she was willing to lie with a demon for the glory of Ahriman's power."

"But why?" Cressida protested. "The wedding of a witch and a demon was to *stop* Ahriman, not glorify him."

"In the sacred grimoire, yes. And woe befell the witches throughout the ages who made the attempt. Demons are an untrustworthy lot, and it takes the greatest strength to withstand them when you let them get too close. But the sacred grimoire was not the only ancient tome in the Scepter Coven's library. It was Marcus who found the correct book, Marcus who read it, and Marcus who called the demon Belessanu to him, that he might subjugate her to his will. He took the demoness as his consort years ago, and his power increased a hundredfold."

As Cressida's horror grew, she twisted in the lawgiver's grasp, but the combined power of the lawgiver and the spells from Marcus's foot soldiers were more than a match for her, particularly with her hands covered and the nascent flicker of power she'd gained from Stefan effectively dampened.

"There's no other tome. I would have found it too," she gasped as the lawgiver's hold tightened, though, unbidden, the words of the demoness raked through her mind, mocking and twisting. *"Those who control the present, control the past."*

"You would have had Marcus left it there for you to find. But fortunately, he is no fool. After that, it was just a matter of seeing which of you was stronger. I had actually still believed it would be you. When I stole you from that waiting room at the hospital after I sent both your parents into surgery and you came to me so willingly, I thought you were the fated leader of the Scepter Coven, the one who would clear the path for Ahriman."

"You *what*?" Cressida suddenly felt dizzy, the ground rushing up to greet her, but the lawgiver hauled her back in place.

"Marcus came from such less dramatic beginnings that I felt you had the easy upper hand. But he showed promise early on, always pushing to learn more, always searching for ways to cheat. He yearned for the darkness in a way you simply never did, and so the path was set. And his abilities have blossomed over time while yours, sadly, have not."

Cressida forced herself to keep staring at Marcus and not react, though inside, she wanted to howl. All these recent years, as doubt had slowly crept in to darken her thoughts, she'd thought it was her own doing. But now she saw the truth. The lawgiver had worked to keep her exactly in the lane that she'd mapped out for her. Never allowing her to get too strong, always assuring Cressida that control of those around her was more important than control of her own abilities. How could she have been so stupid? How could she have trusted so much?

Deep within her, rage sparked to life, and with it a flicker of heat along her fingertips, despite the dampening effect of the blankets over her hands.

But it was far too late for her to stop what was happening now.

The skies above Marcus opened in the way that she'd first expected them to when she'd summoned Ahriman. The starlit sky split wide, and smoke and fire billowed, revealing one enormous claw to the right and another to the left. The claws pushed the fabric of the sky apart and revealed a creature easily three stories tall, dripping with blood and gore, his face a mass of spiked teeth and curling tentacles, his body slick with a fluid that scorched the earth. The trees around the sacred grove instantly turned white, their branches and leaves withering away, and the spell casters nearest his presence didn't die—they vanished, incinerated to dust.

"Ahriman!" Marcus shouted. "Keep the promise you made to our ancestors. Stand with us and protect us in your mighty grasp."

"*You...*"

When Ahriman spoke, Cressida couldn't help herself. The tears that filled her eyes and flowed down her cheeks were as impossible to deny as her next breath. She wasn't alone either. The foot soldiers to her right and left staggered back, and even the lawgiver rocked back on her heels, choking on the sudden wave of misery that emanated from Ahriman's voice, misery that he wielded like a weapon.

"You dare to ask me *anything*," Ahriman intoned.

Marcus, at least, seemed prepared to meet the monster. "The terms of your entry into this world are inviolate!" he shouted. "You are summoned here to do the work of the Scepter Coven, and in return, the Scepter Coven is yours to command. I give you the greatest spell casters ever born to do your bidding, and a world filled with demons to be your army. No mortal will stand before you, and all will kneel."

"Starting with *you*."

Ahriman reached out a long clawed hand, pointing at Marcus, but again, the spell caster had learned his lessons well. He lifted his arms high and shouted a spell Cressida had never heard before, let alone one she could follow, and whatever wave of power Ahriman sent his way was deflected into the forest surrounding them—which immediately caught on fire.

"No!" Cressida gasped as the sacred grove went up in flames.

"Protect the trees," Fraya demanded. She wrenched Cressida to her feet, and the foot soldiers freed her hands. Then the lawgiver shoved her forward. "The spell casters will help. There must be no trace of the work we do this night."

Shaking with fury but bound by the compulsion spell the lawgiver was laying upon her, Cressida turned her attention to the burning forest. She glanced at the spell casters by her side, her lip curling in derision. They followed her order now, but had they ever really pledged fealty to her? Or was she simply the tool of Marcus and the lawgiver, a wind-up toy they could set into motion at their desire?

But she wasn't that, she knew. Stefan had seen the strength in her and had coaxed it into the light, shifting her perspective from the inside out to the outside in and back again. She was bleeding and broken and scorched, but she was the high priestess of the Scepter Coven, and there was power in that.

Cressida held up her hands, and, in the shadow of ultimate evil, she began to heal the world.

26

Stefan stared in horror as the woman whose face had haunted him for six thousand years raced toward him, while he stood rooted to the spot. He couldn't escape her. He wouldn't escape her. She had died far away from him—he'd not known of her death, in fact, until he'd realized his body was beginning to change, his heart to wither, his blood to slow. He'd known Fallen angels who'd experienced the same in the midst of becoming a demon, but it wasn't until he was already doomed that he'd realized it was happening to him. And when he'd cried out to the heavens for understanding, hers was the face that he'd seen.

But how could she be here now? How was that possible? She'd been a human, and she'd died at practically the dawn of civilization. Yet her simple shift looked freshly woven, her skin young and supple, and her face...

Stefan realized his error a second too late. As the woman approached—her eyes wide, her face contorted in a mix of agony and fury—she transitioned into an entirely different creature. For a split second, he expected the demoness that had fought Cressida to appear, Belessunu, but this was something else. Something different, but...recognizable. A demon he'd encountered before, somewhere.

And then there were two of them.

"What the hell?" Stefan muttered. "Who are these guys?"

He hadn't expected the question to be answered, but the Archangel Michael's voice sounded in his mind anyway. *"You are a member of the Syx, in great distress—"*

Stefan scowled. "I'm not in that great distress."

"As such, you are the easiest target these demons have faced in centuries. To kill a member of the demon enforcers, even one who is weak, broken, clearly distracted..."

The two demons turned into three, and Stefan squinted with renewed concentration. "Wait a minute, I totally know that asshat. Warrick fought him in the Punic Wars. I thought he'd long since been sent on to his great reward."

"He should have been, but Warrick did not remain to ensure his work was completed, and so Rimush remained upon this earth, never again to be drawn out of his hole if there was any chance a Syx could be in play...until now, anyway."

The demons separated, moving to encircle Stefan. He turned with them, keeping his focus.

"You know, you seem to be a little too certain about this little tableau we've got setting up here. It almost makes me think you're playing fast and loose again."

Michael didn't speak for a long moment, and then all he said was, *"Be careful, demon."*

Despite his predicament, Stefan grinned, continuing to mutter as he judged the space between himself and his attackers, weighing the angles, the area, the humans in the line of danger. He had this, no matter how old these demons were. He totally had this. "You are playing fast and loose! You summoned these guys somehow, didn't you? That's some seriously underhanded shit, you ask me. What is it you got against me, anyway? Is it the hair? Because I do have great hair. My ability to actually maintain a sun tan? My dashing good looks?"

He paced the demons as they shifted, and the electricity built as the creatures drew upon the power rocketing around the sacred grove. "Okay, okay, okay," he muttered. "One against three, and they're not rushing me, so that means, what, they know I can take them out? They know I can kick their asses?"

"Keep going," Michael said drily, and Stefan pursed his lips. Because the truth was, the demons facing him *should* simply rush him. It would make the most sense of any move, and they should do it all at once. Demons did not have a sense of advanced strategy, not in the traditional sense. Their game was simply to end someone, and getting the drop on a member of the Syx was heady stuff indeed.

"That what's got you so jacked up?" Stefan demanded of the three. "A chance to take out a Syx? You guys have spent all this time in Ahriman's back pocket, but now you're ready to stretch your legs and play Whack-an-Enforcer?"

They didn't respond, but, to Stefan's surprise, they didn't *not* respond either. Once again, he'd expected them to rush him during his statement, but they didn't.

"You guys just going to stand there and stare at me all day?"

"You've changed," growled the closest demon, one of the throwback demons who could have been one of Botticelli's muses for his Divine Comedy illustrations. Smaller than the others but nevertheless imposing, his copper-colored skin stretched over an animalistic, horned head and down over a thin chest, bulbous belly, stocky legs, and huge taloned feet. Wings stretched out behind him at sharp angles, twitching uselessly in agitation.

A second demon shifted, the one Stefan recognized as Rimush. He was a heavily built bull of a demon with the face of a rat and long-fingered hands and feet, who sniffed the air, his teeth hanging over his lower lip. "I smell a witch."

Stefan's brows shot up, but of course he should have thought of that. The fact he hadn't merely proved he was almost as dumb as the demons he was facing. He couldn't have experienced all he had with Cressida without having some of the starlit magic of the human rub off on him—he had breathed her in, reveled in her, body and soul.

But had he really changed?

Cressida had transformed, certainly. He'd seen the purplish-red fire dancing over her skin both when they'd been wrapped in each other's arms and now, deep in the fight. It marked their connection and perhaps even spoke to a source of power she could now access, even though he hadn't had time to understand what that power might be, exactly. He couldn't see her now because a curtain of mist now hung heavily between him and the coven leadership, who were no doubt dealing with the arrival of Ahriman, but because it was looking so quiet, he suspected the major fire-works hadn't started happening yet.

Which was good, because he kind of had his hands full at the moment.

"Witch," rumbled the third demon, a long, skinny crea-ture who looked almost human if you didn't count the horns and tail or bright red, glistening skin. That level of body oil almost always indicated poison, and that meant he was the demon most likely to attack first. But he hung back, assessing and watching, and finally, Stefan caught on.

They wanted him to make the first move.

Why?

Then the last demon split again, and a new terror emerged.

"Oh, for fuck's *sake*, are you kidding me?" Stefan rolled his eyes, then slanted his gaze toward the final demon, this one a very familiar-looking demoness. Most demons chose to manifest as male for the simple reason that males tended to scare humans more. It took a real nightmare of a demon to manifest as female and still command the respect of mortal nightmares.

Belessunu managed to carry it off. "Looks like they've got you both on human *and* Syx duty, today. You pull the short stick?" he taunted as the dragon-shaped demon coiled in obvious irritation. Her tail swept around her, flicking and twitching. No witches remained in this section of the clearing, which was a good thing, since with four archdemons ready to tango, Stefan was pretty much going to have to set the place on fire.

But Belessunu didn't say anything, just seethed at him, and he leaned forward. It was his turn to sniff the air, and the scent he picked up was...jealousy?

And another scent too, which made his eyes flare wide. He didn't understand it, but Belessunu was by far the strongest demon of this set. That she wanted him dead was no great surprise. But the reasons why she wanted him dead bore some investigation.

"You were summoned here by Marcus, weren't you?" Stefan challenged, and Belessunu hissed, even as the other demons turned and growled at her, showing fangs and forked tongues.

"I was summoned by no human," she snarled back. "I am here for one reason. To kill you. It will be my pleasure to remove one of the Syx from this world. It is a death that is long overdue."

During her speech, however, Stefan's brain was working overtime. He'd edged toward her, and his knowing grew more overwhelming the closer he got to her. Surely he couldn't be mistaking this. It almost reminded him of Cressida and yet—

And then it came to him. Belessunu hadn't been summoned by Marcus, exactly, or at least not solely to fight.

"Son of a bitch," he exclaimed, barking a crack of laughter. "You're *porking* him!"

The deliberately crass language struck the female demoness exactly the way Stefan wanted it to. The demoness stretched her lips back from her fearsome jaws and roared, fire leaping from her throat to shoot across the open space. Because he was expecting it, Stefan ducked quickly, but the other demons weren't idiots. They too avoided the blast of fire, and as if on cue, they all rushed forward, finally taking the fight to Stefan, as he needed. If he'd acted first, they would be reacting to him and able to move against him. With all four of them lunging forward, however—

Stefan realized his mistake too late. They weren't all rushing together. The Botticelli demon came in with a wail of fury, even with the slender-horned demon, but Belessunu and Rimush held back. Stefan brought his hands together in a mighty clap as the smaller demons attacked. Unfortunately, they were far different from the usual members of the horde that he faced. Their powers were deep and strong, and well honed through millennia of effort. It wasn't a question of him dispatching them—of course he could and did —but the effort cost him more than he anticipated.

And then, even as they exploded into fire and tarry black goop, Rimush and Belessunu struck.

Pain exploded along Stefan's right shoulder and left hip,

so intense that he suspected Cressida either no longer was feeling the impact of the damage done to him or she was dead. Because he'd never felt pain like this in his entire immortal existence. Belessunu bathed him with fire as she turned, scorching his skin black, while Rimush somehow got his head down enough to gore Stefan's side with a thick, razor-pointed horn. Stefan grappled for Rimush's skull with his right arm, his blistered left arm flapping uselessly at his side, and managed to secure him well enough to ride him as Rimush bucked and jumped like a frenzied bull.

Meanwhile, Belessunu screeched at Rimush in a language Stefan hadn't heard in far too long—the base language of demons, which was also the base language of humans before the Father had set their tongues alight with multiple languages to forestall their ambitious climb to heights they did not seek to understand, merely conquer. The famed Tower of Babel, in mortal myth. Too much knowledge too soon had caused the downfall of humans— and had brought about the demise of the Fallen as well. Because once the Fallen had become entangled with the humans, in far too many cases, they'd lost all sense of reason.

All sense of reason.

Belessunu bellowed another wave of fire, this one close enough to Stefan's head that he felt his hair singeing. But it was Rimush beneath him who screamed, clearly feeling the heat of the close call as well and not liking it. It was obvious to Stefan that Belessunu no longer cared who she hurt in her attempt to take him down, and also that she preferred to do so from a distance. That was important too.

Rimush had figured out the same thing. He flung Stefan off him with a mighty roar, and Stefan hit the ground hard, scrambling up in a crouch. Then Rimush raced at Belessunu in a blind rage. Stefan, clamping his hand on his gored side and willing himself to heal, watched in a momentary daze. The sheer fury of Rimush's attack gave him the few critical seconds he needed to blast himself back together again, and he drew in a shaky, cleansing breath.

But the bullheaded demon seemed to underestimate Belessunu's sense of self-preservation as well. She didn't even let him get within ten feet of her before opening her gaping jaws wide and unleashing a fiery blast that caught Rimush full in the face.

Only... the demon kept going. Stefan staggered to his feet, staring at the demon in shock as he windmilled his arms, the plate-metal thickness of his skull apparently more than enough to withstand the demoness's raging fire. It was like watching a bull fighting back a fire hose of water, and the bull was gaining ground. When Belessunu's spurt of flames petered out, Rimush roared his fury and crashed directly into her, the two of them tumbling end over end.

Stefan blew out another long breath, the extra moments of reprieve all he needed to restore himself more or less to full capacity, but he didn't miss the irony of the carnage in front of him. This was the sort of demon-on-demon battle that Marcus and even Cressida had banked on when she'd chosen three demons to play their parts in her sham of a harem. Demons were undoubtedly the scourge of the universe, but seeing them set upon each other for strategic abuse didn't sit well with him. Something to contemplate when all this was done and order had been restored to the universe once more—or at least his little corner of the universe.

Stefan straightened as Belessunu regained her feet first, and he braced himself for another rain of fire as the demoness returned to her scorched-earth attack—but the dragon surprised him once again. With a twisting wrench, she whipped her tail around and caught Rimush at the midsection, the whipping tail circling him once, twice, and then a third time. With the final coil, Rimush finally reacted, but the moment he put his hands around the tail—

It exploded, littering the clearing with Rimush parts.

"Holy shit!" Stefan barked, scrambling back a few steps. The gory stump of the tail whipped back around to the other side of Belessunu, where, even as he watched, it began regenerating, coil by mirror-bright coil. Meanwhile, Belessunu turned, finding Stefan quickly, and reared back— then roared with six thousand years of pain, loss, hatred— and rage.

Stefan took off directly for her.

27

Cressida jerked back around, hearing the roar of the demons on the other side of the curtain of mist that Ahriman had dropped over them. It sounded as if a veritable army was engaged in battle, but with a deep bass that couldn't be the same horde she'd already fought. She knew—*knew* that Stefan was in the thick of it too. She no longer felt the pain of his every wound, but she could feel the leaping rage of his energy, the delighted rush of his power as he threw himself into the fight.

But though she yearned to rush to Stefan's aid, she was still collared by Marcus's power. Marcus's and the lawgiver's too.

She swept her gaze over the trees that ringed the sacred grove—the side of the grove she could see, anyway. They were all restored to their original form, reaching into the sky in a verdant mass of leaves and boughs, their rustling foliage creating a magic all their own. They were beautiful, but they were alone in their triumph, silhouetted against the bright lights of the city. There were no longer any spell casters remaining to share in their healing grace.

Cressida frowned, turning around further as the spell of healing still flowed from her lips, her cadence unbroken—and then she understood.

The other spell casters had been gathered into a small knot of humanity behind Marcus. And they were also kneeling now.

Anger surged within Cressida, and it was all she could do not to stop speaking her spell entirely. But she knew instinctively that her calm, flowing voice, dedicated to the healing of the earth, rendered her almost invisible to Marcus and the lawgiver. As long as she spoke, they believed she was totally focused on the task they had allotted her. And why would they think any differently? Since she'd been very small, she'd always striven to do whatever the lawgiver had asked of her. She'd studied, she'd learned, she'd memorized, she'd deferred.

Mostly deferred, she realized now.

Despite her best efforts, her voice rose and grew more forceful, the leaves of the trees seeming to swell with the intensity of her emotion. She'd learned everything that Marcus had, except for the dark arts of spell casting. She'd grown up alongside him, reading the same books, researching the same history, absorbing the same lessons. Why shouldn't she have gone on to become a master spell caster as well? Why had she been turned—and allowed herself to be turned—to the role of nurturer and empath and leader?

Leader. Cressida curled her lip. She was no leader. She was a puppet on strings carefully controlled not only by the woman who had apparently kidnapped her from the bosom of her family, a family Cressida suspected with chilling certainty had then passed on to the Goddess, but she'd also been manipulated by Marcus. Her dearest childhood friend.

How long had he been part of Fraya's plan? She'd said he'd shown greater promise than Cressida had, more willingness to explore the darker paths that would be needed to engage with Ahriman. But those paths weren't necessary. Not if they maintained their plan to destroy the archdemon.

Another arc of anger simmered through her, and once again, the trees she stood beneath responded. Their rush of rustling branches took on a melody as well, a melody that sounded almost like a thousand voices murmuring in the shadows—and then a dozen—and then one. Hers.

The sacred grove sang back to her the song of healing she had given it, returning to Cressida the power she'd gladly given up...and something more as well.

Cover.

Cressida's eyes flashed wide, and she took a long step backward, her arms still raised high, her hands outstretched. No one stepped into place behind her, to keep her at her task. Her voice still ran strong, but now it was mingled with the sound of the trees, the trees that were calling back to her, singing her song of healing. She began a new cycle of the spell, and then, abruptly, cut off her voice. Her lips still moved, but no sound came from her anymore. Instead, the voice of the sacred grove soared into the sky, matching her voice exactly.

Cressida pivoted in a dreamy, swaying motion, the picture of the healer witch in the thrall of her spell, and her gaze took in Marcus, the enormous creature before him, the kneeling, broken spell casters—and Fraya, who stood off to one side, her face alight with an almost feral joy. Not merely joy either. Pride. Satisfaction. Accomplishment.

The face of a woman who'd done what she'd been born on this earth to do.

Cressida could understand that feeling. It was swelling within her too—fueled by the song of the sacred grove, the fire of a demon's love, and something far more than that, something that she had discounted and cast off, dismissed and ignored for most of her twenty-three years with the Scepter Coven...

It was fueled by herself. She was the generator for the energy that now crackled through her blood and along her skin. She was the one who could put fire into the ancient spells of the sacred grimoire.

She was the one who would fight Ahriman, and she would be enough.

"Ahriman!" she cried, her voice rising above the melodic healing music of the sacred grove. The enormous demon twisted toward her, searching at once for the irritant far below him who dared call his name. He roared in anger as he fixed on her, but Cressida kept going. "You are a demon summoned to obey the will of the Scepter Coven. You will bend to my command!"

Then she was off and running again.

What happened next seemed to progress almost in slow motion, at least in Cressida's mind. She had the curious sensation of being able to leap forward when all around her could barely turn and gape, to strike before anyone could even draw breath.

This was the power that had been accorded her when she'd become high priestess of the Scepter Coven. *This* was the power to lead and to strike down her enemies. It was power that was rarely called upon, but that didn't mean it wasn't there. She had learned it, she had mouthed all the spells, absorbed all the lessons—and now she would use it

in a way the original writers of the grimoire had undoubtedly never intended.

Against her own consort.

Marcus recovered from his shock before the rest of the
spell casters—even before the lawgiver—and thrust out his
hands as Cressida reached him. With the skill of a master
spellcaster, he struck her with a flood of images that made
her stagger back, horrifying in their truth—images playing
in sharp relief of the earliest moments Cressida could
remember, a loud, crashing hospital emergency room, shiny
black shoes and a pretty dress—and more images too,
impossible images, harrowing and awful—no, no, no!

She shoved his gut-wrenching spells of illusion away. He
didn't know that Fraya had already betrayed his secrets, and
she had no time for his petty tricks. Not now. The fate of her
coven was in her hands, as well as the fate of witches everywhere. Ahriman was even now struggling against the
combination of spells she'd thrown up at him, and that
magic wouldn't hold.

"Stand down, Cressida," Marcus seethed, and then his
mouth was working to speak the spells he'd learned not in
the sacred grimoire they'd studied since their youth, but in
the dark grimoire the lawgiver had led him to. He was
complicit in his crimes against the coven, she thought, but
he wasn't wholly to blame.

Then again, because of Marcus, witches had died.
Because of Marcus, more were about to be sacrificed. All to
ensure his vision of a greater glory, subjugating the world of
witches and humans at Ahriman's side.

It was not to be borne.

Cressida swept her hand forward, the arc of her fingers
stopping three feet from Marcus's body, just out of range of
his own hands—but her fire extended well beyond her

grasp. It sliced out in a sparking arc of red-and-purple fire, its edge honed to a razor-sharp tip, and slashed across Marcus's throat so quickly, his eyes flew wide only after the deed had already been done.

Marcus's spell stopped midbreath—because his voice stopped midbreath. His hands shot to his throat as he toppled forward, but his neck had not been severed...only his vocal cords. The betrayer of the Scepter Coven wouldn't speak a new spell again, not if Cressida had anything to say about it.

Then she turned to Ahriman as he thrust his enormous arms wide. The impact of his energy staggered her, and she cried out in pain. The spell casters were thrown onto their backs, Marcus began scrabbling away on his knees, one hand on his throat, the other on the churned-up dirt and grass of the trampled grove. The curtain of mist between her and the rest of the grove fell away, and Cressida noticed with surprise that the trees were healthy and lush all around the grove, her spell extending far into the forest of Central Park. There were no spell casters at all on the far side of Marcus's curtain, however, and Cressida blanched in sudden dread. Were so many already gone, burned to ashes with Ahriman's arrival?

She searched the far side of the grove for a precious moment more, alarmed to see a fireball of energy twisting and writhing across the scarred ground, but very little else.

Then Ahriman struck, and the sky rained down fire.

STEFAN SUCKED in a startled breath as he ran, realizing he could see all the way across the grove—which he was sure he would appreciate the moment after he pounded

Belessunu into the ground. A moment later, however, he connected with the dragon-bodied demon, her wings spread wide as if she was batting back an unseen storm. Stefan was that storm, and he raged with all his might, combating Belessunu's anger with his own deep stores of fury. The archangel wanted this creature sent back unto the Father, and Stefan was more than willing to do the deed.

As he connected with the demon and the two exploded into a fiery conflagration, however, he learned something else from the ancient beast.

The true depths of Marcus's betrayal.

Belessunu's thoughts were an open book to him, and as he barreled into her, sending her sprawling, he took an equally harsh dive into her memories. And there he found Marcus, at almost the same time that Cressida had begun awakening to her own confused thoughts about her child-hood friend. While Cressida had thought Marcus was forming a deeper attachment to her, he was actually begin-ning a dark and twisted affair with the demoness, summoned by his own hand. He cut his teeth against her scales, learning from her and subjugating her to his demands by turns. And Belessunu had returned to him will-ingly, again and again, ravenously and almost desperately in the end, as she sensed Cressida becoming a true threat...not for her lover's heart, but for the position she felt Marcus truly deserved. The position of high priest by Ahriman's side.

"You dare!" Belessunu screeched, whipping her snout around and blasting Stefan back with a swath of fire. As he tumbled, he saw Marcus scrabbling away from the battle between Ahriman and Cressida. The spell caster crawled on his knees, one hand pressed to his throat, the other bracing him as he fled, and then Stefan's gaze lifted up—and up farther still—all the way to the roiling fury of the demon Ahriman—

Who Cressida now faced alone.

"Oh, for the love—Belessunu!" Stefan shouted, drawing the demoness's attention as he flung out his right arm. "There's your human now, beat to shit—you want me? Or do you want to save him?"

The dragon's entire body bucked, her snout coming around again as her gaze followed Stefan's gesture—and she saw Marcus on the ground. She recognized immediately the witch's distress, but she didn't go to him. Instead, her eyes narrowed and she swung her head back to Stefan—

"Wrong answer," Stefan growled. He honestly wasn't sure what he would have done if Belessunu had chosen the human over her own killing rage, and it was just as well she didn't force him to choose. Instead, he used the demoness's momentary distraction against her and thrust his hands out, purple-red flame bursting from his fists as he clocked her snout in a two-handed punch. The demoness didn't just fall back, she burst upward, her wings lifting her in a mighty rush to send her soaring into the sky—

Straight into a burst of fire emanating from the claws of Ahriman.

The explosion made Stefan flinch away, and he immediately sought out Cressida, who was also bent beneath those flames. Unlike Belessunu, however, Cressida had clearly been expecting the blast. She held her hands high, a shield of purple and red radiating from her palms, and Stefan felt great tides of his own energy leave him as she pulled his strength to her cause. He grinned, his heart swelling with triumph. She was doing it! She was using him exactly as her sacred grimoire had dictated, drawing on his power as her consort, channeling it—

Stefan saw the lurching rush of the lawgiver from the corner of his eye, and panic leapt within him. He couldn't take out the human himself, couldn't touch a child of God, but how would he ever—

"No!"

It was another female whose scream filled the sky, another form that burst onto the battlefield, wielding a mighty spiked cross, and suddenly, the lawgiver sprawled to the left, Cressida's captain of the guard laying her flat. The lawgiver struggled to rise again, and Dahlia didn't hesitate, cracking her with a solid punch the second time, then balling up her fist and leaning forward in one of the most threatening poses Stefan had ever seen anyone, male or female, take against a fallen foe.

The lawgiver stayed on the ground.

Cressida raised her voice in another spell and—and if Stefan was hearing correctly, he would almost swear the trees were taking up her cry as well. The trees and the remaining spell casters, staggering to their feet to raise shaky hands and trembling arms—but singing. Once again singing the song of the Scepter Coven, first among all witches, calling down the very stars to defeat their ancient enemy.

Ahriman didn't even pause to register the combined might of the Scepter Coven beneath him. He drew in a mighty breath, ready to rage anew, and barely seemed to notice as the first star of heaven rained down upon him—and exploded.

Stefan was knocked flat by the sonic boom that shot out in all directions from the ancient demon as he blew into a million pieces, and he curled over on the ground, barely coming up to his knees against the raging fury of light and sound. The entire grove had taken on an air of unreality, the spells of the coven mingling with the energy of earth and sky to reverberate in endless, undulating waves of power. Not sure whether he should laugh or cry with exultation, he drew in a shattered breath...

And then he saw her again.

The woman—the human woman—who'd died for loving him.

"Elisha?" he gasped, not believing his eyes. But while before the distracting illusion of the demons had shimmered and varied, a construct of magic that could not hold its place, this young woman looked solid. Real. As perfect in this moment as the day he'd left her, six thousand years before. The day she'd cursed him for eternity, then died without Stefan even realizing she was placing herself in danger, all for the distress of losing him. "That can't be you. You...can't be here. You *can't*."

Elisha stared back at him, her eyes haunted with sorrow, her smile infinitely sad. "My beautiful Fallen," she said, her words no more than a whisper, but carrying to Stefan as clearly as if she were shouting down at him from on high. "You were my heart, my love, my life, and my—"

"I know," Stefan moaned, reaching for her in death the way he could have in life—should have, and didn't. "Your death. Beautiful child of God, I was your death, and I have never forgiven myself for it."

Elisha shook her head and took his outstretched hands in hers.

"No, Fallen," she said solemnly. "You were my lesson. I know that now. Nothing more, and nothing less." She squeezed her hands. "And I forgive you."

28

Cressida stood in the shadows, beneath the trees she'd brought back to life and who'd then become her own living, singing army, tears trickling down her face.

Her ears ringing with the explosion, her body still vibrating with the waves of power coursing across the sacred grove, she could see nothing but Stefan and a woman of almost transcendent beauty speaking together, Stefan on his knees, the woman standing. She watched Stefan bow his head as the woman placed her hands upon him, almost in benediction. It was perhaps the most beautiful and devastating thing she'd ever seen.

"The picture of grace, I would say."

Cressida jumped, then cast a sidelong glance at Jim Granger. The exorcist's gaze was on the scene in the clearing, and his smile was weary but relieved. The smile of a man who'd seen too much, and who would take any grace he could.

"How is she here?" Cressida asked.

"She's here because Stefan needed her to be, more than

he needed life itself. You could say he needed that young woman's forgiveness even more than he believed he needed the Father, and so the Father, in his generosity, brought her to him."

Cressida slanted the man a skeptical glance. "The Father? Or would it be more likely his boss, the archangel he spoke about. This seems like a trick he would pull."

Jim Granger chuckled, not unkindly. "You're as cynical as Stefan is, but perhaps understandably so. You've been treated even less well by your mentors than he has."

She twisted her lips. "I don't know, I haven't been forced into battle for the past six thousand years for a shot at redemption. A redemption it now seems he's received." She couldn't help the way her voice shook when she looked back to the center of the clearing, or the choked gasp in her throat when she realized Stefan had gone. He deserved to be wherever his redemption had earned him, she knew. Whether that was back with his fellow enforcers or in the exalted tiers of heaven. She refused to look at the sky, though the urge to do so was powerful. Would it be enough to know that Stefan would be up there, gazing down upon her? Would it be enough never to see him again?

"No. But what have you faced?" Granger's words were quiet, gentle. But he knew, Cressida thought. During the highest point of the battle, the information that Marcus had spewed out toward her had flowed on the circuits traveling between all the consorts caught up in their sacred bond— including Stefan and Granger. He knew.

Still, there was healing to be found in speaking the truth aloud. A truth she'd both never and always known on some level, she supposed. A truth that both shamed and exalted her.

A truth that was curiously hard to admit, in the end.

"Lawgiver Fraya didn't rescue me, that day in the hospital," she whispered. "She stole me. My parents were witches who'd fled the coven."

"Their accident?"

"Was no accident." She shook her head, her throat constricting. "It was all arranged. All because they didn't want me to grow up a witch. They wanted it to be my...my choice. But Fraya had seen something within me that she craved, even when I was a baby. A strength she could twist. Use."

"And she was right about that strength." Granger nodded. "For all that she was wrong about everything else."

Cressida pursed her lips together for a long moment, unable to speak. In her minds' eye, she could see only her shiny black shoes, her pretty dress. She could only remember the need to be quiet—so quiet. To not say a word. Now she knew why that silence had been necessary...and why she hadn't objected when the familiar, kind-eyed lawgiver had come for her on that terrible morning, holding out her arms, telling her it would all be okay. Smiling at her.

"Where will your path take you, High Priestess?" Granger murmured at length, recalling her attention. "Your coven needs you too."

"I know it does," she sighed. "Marcus is—I don't know. Caught up in the destiny of his master, I suppose. I don't know how long he's been under the sway of Ahriman, or who was the first to lead whom between him and Fraya. They both led critical elements of the coven, though. Most of the elder lawgivers died from the effort of protecting the coven. Those who remain are all quite junior. It will take time for them to adjust, to step up into their new roles."

"It will take time. And it will take leadership. You'll be there for that."

"Yes," Cressida agreed. "I'll be there."

Once again, she felt an unreasonable urge to glance at the sky, though there was no more reason for Stefan to be there than here beside her. Instead, she turned to Granger, her own smile wry. "And where will you go? You're my husband, you know. I need to know these things."

"I never expected to be married." Granger chuckled. "It was...an education. But I'm not meant for coven life. I'll retrieve my cross, then be on my way."

Cressida blinked, noticing for the first time that Granger didn't have his trademark weapon. "But where—"

"Exorcist!" From the crowd of coven spell casters and soldiers, a witch broke free, covered nearly head to toe in black goop. She held a staff in her hand equally covered, and she lofted it high. "It worked! She was throwing spells to help the demon, and this worked!"

Cressida didn't even bother to hide her grin. "You let her use your weapon?"

"She believed in it more than any who touched it, and she was being set upon mercilessly by the horde. In the end, I don't need any instrument forged by man to do God's work. If He wills it, it is done. The rest is party tricks."

"Uh-huh. And yet you gave your party favor to a woman you barely know—a witch, no less, who doesn't believe in your God."

"My God isn't so small that he begrudges those who would find their own paths to Him, no matter how twisted those paths may be."

Cressida nodded as Dahlia started heading their way. She didn't envy her friend the exorcist's goodbye, as gentle as she knew Granger would be. Being left was never easy, no matter how good the reason.

Cressida turned and headed deeper into the trees,

giving Granger and Dahlia their privacy. She didn't stop moving until she reached a small break in the forest, and sighed as she stepped into a soft spill of moonlight. Almost against her will, she found her gaze lifting past the tops of the trees and into the starry night. Through some trick of the shadows, the eternal brilliant light smog of New York City couldn't quite hide the starlit sky. She sighed, angrily rubbing away the few tears that dared make tracks down her smudged cheeks, and tried to center herself, so that she might hear the quiet, grace-filled voice of the Goddess.

"You really make a guy work for it, don't you, princess?"

That wasn't it.

STEFAN STOOD motionless as Cressida made her way through the trees. He'd felt her every movement, his lungs expanding with hers as she took in a steadying breath, his own eyes itching as she'd wiped tears away. He didn't know how long the symbiotic connection was going to last between them, but he found he didn't hate it as much as he would have expected.

"How long have you been there?" she demanded, clearly working to keep her voice steady. She still refused to look at him.

"Long enough to see Granger practically get knocked down by your new head of security. You guys are going to have to do a better job getting into the city, though. I don't think Granger is an upstate New York kind of guy."

"And what kind of guy are you?"

As soon as the words were out of her mouth, Stefan knew she regretted them—but he didn't. He grinned alongside her and looked up at the stars. "I don't know. I guess I'm the kind of guy who gets around a lot."

She snorted, but before she could pass him off with a witty retort, he kept going. "I'm the kind of guy who's spent six thousand years trying to make up for being an asshole, not realizing that sometimes, it's not all about me. It was mostly about me, and that's why the sin was laid at my feet, but there was also a little matter of free will that I conveniently forgot, and lessons for us all to learn. Which doesn't excuse what I did, but..." He rubbed the edge of his jaw where Elisha had touched him. "It does make it a little easier to sleep at night."

"Will you see her again?" Cressida asked, and he didn't miss the hollowness to her tone. Her dismay should have dismayed him, but it didn't—far from it. He felt an almost unbearable lightness in his heart unlike anything he'd ever experienced before.

"Elisha? No," Stefan said.

"How can you know that for sure?" Cressida looked at him for the first time. "If I'd fallen in love with you and had the chance to see you again, I'd find a way. She did once. She easily could again."

"She could, except that wasn't Elisha standing there."

That caught her. "It wasn't?"

Stefan smiled. He always forgot this about humans. They could believe in the most unreasonable thing, yet consider the slightest of divine acts the stuff of myth and fairy tales. "No, Cressida. The image you saw wasn't Elisha but my memory of her. Beautiful and strong and full of life. That's what I needed to let go. Elisha fell in love with me and I left her, not realizing the impact of my actions, not realizing the frailty of the human heart. And so I hurt her— more than she could bear."

"And you paid for it," Cressida said, her words barely audible.

"I learned from it," Stefan countered. "And I was blessed by it, in the end, though I would never have seen it that way."

Cressida's lips twisted. "I wouldn't see it that way either." She cast her gaze heavenward again, her mouth twisting into a grim smile. "You follow a harsh taskmaster."

"Oh, I don't know. He has a sense of humor too," Stefan murmured. He lifted a hand, and a spark of flame jumped from his fingers, lighting the shadows between them in a flicker of purple and red. Cressida glanced over, a smile teasing at her lips as she watched the flame, and Stefan leaned closer. "And after all, he brought me to you. That has to count for something."

CRESSIDA COULDN'T HELP IT. As always, the demon found a way to make her laugh, and she hiccupped a choked breath and shook her head. She lifted a hand to wipe away a tear, then shivered when Stefan caught her fingers and held them close. The touch of his hand against hers was an indescribable feeling, but she *wanted* to be able to describe it, wanted to somehow freeze this moment and remember it for the rest of her life.

"What are you thinking, princess?" Stefan murmured, and Cressida blinked at him, surprised to find her vision still blurred with tears.

"I'm thinking how lucky I am," she said, her voice wobbling as Stefan's brows shot up.

"Lucky?"

She smiled ruefully. "Yeah, lucky. How many women, witches or otherwise, can say they fell in love with a demon, who then turned around and helped her find the strength to defeat the ancient nemesis of her people, a creature of great and terrible power? I mean, that's—"

"Whoa, whoa, whoa." Stefan tightened his grip on her hand. "Back up there a second. Say that again?"

Cressida sighed, her pulse leaping as Stefan stared at her with his dark eyes limned in fiery red. "Well, see, there was this demon, and he ended up helping me defeat—"

He cut her off, his gaze impossibly intense. "Before that."

"Oh," she said softly, her heart thudding a bit more heavily as heat skated through her. "You mean the part about how much I've fallen in love with him? How I plan to look up at the sky every night and count a million stars, hoping that one of them will be one he looks up and sees too? How I hope I can remember every tiny little detail of his smile, his laugh, his stupid jokes—and the way he literally set me on fire? That part?"

"That part's a good place to start," Stefan said. He shifted closer to her, not letting her drop her gaze. "You might want to add the bit that it's the high priestess of the Scepter Coven who's given this demon back his heart, though—his heart, and his reason for living. And that she might as well let go of her dreams to watch the stars at night. Because she's going to have to keep her focus on leading the coven that killed that ancient nemesis of hers. I understand that's kind of a big deal in witchdom."

Cressida nodded, tightening her jaw as he recalled her to her responsibilities. "I know—"

"And besides all that, this demon of yours, he's going stick right by your side, princess." He held her hands tight, another burst of red-and-purple flame flickering high. "Not just in your memory, not just in your heart. But here, with you. Whenever you need me. As long as I'm not in the midst of pounding some demon into the ground, I'm completely yours."

Cressida sucked in a quick breath, searching his eyes. "But how can you make that promise? You're sworn to the enforcers, to the archangel. That doesn't all change because of me."

But Stefan merely gave her a crooked smile, his eyes dark and unrelenting.

"I think you underestimate the powers of the high priestess of the Scepter Coven," he said softly. "*Everything* changes because of you."

He pulled her into his embrace, and Cressida felt the strength of his arms around her, the heat of his skin against hers. And somewhere, far off in the heavens, a soft laugh drifted among a million stars, and words were spoken that Cressida could barely hear, framed as she was in the prism of Stefan's love. "*She is your redemption, Nur-ayya Dadanum. Accept, and you are forgiven...*"

"Oh, I accept," Stefan sighed into the stillness that followed. "I totally and completely accept."

Then his lips came down on Cressida's, and spectral fire leapt and danced around them, brightening the sacred grove once more.

THANK you for reading **Demon Bewitched!** I sincerely hope you enjoyed Stefan and Cressida's adventure. If you did and you'd like to help other readers find them, I truly appreciate you leaving a review for the book wherever you purchased this copy!

WHAT'S **next for the Demon Enforcers?** Continue their story with Demon Ensnared. Visit my website at www.jennstark.com and sign up for my newsletter to learn more about the Demon Enforcers!

BOOKS BY JENN STARK

The Demon Enforcer Series

Demon Unbound

Demon Forsaken

Demon Bewitched

Demon Ensnared

Immortal Vegas Series

(series complete!)

One Wilde Night (prequel novella)

Getting Wilde

Wilde Card

Born To Be Wilde

Wicked And Wilde

Aces Wilde

Forever Wilde

Wilde Child

Call of the Wilde

Running Wilde

Wilde Fire

Wilde Justice Series

The Red King

The Lost Queen

ABOUT JENN STARK

Jenn Stark is an award-winning author of paranormal romance and urban fantasy. She lives and writes in Ohio. . . and she definitely loves to write. In addition to her Immortal Vegas and Wilde Justice urban fantasy series and Demon Enforcers paranormal romance series, she is also author Jennifer McGowan, whose Maids of Honor series of Young Adult Elizabethan spy romances are published by Simon & Schuster, and author Jennifer Chance, whose Rule Breakers series of New Adult contemporary romances are published by Random House/LoveSwept and whose modern royals series, Gowns & Crowns, is now available.

Visit her online at www.jennstark.com and sign up for her newsletter to keep up with all the latest information about upcoming releases and special events!

facebook.com/authorjennstark

twitter.com/jennstark